THE GIRL WHO COULDN'T LIE

Radhika Sanghani

To my younger self

First published in the UK in 2024 by Usborne Publishing Limited, Usborne House, 83-85 Saffron Hill, London EC1N 8RT, England, usborne.com

Usborne Verlag, Usborne Publishing Limited, Prüfeninger Str. 20, 93049 Regensburg, Deutschland, VK Nr. 17560.

Text © Radhika Sanghani, 2024.

The right of Radhika Sanghani to be identified as the author of this work has been asserted by her in accordance with the Copyright, Designs and Patents Act, 1988.

Cover art by Saskia Bueno © Usborne Publishing, 2024.

Author photo by SEBC Photography.

The name Usborne and the Balloon logo are Trade Marks of Usborne Publishing Limited.

A CIP catalogue record for this book is available from the British Library.

ISBN 9781805316749 9440/1 JFM MJJASOND/24

Printed and bound using 100% renewable energy at CPI Group (UK) Ltd, Croydon, CR0 4YY.

MIX
Paper | Supporting responsible forestry
FSC® C171272
www.fsc.org

RADHIKA SANGHANI

THE GIRL WHO COULDN'T LIE

USBORNE

Chapter 1

Priya Shah jolted awake. She was having a terrible day. But that wasn't really a surprise because lately, all her days were slightly terrible. They had been ever since *that* day. The 13th of August. Almost a year ago. The most terrible of all the days. She felt a lump rising in her throat at the thought, but she forced it down with a heavy swallow. Now was not the time to think about the worst day of her life. She had enough problems happening this very second.

"Excuse me. Earth to Priya!" Mrs Lufthausen glared at Priya over the tops of her gold-rimmed spectacles. "For the last time, please can you explain to me why you thought that double maths was an appropriate time for a morning nap?"

Priya gulped. She felt a soft, cool hand slip into her right hand. Mei. Her best friend was telling her she had her back. She smiled.

"Do you think this is FUNNY?" demanded Mrs Lufthausen. "This is the *third* time that you have been caught napping in my lessons this term!"

"*Of course* she doesn't think it's funny!" cried a voice to her left. "She has a weird thing where her apologetic face looks like her happy face. It's, like, genetic. Right, Priya?" Sami. Her other best friend. Standing up for Priya like she always did. "And she wasn't *asleep*! She was thinking, obviously. Everyone knows you do the best thinking with your eyes closed. It's the only way to solve a quadratic equation, in my humble opinion."

"Samantha Levin, does it look like I was speaking to you?" thundered Mrs Lufthausen. "Get back to your equations. And Priya, it is completely unacceptable for you to keep falling asleep while I try to teach you basic mathematics. If you don't explain yourself now, I'm going to have to ask you to leave and wait outside."

Priya's cheeks burned with humiliation. She was a good student. She didn't get sent out of lessons! That was the kind of thing that happened to Katie and Angela. Not top students like her. But now she was going to get sent out for the first time in her entire school history and there was nothing she could do to stop it. It wasn't like she could tell Mrs Lufthausen the truth – that she was exhausted because, unlike her younger sister Pinkie, she was physically unable to fall asleep while her parents were shouting, and that when she finally *did* get to sleep after they'd stopped arguing, it was time to wake up for gymnastics practice. Of course she was tired – she'd slept less than a gamer who stayed up all night playing people in Korea.

But Priya knew exactly what would happen if she said all that out loud. Mrs Lufthausen would tell the school counsellor, who would tell her parents, and Priya would end up in big trouble. Because her parents' golden rule was *Don't Air Your Dirty Laundry in Public*, which basically translated to: *pretend everything is perfect at all times*. And if Priya admitted that her gymnastics practice was affecting her schoolwork, her teachers would want her to quit – especially because gymnastics was totally separate to school. Her parents would feel shamed into making Priya quit the team, which meant her chances at getting into the Teen Olympics would be over for ever, even though she'd been training for it her whole life. And worst of all, it would mean she'd never get to watch Dan Zhang do pull-ups ever again.

Priya looked up at Mrs Lufthausen and took a deep breath. "I'm so sorry, Mrs Lufthausen. I guess I stayed up too late watching videos of dancing baby goats. It's my fault."

The teacher shook her head. "I'm disappointed in you, Priya. Please go outside for the rest of the lesson. And next time you want to watch a goat dance, try to think about the consequences."

Priya got up and left the classroom. She stood outside

feeling a burning mix of shame and anger. It wasn't her fault any of this had happened. She hadn't *meant* to fall asleep. She knew Mrs Lufthausen took it personally, but if anything, it was a big compliment that it was only in *her* lessons that Priya fell asleep. It was just so warm and cosy in that classroom, with the sun streaming in from outside, Mei and Sami sitting on either side of her, and Mrs Lufthausen's monotonous voice explaining the wonderfully stable predictability of algebraic equations. It was a complete contrast to Priya's morning – her parents arguing as per always, Pinkie making everyone late, and Priya panicking because she couldn't find her brand new trainers. It turned out Pinkie had decided to "decorate" them with a permanent black marker and when Priya had shouted at her, their mum had rushed in to console *Pinkie,* not Priya. If that wasn't bad enough, she'd then told Priya off for "upsetting her younger sister". The unfairness of it all had left Priya speechless, and by the time she'd found her voice again, nobody had time to listen to her. They were late to drop her off for gymnastics. Which meant that when she arrived, her coach Olaf had told her off for her poor punctuality in front of everyone. In front of Dan Zhang.

Priya thought that would be the most humiliating moment of her day – until she was kicked out of maths. How was Dan ever going to realize he was the love of her life when the only time he saw her she was being told off like a schoolgirl? Okay, she *was* technically a schoolgirl – and he was also a schoolboy, at the boys' school next door to hers – but that wasn't the *point*. Dan was in Year Nine – a whole year above Priya – and everyone knew boys liked sophisticated girls. Priya was going to have to try extra hard to prove her maturity if he was ever going to fall for her. She looked forlornly down at her bright purple and white New Balances, which were now decorated with wobbly smiley faces. This was not a good start.

Priya's stomach lurched as she inspected the invitation that Sami had just given her. It was thick, purple and sparkly. On the front, big capital letters proclaimed: *YOU'RE INVITED TO SAMI'S BAT MITZVAH!!!!!* But on the back, it said something so awful that Priya wanted to cry. She read the three words one more time – *Saturday 30th June* – and swallowed. Hard.

"Don't you just LOVE it?" cried Sami. "It's going to be the party of the year."

Mei raised an eyebrow. "Katie's parents hired out an actual nightclub for her party last month. And everyone got free iPhones. I think *that* might have been the party of the year."

"Uh, yes, but we're actually invited to this one," pointed out Sami.

"That's true," agreed Mei, glancing down at her phone that was definitely not a free iPhone. "It's going to be amazing. Right, Priya?"

Sami waved her hand in front of Priya's face. "Helloooo, Priya? Why are you still staring at the invitation?"

Priya looked up with a wide fake grin plastered on her face. "Because it's only the coolest invitation I've ever seen! And I happened to see one of Katie's invitations up close when it fell out of her bag."

"Why, thank you," said Sami proudly. "I designed it myself."

"But is your bat mitzvah *definitely* happening on the 30th of June?" asked Priya. "As in, that Saturday? For sure?"

Sami's green eyes narrowed. She scrunched up her nose suspiciously and tucked her bright red hair behind her ears. "Priya Shah. You had *better* not be telling me that you cannot come to my bat mitzvah, aka the biggest day of a Jewish girl's life. The day I go from girlhood to womanhood."

"I thought you reached womanhood when you got your period last year?" said Priya, desperately trying to distract Sami from her original line of questioning.

"That is not the point," declared Sami. "The point is that you're my best friend in the entire world – I mean, you AND Mei are my best friends in the entire world."

Mei rolled her eyes beneath her block fringe. "It's cool. I'll be the afterthought."

"And," continued Sami, undeterred, "not only did you miss my starring role as Katniss Everdeen in Heartland Secondary School for Girls' performance of *The Hunger Games: The*

Musical, but you missed Mei's *major* AquaSplash birthday takeover."

Priya's face fell. "I still can't believe I didn't get to swim down the space bowl. It's meant to be a twelve-metre drop."

"Fourteen," amended Sami, starting to count out all the things Priya had missed on her fingers. "On top of that you've also missed countless play rehearsals I've asked you to come to for moral support, basically *every* birthday party anyone in Year Eight has ever had, and ninety-eight per cent of our sleepovers."

"You know I want to come to everything," said Priya. "It's just—"

"Gymnastics," chorused Mei and Sami. "We know."

"Olaf thinks I could be the only person from our club to make the new Teen Olympics team," said Priya. "Which is major! If I get onto it, it's basically guaranteed that I'll be in the real Olympics when I'm older! I just have to make sure I keep up with all the training sessions and go to all the competitions. I hate that they're always on weekends – you know I do. It would be so much better if they happened on Tuesdays and I could miss double maths."

Sami cocked her head to the side, conceding Priya's point. "Fine. But all I'm saying is, you owe it to me. To come to my bat mitzvah. It's super important. You absolutely have to be there. No excuses. At all."

"I think she's trying to say she hopes you can make it," said Mei.

"No," corrected Sami. "I'm saying that if Priya tells me she can't come, I will officially have a fully-fledged breakdown right here in the school canteen. And then spontaneously combust."

Priya laughed nervously. "Okay, there is no need to be so dramatic. I never said I couldn't come."

Sami's eyes lit up. "Wait, do you mean—"

"Yes, of course I can come to your bat mitzvah," said Priya, despite a little voice in her head telling her that now would probably be a good time to STOP TALKING.

"Seriously? You don't have a competition that weekend?" asked Mei eagerly.

"Nope," said Priya, actively blocking out the voice that had now dramatically crescendoed to shout about the major competition – the Nationals – Olaf had told her about that exact morning. A competition that the Teen Olympics scout would be at. A competition where the prize money would pay for her entire next year's training. A competition that could change her life – and was happening on Saturday 30th June. She swallowed one last time. "No competitions at all!"

Sami and Mei high-fived and whooped loudly. Priya forced her face into something she hoped looked like a smile and ignored the plummeting feeling in her stomach. Today really was an absolutely *terrible* day.

Chapter 2

"I'm home!" called out Priya as she opened the front door, kicking off her ruined trainers. She looked at them in annoyance one more time. The smiley faces were drawn so badly that all the faces looked mildly anxious instead of happy. Pinkie had unwittingly captured Priya's permanent mood.

"Hi, *beta*! We're in the kitchen!"

Priya followed her dad's voice into the kitchen and gasped. There were five pans on the cooker, discarded onion skins and okra ends on the chopping board, with an overpowering garlic odour pervading absolutely everything. Her dad was standing by the cooker, trying to stir all the pans at once, while Pinkie was sitting at the dining room table making a huge mess with a bunch of paintbrushes, a chocolate bar dangling precariously out of the side of her mouth.

"Oh no." Priya exhaled. "When's Mum coming back?"

"She should be here any minute," said her dad happily, adding way too much chilli powder to the curry.

Priya winced. This was not good. The top three things her mum hated were: mess, strong smells and refined sugar. If she walked in the door right now, there would be an argument that would last at *least* two hours. And from the sound of things, Priya had precisely one minute to fix everything.

She quickly turned on the ventilator fan and started tidying up the kitchen counters. She had no idea why her dad couldn't make a bit more of an effort. It was nice he tried to make dinner for their mum, who always came home exhausted after spending all day "managing complete morons", but it wasn't so nice when he forgot to do all the things her mum specifically asked him to do. Like avoiding messes, strong smells and refined sugar.

"What would I do without you?" Her dad beamed as Priya rescued the rice from burning while simultaneously wiping down the counter.

"I have absolutely no idea," muttered Priya.

"What's that?" asked her dad.

"Nothing, Dad! Happy to help!"

"Pinkie, can you tidy up your things?" he asked. "So we can lay the table?"

But Pinkie ignored him and carried on painting what looked like a multicoloured explosion.

"Pinkie?"

"I'm doing my homework, Dad."

Their dad turned to Priya apologetically. "Do you mind, Priya?"

Priya sighed and started to tidy up around Pinkie. Her sister was only two years younger than her, but she had ADHD, which meant that she was hyperactive, inattentive, impulsive – and that, according to their parents, nothing was ever her fault. Sometimes, if her parents wanted to blame a human being and not a neurodevelopmental disorder for something that had happened, it became Priya's fault instead. Priya knew that none of this was in Pinkie's control, but it still wasn't easy being her older sister.

"What exactly is that meant to be?" asked Priya.

"It's an abstract portrayal of our family," explained Pinkie. "Me, Mum and Dad are the swirls. You're the square." She pointed to a tiny box in the corner of the painting.

Priya frowned and opened her mouth, then changed her mind. "Whatever. Can you just tidy it away? And you need to finish your chocolate before Mum comes back. Where did you even get it from? I haven't seen chocolate in this house since the Lakhanis brought that box of Ferrero Rocher over in 2019."

"School. If you hit the vending machine hard enough, free Kit Kats fall out."

Priya thought about asking her sister to get her one too,

then remembered that gymnasts who were in the country's top ten for their age group were not allowed to casually eat chocolate bars. Unless they were full of protein powder. "Okay, but hurry up and finish it. Or let me throw it away?"

Pinkie didn't reply – she looked very engrossed in colouring Priya's square blue – so Priya picked up her half-eaten chocolate and threw it into the bin. "Done."

"Oh my god! I can't believe you threw it away!" cried Pinkie. "Give it back!"

"You weren't even eating it!"

"It was *mine*. I want it back!"

"What do you want me to do? Climb into the bin?"

"Yes!"

"Girls, please…" begged their dad. "Just…"

Pinkie clambered across the table towards Priya, who batted her arm away. Suddenly there was a loud crash and they both froze. One of the bottles of paint had fallen off the table, splattering bright red paint all over the wooden floor.

"WHAT is happening?!"

Priya, Pinkie and their dad all turned in slow dread. Mum was standing in the hallway, clutching her shiny leather handbag, staring in horror at the crime scene in front of her. Priya closed her eyes and swallowed, hard.

Two hours later, their parents were still shouting.

"I just wish they'd *stop*." Priya sighed. She was sitting on the sofa in the living room with Pinkie. They were both eating bowls of rice and okra curry in front of the TV. This was technically strictly forbidden – all meals in the Shah household were meant to be eaten at the kitchen table. But if their parents were arguing in the kitchen, this rule was disregarded. Which meant Priya and Pinkie now ate in the living room on a daily basis.

"Uh huh," said Pinkie. She stared intently at the screen, and then howled with laughter as a cartoon rat bowed with a flourish.

Priya rolled her eyes. "You've seen that film a hundred times. Can't we watch something else?"

"*Ratatouille* is a classic."

Priya sighed and spooned more curry into her mouth. She winced at the spiciness and tried to block out the sounds of her parents' fight. But unlike her sister, she couldn't lose herself in watching rats make dinner. Instead, she couldn't help listening to the real-life drama going on in the kitchen.

"You *know* you have to watch them," her mum was saying. "Pinkie needs extra attention! And Priya has to focus on her schoolwork. I can't do everything around here! I'm the one who—"

"Pays for everything," finished her dad flatly. "I know. You remind me of that every single day. But it was your idea that

I go part-time so I can be around more for the girls, and take Priya to her gymnastics, and Pinkie to her appointments. I'm doing what you wanted, but it's never enough, is it?"

"Yes, because I thought you'd actually *help*," cried her mum. "Not make a huge mess every single day – a mess that I have to clean up after spending all day managing those complete morons."

"If you hate your job so much, why don't you go part-time instead?"

"Because I earn more than you ever could!"

Priya closed her eyes. She couldn't bear it. It wasn't her dad's fault that he wasn't as clever as their mum. She didn't understand why Mum had to rub his face in it all the time. But it was also undeniably annoying that Dad always made such a mess – or at least, failed to stop Pinkie from making a mess. She frowned and decided this argument was sixty per cent her mum's fault and forty per cent her dad's. Last night's fight had been 70:30 to her dad. And the night before had been 55:45 to her mum. It turned out that the ratios and percentages Mrs Lufthausen had taught them were actually quite useful for keeping track of which parent was to blame.

But the boring truth was that, on average, they were both equally at fault. Her mum got stressed all the time and criticized her dad way too much. Her dad made endless silly mistakes and wasn't very good at all the things her mum wanted him to do. Priya tried to help him out, but it wasn't enough. And it didn't always go well – tonight's efforts were a case in point. She just wished that both her parents would hurry up in realizing they'd married the wrong person and get a divorce, like Sami's parents had. But they never would. Because they were Indian.

In Priya's opinion, being Indian was not easy. Sure, you got to eat delicious food and celebrate Diwali with fireworks. But you also had to wear uncomfortable outfits whenever a relative got married, make sure your bra straps were *never* showing and – most importantly of all – pretend that absolutely everything was fine when it was the exact opposite of fine. Being Indian was the reason her parents didn't get divorced, the reason they never told anyone they were struggling with money and the reason that Pinkie's ADHD had to be kept secret from everybody in the community.

Worst of all, it was why Priya wasn't allowed to talk to Sami and Mei about anything that was going on at home. Like her parents' constant fights. Her mum relentlessly lectured her that "blood was thicker than water", which apparently meant you could only trust family, and not friends. This made no sense to Priya because she was so much closer to Sami and Mei than the dozens of Masis and Masas she only ever saw once a year. But her mum was adamant: any family secrets had to stay within the family. Except she didn't seem to ever want their relatives to know either. Not the cousins, because they would gossip. And it was best if Priya didn't tell Pinkie either, because she was only ten and it wasn't fair to stress her out. Which meant there was nobody else Priya was allowed to speak to. Not since August 13th last year.

"Girls?" Her mum walked into the living room, looking apologetic. "You really shouldn't eat in front of the TV."

Priya decided not to point out the obvious. "Sorry."

"You...didn't hear any of that, did you?"

Priya shook her head. She turned to Pinkie who was watching the movie, oblivious. "We didn't hear a thing."

Her mum's face relaxed in relief. "Okay. Good. And...um, how was your day, *beta*? Did gymnastics go well? And school?"

Priya thought about every single thing that had gone wrong that day. She felt the lump come back in her throat and the tiniest of tears prick her eyelids. She swallowed it all away, shook her head and forced herself to smile. There was no point upsetting her mum when she was already so tired. "Everything was great, thanks, Mum. I had a...great day."

Her mum smiled at her. "Of course, you did. You always do. I'm so lucky to have you, Priya. I don't know what I'd do without you."

After dinner, Priya sat at her computer finishing her homework. She was so glad the day was almost over. All she had to do was add one last paragraph to her history essay and she could finally go to bed. As long as her parents didn't start arguing again. She yawned as she typed out her conclusion to: *Which of Henry VIII's wives was the most sympathetic?* She'd spent ages proving it was Catherine of Aragon and she was quite proud of it. She felt sorry for the first queen – she'd just been living her life and trying to do everything as best as she could when suddenly Henry had brought Anne Boleyn into their lives, overcomplicating everything. Priya wasn't sure who the Anne Boleyn in her life was – her parents' money problems? The Olympics? – but somehow, she still felt she could relate to the Spanish queen.

Suddenly, the screen went blank and the lights went out. Priya clicked the keypad in confusion, but nothing happened. Her laptop was so old that it needed to be plugged in all the time, and if the power went off, it switched off too. She got up and tried to turn the light on, but blackness remained.

"Hello? What's happened?!" She opened her bedroom door and saw the whole house had fallen into darkness.

"Your sister thought it would be a good idea to turn all the kitchen appliances on at the same time," called out her dad. "A fuse tripped. But don't worry! I'll have it all fixed in a second!"

"I was *experimenting*," clarified Pinkie. "It was our physics homework."

"I think I'll need to have a word with Mr Jarvis." Her dad sighed. "Your homework is not conducive to me watching the Champions League."

"Dad! Are you saying my education is less important than football?"

Priya drowned out their voices and sat in silence, waiting for the electricity to come back on. When the lights flashed, she restarted her laptop. She opened up the file with her history essay on it, desperately wishing that this wouldn't be yet another thing she had to add to the list of things that had gone horribly wrong that day. But as the file opened, Priya's remaining hope died. The file was empty. There was nothing in there at all. Her entire essay was gone.

Chapter 3

Priya lay in bed doing the one thing she'd spent all day resolutely trying not to do: crying. With the duvet over her head, and a pillow muffling the sound, she finally sobbed. She was just so tired. Everything kept going wrong and she didn't know how to fix it. It wasn't just her essay, or missing Sami's bat mitzvah, or Pinkie being Pinkie, or even her parents arguing. It was *all* of it. Everything was so hard and it had been ever since... Priya tried not to let herself think about August 13th but then she gave up. She was already crying. She may as well cry about the one thing she really wanted to cry about.

Ba.

She'd been the one person Priya could talk to. The best grandma in the world. Priya had loved her so much. But then she'd died. And now she was gone. For ever. Priya cried as loud as she could into her pillow and felt the lump in her throat finally dissolve. It was so hard pretending everything was fine all the time when on the inside, she was the saddest she'd ever been. But there was no other choice. If her parents knew how sad she still was, they'd worry more – and the more they worried, the more they argued.

They hadn't always been that bad. Of course, they'd never actually had anything in *common.* Her dad was the world's most easy-going man and her mum was a total perfectionist. But in the past her mum had managed to laugh off her dad's mistakes. And he hadn't been so defensive back then; he'd been more understanding and considerate. But when Ba had died, it felt like her parents had decided to channel their grief into arguing. While Pinkie had channelled hers into being more annoying than usual. And Priya had channelled hers into...well, nothing. She'd just swallowed it. Which was why she now had a semi-permanent lump in her throat. None of it was ideal, but neither was Ba's death.

Priya wished her parents would at least speak about Ba, but every time she tried, they just changed the topic. So Priya had stopped trying. She knew it was probably their way of processing their grief, but it made her feel lonely. Her grief didn't want to be silent. She wanted to reminisce about Ba, and laugh over Ba's best jokes, and dance to Whitney Houston (Ba's favourite singer) in her honour. She'd hoped that they might even be able to have a memorial service for Ba this

August for the first anniversary of her death, but when she'd asked her mum, she'd snapped at Priya and told her she was busy with work. So Priya had asked at another more opportune time, when her mum had been scrolling through social media. But this time, her mum had shut down the conversation, saying they didn't need a big hoo-ha to remember Ba. Priya hadn't asked again.

If only her grandma was there now to give her some advice. Like when she'd messed up her beam routine in the Junior Nationals two years ago, and Ba had told her she deserved a gold. Priya had been confused – how could she, when she'd messed up her split jump and fallen right off the beam? But Ba had pointed out that the others hadn't had to pick themselves up and get right back onto that beam. In her opinion, it was Priya who deserved a gold medal for her bravery.

Or when Priya had heard her parents arguing about money for the first time. Back then, she'd naively worried they'd get a divorce. When she'd told Ba, she'd clapped her hands together in excitement. "A divorce! Wouldn't that be wonderful? They'd both be free to live their own lives without arguments!" Priya hadn't really understood what she meant at the time, but now it made total sense. That was the thing about Ba – she was so wise that her advice lasted all the way into the future.

Priya squeezed her eyes shut and tried to imagine what Ba would say right now. "There's no point crying over things you can't change. What would Henry VIII do? Get a new wife? Exactly! So go get a new essay!"

Priya sighed. Ba definitely would have said something better than that. But even trying to think of what she'd say was better than nothing. So, Priya kept going.

"The gymnastics competition is on the same day as the bat mitzvah? So go to both!" If only. Priya had been to enough gymnastics competitions to know that they took up the entire day with all their events and the most important ones – the individuals – were always in the afternoon. Right when Sami's party began. "Okay, well, pick the one you want to go to the most!" But it wasn't that simple. Priya *had* to go to the Nationals. The Olympics scout would be there! It was what she'd been working for since she was six, and everyone would be so disappointed if she didn't go. Not to mention how stressed her parents would be if she didn't win the prize money; with bills getting higher, they were planning on using it to pay for her training. She didn't *have* a choice – she refused to contribute to any problems that would lead to more arguments for her parents.

"Oh, your parents arguing isn't a bad thing!" Ba would say. "It might help them finally get that divorce!" But Priya now knew that her younger self had been wrong in thinking her parents might ever divorce. That was never going to happen because her parents' worst nightmare was not being stuck in an unhappy marriage – it was people *finding out* they had an unhappy marriage. It all came back to their number one rule: Don't Air Your Dirty Laundry In Public.

What would Ba say to that?

Priya tried desperately to imagine her response, but no matter how hard she tried, she couldn't conjure her up again. It was too difficult. Her face crumpled with the effort, and in the end, she gave up and let herself relive the last time she'd spoken to Ba instead.

It had been in hospital. Priya's mum was sobbing in the hallway with her siblings. Nobody was paying attention to an eleven-year-old Priya, so she slipped through the open door alone and found her grandma lying on the white bed. She looked tiny and scarily fragile. For the first time in Priya's life, she realized that her grandma was actually old. Priya stood, frozen in the doorway, until Ba looked up and winked. Priya sighed in relief. Ba was still Ba.

"Come on in! I'm not dead yet!"

Priya gave her a watery smile. "I really, *really* don't want you to die, Ba."

"And I don't want lumpy custard with my pudding, but it looks like that's what I'm getting." Ba scrunched up her face at the pudding on her tray.

"I don't know what I'll do without you," Priya whispered. "Please don't go."

"Even if I have it on good authority that the custard in heaven is completely lump-free?"

Priya laughed despite herself. "You're not meant to make jokes about death."

"Are you quoting your mum again? I'll never know how my daughter managed to come into this world without a sense of humour. Thank goodness you have one." Ba reached out for Priya's hand. "I know it's not going to be easy, *beta*. I'll hang on for as long as I can. But…that custard is calling me."

"Ba!"

"Sorry, sorry. But you'll be okay, Priya. You always are."

Priya paused and then spoke very quietly. "I'm not though. I just pretend I am."

"I know, my darling, but you don't have to pretend. It's okay to cry and be sad and get things wrong! It's all part of life. That *is* being okay. It's okay to not be okay."

Priya looked doubtful. "I just know I'm going to miss you so much I can't even breathe when I think about it."

Ba squeezed her hand. "Me too. But I promise you I will be up there looking down at you every single day."

Priya raised an eyebrow. "I'm not sure I feel comfortable about you looking down at me while I'm on the loo."

"I'll avert my eyes a few times a day but otherwise, I'll be there."

Priya laughed as she wiped her tears away. "Promise?"

"Promise."

"I just don't know who I'll be able to speak to without you," said Priya quietly. "You're the only person I can be honest with."

"You can still tell me everything. You just might not be able to hear my replies in the same way."

"But I need you. How will I get through life without you?"

"You'll be just fine, *beta*," said Ba. "But I do have something that might help when it all feels a bit too much..." She coughed loudly, causing Priya's face to wrinkle up in concern, then slipped her hand under the bedsheet. When she brought it back out, she was holding a small gold bangle. It was made of pure gold, a simple round band that was studded with large gleaming rubies and tiny diamonds dotted between them.

Priya gasped in recognition. "Your bangle!" She'd admired it every single time she went over to visit her grandma. It was so shiny she couldn't help being drawn to it. But the clasp was broken, so Ba never wore it, and neither could Priya. The bangle was stuck shut, and no matter how much Priya tried, her hands were just too wide for the bangle to slide over them.

"It's for you," said Ba. "It'll help you when you need me the most."

"Help me remember you?" asked Priya in confusion. "I'll never forget you – *never*!"

"I know, *beta*," said Ba. "But the bangle will help you when you feel lonely. You see, loneliness comes when we can't be honest with people."

"Okay," said Priya, frowning. "But what does that have to do with the bangle?"

"The truth," began Ba, but then she started coughing again. "The truth is the—" Her coughing increased so much she couldn't finish her sentence.

Priya reached out to touch her arm. It felt thinner than usual. "Ba? Are you okay?"

Just then the door opened. It was Priya's mum.

"Priya!" she cried. "You need to let Ba rest. Come on out."

"But we were just talking."

"You can talk to her later, go on."

Priya rushed to give Ba a big hug. "I love you, Ba. Always."

"I love you too, Priya. And remember...the bangle."

Priya had never spoken to her grandma again. She'd died an hour later. All she had left of her was a shiny gold bangle with a broken clasp that made her cry every time she looked at it. *The bangle.* Priya suddenly needed to feel its cool metal on her hands. She pushed the duvet off and rushed straight over to the Box of Important Things on her dresser. She took the lid off the shoebox (covered in glittery wrapping paper) and there, underneath a photo of her, Mei and Sami, next to her collection of gold medals, was Ba's bangle. Priya clutched it tight to her chest. It was still so beautiful. She'd never seen a bangle like it – on first look it wasn't so different to some of her mum's bangles, gold and decorated with precious stones, but when Ba's bangle caught the light, the whole thing *glowed*. It was designed so that there were hidden hinges in between the stones so that the bangle could open up right in the middle. But they were stuck shut. Every time Priya had flicked open the simple clasp on the other side and then tried to gently ease open the hinge, it refused to move. If only she'd had smaller hands, it would have just slid onto her wrist. But she didn't, and neither did Ba.

Priya remembered once asking Ba why she didn't get it fixed. Ba had smiled mysteriously at her. "If the bangle wanted me to wear it, it would let me." At the time, little Priya had decided this meant the bangle was magic and had made up countless stories about its powers as she'd run around the house, making dens out of Ba's sarees. Ba had encouraged her, inventing a story all about how the bangle had once belonged to the most intelligent princess in India. Priya still remembered the whole tale.

The princess was so smart that she'd discovered the secret of magic and alchemy, and she was well aware of the danger of her knowledge getting into the wrong hands. When the conquerors came, she knew they'd come straight for her magic. So she hid it all inside her jewellery, transforming the powers into gold, and then gave the precious trinkets away to her most trusted servants. The princess was smart enough to know that conquerors always underestimated people they saw as beneath them. Which was why her jewellery survived for centuries, in the hands of her servants and their families, being passed down from generation to generation. According to Ba, their family was directly descended from the princess's most trusted maid.

Little Priya had lapped all of this up. She adored the story of the smart princess and the magic bangle. But now she was twelve, she knew it was all childish nonsense that Ba had created to entertain her. The bangle wasn't magic. If it was, it would have saved Ba. Or at the very least, opened its clasp so that Priya could put it on. Priya tried once more just to prove to herself that she was right. Nothing happened. The hinge stayed obstinately shut. As always. Priya felt a tiny flicker of hope die out inside her. She didn't know what she'd been thinking – that the bangle would suddenly open and Ba would appear out of nowhere? She was being ridiculous.

Priya felt the shreds of her optimism dissolve, replaced by a desperate urge to cry again. She pulled the duvet back over her head, and let her quiet tears wash over the bangle. She was so tired of pretending everything was okay all the time. But she had to. Ba was wrong when she'd told Priya that it was okay to not be okay. When the most popular girl in school had suddenly decided to stop ignoring Priya a few months ago, and instead, forced her to do her homework, Priya had tried to tell her parents. But she'd only got as far as admitting she'd had a bad day when her parents completely freaked out.

Her mum's face had tightened in panicked anxiety – her biggest worry had been that Priya had failed an exam. While her dad had asked her five times in a row what had happened, his voice rising each time, not even giving Priya time to reply. It had been so obvious that neither of them could handle anything going wrong in her life that Priya knew she couldn't tell them the truth. They'd probably just end up arguing about it anyway, and if they told the school, it would make things so much worse. Telling on Katie Wong was *not* an option. So instead, Priya had just rolled her eyes and told her parents to relax: it was only a bad day because she'd forgotten her gym kit! They'd both looked so relieved by the lie that she'd decided to never bother trying to tell them the truth again.

Priya cried louder at the memory. She was so tired of everything being so hard. Just then, she heard a small click. She lowered the duvet and dried her face quickly. Was that Pinkie at the door? She called out "hello?" but it was met with silence. Priya looked back down at the bangle. It was damp with her tears. She carefully dried it on her UK GYMNAST T-shirt and then gasped aloud. The bangle was bent in two halves! Had she broken it?! She held it up to the light and this time she froze in total shock. It wasn't broken. The hinge had opened.

Without thinking, Priya immediately slipped the bangle onto her right wrist. She used her left hand to close the clasp and there was another click as it locked into place. She inhaled sharply. She couldn't believe it. She had absolutely no idea how this had happened – perhaps her tears had loosened the clasp? – but she didn't care. Because finally, after months of feeling alone, she knew that Ba was with her. Okay, she couldn't see her. Or hear her. And nothing had actually changed since she'd put the bangle on, but that was irrelevant. Because after thousands of failed attempts, Priya was *wearing the bangle*. Maybe things were finally starting to get better.

Chapter 4

Priya yawned as she trudged down the stairs into the kitchen. For once, she'd had a good night's sleep and she felt better than she had in weeks. She hoped her mum would be downstairs – when it was her turn to do mornings, the girls had cereal for breakfast. Coco Pops for Pinkie and Weetabix for Priya. Not exactly the dream breakfast, but *so* much better than when it was her dad's turn and he tried to make them something from scratch. Which meant they had to pretend to eat burnt scrambled eggs or undercooked pancakes – then eat cereal anyway. And leave the house twenty minutes late.

"Morning, Priya! We're having eggs!" Her dad beamed at her from the other side of the kitchen. "Poached or scrambled?"

Priya tried to think of what was harder to ruin. "Uh... poached? Actually—"

"Poached it is!" cried her dad. "Toast is in the toaster.

Or should I say, 'bread' is in the toaster. Because technically it hasn't become toast yet, has it?"

"Right... Where's Pinkie?"

Her dad turned to face her with a guilty expression. "I suppose she's still resting."

"Dad! We need to leave in ten minutes!"

He ran a hand through his bushy greying hair. "I know, Priya. She just...refused to get up. You don't mind waking her for me, do you?"

"Yes, I do mind!" Priya's hand flew to her mouth. She hadn't meant to say that aloud. She was probably still half-asleep. "Uh, sorry. I'll go wake her up."

She ignored her dad's confused expression and trudged back up the stairs to her sister's room. She didn't even look at the lump that was Pinkie, curled up in the middle of the bed. Instead, she went straight over to the windows, opening the curtains wide so bright light streamed into the room. Pinkie muttered protestations, rolling over to face away from the window. In response, Priya yanked the duvet off her body.

Pinkie shrieked, sitting up in alarm. Her short hair was stuck up in tufts, making her look like an annoyingly cute alien. "What are you doing?!"

"We have to leave the house in...precisely nine minutes. Dad has eggs on," said Priya, looking in disdain at the explosion that was her sister's room. The walls were bright blue, the bed was lime green and there were multicoloured beanbags in the corner. Not to mention the piles of clothes and books overflowing on every beanbag. There were even clothes draped over the gorgeous wooden chest that Ba had left Pinkie when she died – an ornately carved antique that Pinkie used for hiding her private "treasures". Priya frowned as she removed the clothes from on top of the chest. Pinkie's room couldn't have been more different to the white walls, white duvet (though it did have a border of sunflowers around the edge) and organized bookshelves of Priya's bedroom.

Pinkie sighed loudly and reluctantly stood up, revealing a nightie covered in Yoda's face. "Why does he bother with eggs? We're not going to eat them anyway."

"Because he wants to show us he loves us," said Priya without thinking. She shook her head. That was weird. She never said things like that to her sister – she normally just brushed off her questions with an "I don't know". Where had *that* come from?

But Pinkie just cocked her head as she pulled her school trousers on underneath Yoda. "Huh. I guess that makes his eggs slightly more tolerable."

"Anyway," said Priya, trying not to think about how strange she was being this morning. "Can you just hurry up, please? I need to get to gymnastics."

"Why are you so desperate to get to gymnastics anyway?" asked Pinkie, who was somehow already fully dressed in her uniform. Priya gave her a look of reluctant admiration. "You go every day."

"Because I get to see Dan Zhang," said Priya. She yelped and her hand flew to her mouth. She couldn't believe she'd just said that out loud! What was wrong with her?!

Her younger sister looked at her curiously. "Who's Dan?"

"He's on my team," said Priya quickly, hoping she wouldn't say anything weird. "He's really cute." Oh no. She ran out of the door before she overshared again and raced down the stairs. Priya paused in the hallway in front of the wide mirror. She stared at her reflection – sensible shoulder-length brown hair, matching brown eyes and a look of total panic etched on her face. This was like being in a waking nightmare – *why* did she keep saying the opposite of what she wanted to say? She shook her head and gave her reflection a stern look.

"Priya Shah," she told herself internally, "stop blurting out your every thought. Just...do what you normally do and shut up! Or you are going to RUIN EVERYTHING. Okay? Just... stop it!"

She gave her reflection one final warning look, and then walked into the kitchen.

"Eggs are ready!" called her dad cheerfully as Priya sat down at the table. "Here you go, mademoiselle – eggs à la Monsieur Shah!"

Priya warily examined the watery eggs seeping onto charred toast, wishing she was upstairs brushing her teeth with Pinkie. How did her sister always manage to miss her dad's worst meals? "Uh...thanks?"

"I used vinegar to make sure I got a rounder egg," her dad said proudly, watching her gingerly cut into it. "Isn't it round?"

"Yes," agreed Priya. It was undeniably round, but it was also the wrong consistency and, as she realized the second her fork touched her tongue, so vinegary that it was impossible to eat. She swallowed it anyway, trying not to gag.

"Do you like it?" asked her dad hopefully.

Priya smiled, ready to lie to her dad like she did every single time he tried and failed to cook her an edible meal. She opened her mouth to say yes.

"No."

She gasped aloud. She'd done it again! Why had she said no?! She didn't want to hurt her dad's feelings! She squeezed her eyes shut so she didn't have to see the sadness on his face. "I'm sorry. I meant it's just a little...uh, undercooked."

"Oh." Her dad sounded disappointed. "I'll, uh, put the eggs back in for a minute then! Yes, that's it. They'll taste all right then, don't you think?"

"No," said Priya miserably, opening her eyes despite herself. Her dad's back was turned towards her as he put the eggs back into the pan, and she was glad. Because she knew she really didn't want to see his face when she finished her sentence. She tried to muster up all her strength to stop the words from coming out. She swallowed them back, but she could feel them getting stronger. She tried one last time to keep her mouth clamped shut, but it didn't work. Her lips parted, and the words she really didn't want to say shot straight out of her, right into her father's unsuspecting back. "They'll still be disgusting."

For the first time in her life, Priya was early for school. Because today, she'd skipped gymnastics. By the time her dad had thrown the eggs away, given the girls cereal and got them all into the car, Priya had already missed most of practice. Normally, she would have insisted on going anyway – Olaf wanted her to squeeze in as much training as she could before the big competition. But this time, Priya told her dad there wasn't any point; he should just take her straight to school. Because it was one thing to tell her dad what she thought about his eggs, but another thing entirely to tell Dan Zhang what she thought of *him*.

After this weird morning, Priya couldn't trust herself to be around him. She was becoming a liability. There was a very strong chance that if she saw Dan Zhang, she wouldn't just smile at him from afar like usual – she'd actually *speak to him*. And, judging from how her conversations had been with her dad and Pinkie, it would *not* go well. Right now, the only things Dan knew about Priya were that she 1) was the longest-standing member of the team and had won more gold medals than anyone else, 2) often came to practice late, 3) was very good at backflips and 4) was the top contender for the Teen Olympics team. It was exactly what the rest of the team knew, and Priya had no intention of that changing anytime soon. It was just too risky. If Dan knew anything more about her, he'd realize how uncool she was, not to mention how much of a mess her life was, which would ruin any tiny chance Priya had of him ever asking her out. She knew it didn't exactly make rational sense – how could he ask her out when she never hung out with the team after practice and competitions? But it was safer this way. Besides, she didn't have time to go to all the socials like Dan – she was always too busy trying to finish her schoolwork, fix her family, and if she had any time left over, hang out with Sami and Mei.

So instead of rushing to school from gymnastics, Priya was now early for school, and was sitting in the classroom, googling "illness where you say what you're thinking" and "why do I keep telling the truth?" She'd skipped past a bunch of self-help articles signalling the benefits of honesty – they were total rubbish; as if hurting everyone's feelings and humiliating herself could ever be a good thing! – and she was now panicking that she had some kind of psychological condition. It was terrifying to think this wasn't just a weird blip and could actually be the new her. She dreaded to think what she'd end up doing next – would she tell Mrs Lufthausen she thought her teaching style lacked personality? Would she tell Katie what she really thought of having to do her maths homework every week? Or – worst of all – would she accidentally hurt Sami and Mei's feelings?

Priya was halfway through an online questionnaire to find out whether she had a compulsive mental disorder that made her say exactly what was on her mind when Sami and Mei walked in, munching on pains au chocolat. She felt a pang of FOMO; going to the bakery round the corner before school was Sami and Mei's morning tradition. Priya always had a standing invite to join them – even though they'd both been best friends since primary school, and had only met Priya in Year Seven, they never made her feel like she wasn't an equal member of their trio – but she never got to join in because she was always at gymnastics. Or finishing her homework. Or, as of today, googling truth-telling illnesses.

"Pri to the ya," cried Sami, swinging her schoolbag onto the desk in front of her and shoving the remainder of her pastry into her mouth, as crumbs sprayed everywhere. "What are you doing here so early?!"

"Trying to work out if I'm losing my mind," said Priya, without thinking. She shook her head in shock. "Uh, I mean..."

"Welcome to my life," said Mei, sliding into the seat next to her. "This morning, I started brushing my hair with my toothbrush. It took me a solid twenty seconds to work out why it wasn't getting the knots out." She held out a thick strand of black hair, clumped together. "Didn't help that I'd already put toothpaste on it."

Priya laughed, already feeling her anxiety start to ease. Maybe she wasn't going crazy – or maybe she was, but they all were. Solidarity in madness was something she felt she might be able to handle.

Sami recoiled. "Ew! Why didn't you wash it out afterwards?"

"Global warming. I only wash my hair on Tuesdays. And today is...a Wednesday."

"Gross," said Sami, shuddering dramatically before turning to face Priya. "So, what weird things are *you* doing, Pri? Let me guess... Did you try to brush your teeth with a tampon?"

Priya laughed. "Ew, no! I don't even have my period yet." Her face flushed red and she stared down at the desk feeling sick. This couldn't be happening. No. Please, no. But it was too late. The words had already barged their way right out of her mouth.

"But...I thought you got your period last year?" asked Sami in confusion. "Just after me and Mei did?"

Priya covered her mouth with her hand, hoping it would stop the words from coming out. But they barged straight past her fingers. "I lied."

"Oh, Pri," said Mei softly.

Priya felt her stomach clench in shame. She couldn't bear this. Any of it. She grabbed her bag quickly, refusing to look at either of her friends, and raced out of the classroom.

"Wait, where are you going?" called out Sami. "Priya, it's okay!"

But Priya didn't stop. She was mortified. Hot, angry tears ran down her face as she raced down the hallway. She crashed into something solid and looked up. Mrs Lufthausen.

"Priya Shah, why on earth are you running in the corridor? Where are you going?"

"To cry in the toilet," Priya replied between sobs. She hiccoughed, startled. As if she'd just said that to a teacher! She flushed, brushing her tears away, and darted straight past a speechless Mrs Lufthausen. She didn't stop until she'd reached the safety of the last cubicle on the right of the first-floor girls' bathrooms.

Finally. She was safe.

Priya sniffed sadly, hugging her knees into her chest. She didn't know what was happening. Why did she keep answering everyone so honestly? Why couldn't she just keep her mouth shut and pretend everything was fine in the exact same way she'd been doing for the last twelve years? Why was everything going so wrong?! She held her arms tighter around her, shifting uncomfortably on the toilet lid. Then she winced as something dug into her wrist. She frowned as she pulled up her shirt sleeve, then gasped loudly.

The bangle. She was still wearing Ba's bangle.

She flicked open the clasp and tried to take it off, but it was stuck. She tried again, but it wouldn't budge. The bangle was stuck shut again – only this time it was on her wrist.

Priya's mind started racing. She'd fallen asleep with the bangle on. And this morning, everything had started going wrong. She'd upset her dad, told Pinkie about Dan and revealed one of her most embarrassing secrets to her best friends. She'd told everybody the truth – even when she *really* hadn't wanted to.

And it had been happening ever since she'd put on the bangle.

Priya stared at its gleaming gold in horror. What if the stories Ba had told her hadn't just been made-up magic, but had been *real*?! Could this bangle really have powers? Priya's heart pounded as her memory flashed back to her conversation with Ba in the hospital. She'd given Priya the bangle just after Priya had said that Ba was the only person she could be honest with. And – hadn't Ba been saying something about "the truth" when Priya's mum had walked in? Priya had assumed that Ba wanted to explain the truth about the bangle, but what if it was more literal than that. What if the bangle forced its wearer to reveal the truth?

Oh no. Priya shook her head in panic at the bangle, stuck on her wrist. Was this her grandma's idea of *helping her*? To give her a magic bangle that had put some kind of curse, or spell, or *who knows what* on her? And now she couldn't get it off! She'd be trapped telling everyone the truth for the rest of her life. She'd ruin everything! Olaf would find out how much she hated training right now and would kick her off the team. Her parents would find out how unhappy she was and spend the rest of their lives worrying. Not to mention how much worse their arguments about finance would get when she wasn't winning prize money... Sami and Mei would find out how much she'd hidden from them over the years and stop speaking to her. And Dan would find out how much she— No, she couldn't bear to think about it.

"Priya?" There was a knock on the cubicle door and Priya jerked in fear. Mei. She'd found her. "Okay, I know you're in there. I can see your bag on the floor. It has your name on it."

Priya sighed. She'd forgotten this was yet another item Pinkie had decorated with her marker pens. She really needed to throw those pens away.

"It doesn't matter, you know," said Mei gently. "Whether you have your period or not. Whether you lied about it or not. It's not a big deal. Honestly."

Priya felt her cheeks flush hot. Whoever thought that brown people didn't blush would take it back if they could see her right now. It was just so *embarrassing* that she'd lied to her friends. But not getting her period had been yet another thing that had separated her from them. As if it wasn't enough missing out on every single fun thing that ever happened because of gymnastics, she'd found herself missing out on actual womanhood too. Her body was so exhausted from high-intensity training that it couldn't be bothered to start puberty. Or something like that – she hadn't fully understood the science when the doctor had explained it to her.

"Loads of people haven't got their periods yet," continued Mei. "If anything, you're lucky! It sucks having to deal with blood in your underwear every month. Not to mention the mood swings. And the spots."

Priya stayed silent. She knew Mei had a point, but it didn't matter. She wanted to be able to complain about that stuff too.

"Besides, we all have things we're embarrassed about," carried on Mei, unrelenting. "Like...how I don't even need a training bra, but Sami already buys her bras from the adult section."

"So do Katie and Angela," said Priya softly. "I saw them in M&S when I was with my mum in the kids' section. Not even the teen one."

Mei laughed. "I know that section well. If you come out, I'll show you the knickers I'm wearing. They *may* have the word *Wednesday* written on them."

Priya hesitated and then reached forward to slide open the toilet door. "I'm wearing Thursday's," she said with a small smile. "I couldn't find Wednesday's."

Mei reached for Priya's hand and pulled her onto her feet. "You know we love you regardless of whether your womb lining is shedding or not, right?"

Priya laughed, wiping away a leftover tear. "Thanks, Mei. I'm sorry."

"It's okay. But...why didn't you just tell us the truth?"

Priya opened her mouth, resigned to the fact that this time, she was going to have to tell the truth whether she wanted to or not. "I was tired of feeling left out," she said softly, feeling her shoulders relax. She looked nervously at Mei to see how she'd react.

But Mei just hugged her tight. "Hey, we're your best friends. You can never be left out with us. Even if you wanted to be. Sami wouldn't let you – she'd literally turn up at your house with a foghorn. And she'd make me come too."

"That's a very good point." Priya grinned, still feeling the warmth of Mei's hug as they broke apart. "Where is she, anyway?"

"Trying to convince Mrs Lufthausen that running and crying in a corridor is not a legitimate reason to get a detention, because expressing your emotions is a healthy sign of pubescence."

Priya laughed as she followed Mei out of the bathroom. Everything was still a total disaster – who knew what the bangle would make her say next, or if it even *was* the bangle that was responsible? – but she felt marginally better. Because she had her best friends by her side.

Chapter 5

Four and a half hours later, Priya was back in the far-right toilet cubicle of the first-floor girls' bathrooms. This time she wasn't crying, which was a solid improvement on the last time she'd found herself there, but she was still hiding from the entire school. She'd somehow managed to get through the morning without any major disasters, though it hadn't exactly been plain sailing. She'd told Mr Long she didn't have a Henry VIII essay to hand in because her little sister had cut the power in her attempts to test voltage on kitchen appliances, but he hadn't believed her. It was ironic, really – Priya had been going to tell him a very boring lie that he unquestionably would have believed, but the truth was too far-fetched for him. He'd even given her extra work to do as punishment.

Priya had also found herself admitting to Sami she didn't

think her new hat suited her, telling head dinner lady Mrs Pringle just how gross the shepherd's pie looked, *and* letting Sarah P know that her new perfume did not smell great. Results? Sami had launched into a twelve-minute monologue on how Priya was brainwashed by societal beauty standards, Mrs Pringle had dumped a wrinkly sandwich onto her tray that was definitely left over from yesterday, and Sarah P had revenge-spritzed her perfume all over Priya's bag. But Priya could handle all of this.

What she couldn't handle was the fear of what she'd say next. Which was why she'd grabbed her salmonella sandwich and raced straight to the bathroom before Sami or Mei could ask her what was up. She already felt better in the safety of the tiny cubicle. There was nobody to offend, and nobody to watch her trying to get the bangle off her wrist. She fiddled with the clasp, trying as hard as she could to prise it open. But it refused to budge. Just then she heard the door open as... one? Three? No, two girls walked in. Priya could hear their footsteps, and by the sound of their stomping, they were the kind of girls who ignored the school uniform code and wore Doc Martens. Which meant they were not the kind of girls Priya wanted to discover her eating lunch alone in the toilet.

"I am so bored of life," said girl one with a sigh. "Can't I just be sixteen already so I can go out and be an adult?"

"Don't you have to be eighteen?" asked girl two. "To, like, drink alcohol and do adult stuff?"

"Yeah, if you want to wait to do it *legally*," said girl one. "And I have zero intention of doing that."

Priya's stomach sank. Katie Wong and Angela Sutton. They were the most popular girls in the year and completely ignored anyone who wasn't as cool as them – which meant that Priya, Sami and Mei were officially invisible to them. Or at least they had been, until a few months ago, when that had changed for Priya.

It all started when she got the highest marks in the class on their maths exam. Katie had come up to her afterwards, deliberately waiting for a moment when Sami and Mei weren't there, and had told Priya to do her maths homework for her. Only she hadn't said it like that. She'd made it sound like Priya would be doing her a huge favour, and it was just a one-off. So Priya had done it. But then Katie had expected her to do it every week. And whenever Priya had hesitated to say yes, Katie had smiled sweetly and told her that if she didn't do it, she'd tell the teachers and get her in major trouble.

Priya had been doing Katie's maths homework ever since. The whole thing made her feel so stupid. She wished she was brave enough to stand up to Katie and tell her no, once and for all. But she couldn't. Instead, she just found herself meekly nodding whenever Katie asked her to do something, pretending she didn't mind. It was why she'd kept it all from Sami and Mei. She hated having to keep yet another secret from her best friends, but it was just too embarrassing to admit that she wasn't courageous enough to stand up for herself. It was probably why Katie had chosen her to do her homework in the first place; Sami and Mei got good marks in maths too, but unlike Priya, they were strong enough to say no. Katie had probably sniffed out Priya's weakness, like a DM-wearing hyena. It made Priya feel so bad about herself that she couldn't bear to think about it.

She quickly lifted her feet up onto the toilet seat so that Katie and Angela wouldn't spot them from underneath the door and went back to silently trying to unlock her bangle. She needed to get it off urgently. Imagine having to face someone like Katie whilst wearing it! She struggled silently with the clasp. She didn't understand why it wouldn't come off, when it had opened just the night before. She yanked at it vigorously in frustration and then watched with horror as her sandwich fell off her lap and skidded across the floor, ending up *outside* her cubicle.

"Oh my god, gross," said Katie. "Is someone trying to eat their lunch in this bacteria hellhole?"

Priya prayed the cursed bangle would recognize this as the rhetorical question it obviously was. But no such luck. "Yes," she found herself saying. She squeezed her eyes shut – oh no. This was not going to go well.

"Who is that?" demanded Angela. "And do you want your sandwich back? Because it's fallen in a puddle of...I'm not sure what."

Priya kept her eyes closed tight and tried to imagine she was about to do a triple jump. She felt her breath steady. If she just pretended she was on the mat, then she'd be fine. She could do this. Slowly, she opened her eyes and unlocked the cubicle door. It was better to just get it over and done with. Maybe it wouldn't be as bad as she was imagining.

"Hi," she said awkwardly, coming face to face with the insanely beautiful Katie and her slightly less beautiful but equally terrifying sidekick. She reached down to gingerly pick the sandwich up, dropping it into the bin. "And no, I don't want that sandwich back."

Katie wrinkled her flawless brow and flicked her long, dark hair over her shoulder. "Weird. Why were you eating your lunch in the loo?"

"I was hiding." Priya winced at her words. She sounded like a total loser. Maybe the truth curse would let her say something else that was both true and less insane? Like... "I was avoiding people," she blurted out. Or maybe she should have just stayed silent.

"Avoiding your little buddies?" asked Katie, looking mildly curious. Her perfectly made-up face lit up. "Oh my god, I lurrrve drama. Have you had a big fight?"

"No," said Priya. A wave of relief washed over her as she realized she'd only said the one syllable. Perfect. But she needed to get out of there before they asked her anything else. Especially something she wouldn't be able to answer with a yes or no. She hurried towards the door, but Angela blocked her with her strong lacrosse-playing shoulders. She scowled from beneath her mass of blonde curls.

"So, why are you hiding from them?"

Priya sighed miserably. Was it just her, or were people asking her very specific questions today? "Because I'm scared I'll say something that will hurt them," she said quickly. She exhaled slowly. That could have been worse. "Anyway. I have to go. I need...a new sandwich."

"Wait!" called out Katie. "You're acting...odd. Something's up. And I'm going to find out what it is."

Priya let out a silent prayer of gratitude. It was a miracle that Katie hadn't phrased any of that as a question.

"I don't like drama going on that I don't know about," continued Katie. "But I *do* like finding out people's secrets." She smiled pleasantly at Priya. "Oh, and I'm going to need my maths homework a day early this week. That's not a problem, is it?"

Priya tried to shake her head, but she found herself nodding. She bit her bottom lip as her eyes widened in fear.

"Excuse me?" asked Katie, her dark eyes narrowing. "Do you have a *problem* with doing my homework?"

"Yes," mumbled Priya wretchedly, feeling her palms go clammy with sweat. "I do."

"And what exactly is that problem?" demanded Katie.

"It's not fair," whispered Priya as quietly as she could,

hoping that Katie wouldn't be able to hear her.

"Riiiiight," said Katie slowly. "Well, what's also not fair is that the whole school is going to find out you eat your lunch in a toilet like a total weirdo. And that you've been copying *my* maths homework for the last few months. Mrs Lufthausen really isn't going to like that."

Priya stared at the ground helplessly.

"Unless doing my maths homework stops being a problem for you," said Katie, her voice dripping with faux honey. "Oh, and I also need a history essay. On Henry VIII's wives. One of them, anyway. Your choice. If I get that before the weekend, maybe I'll keep my mouth shut."

Priya nodded. "I'll do it. It's f—" She tried to say the word "fine" but it wouldn't leave her mouth. "It's not fine, but I'll do it." She barged past Angela before she could say anything worse and dashed straight out of the bathroom.

Priya couldn't believe she'd managed to get through the entire day. Thank god it was almost over. She just had to survive gymnastics now... She took a deep breath, then pushed open the changing room door and strode into the gymnasium, hoping nobody could hear the panicked beating of her heart. She could do this. She just had to avoid absolutely everybody and make sure not a single person asked her a question. Especially Dan Zhang.

Everyone was already practising and warming up. Dan was with James and Kieran, flying over the vault. Priya couldn't help smiling as she watched him, laughing when he wobbled in his landing, high-fiving Kieran after he did a solid handspring and offering James a hand when he fell back in his roundoff. He was so kind, so generous, so— Dan turned to look at Priya, interrupting the flow of her thoughts, and she quickly turned away. She did not want to get his attention, especially today. She slipped out of her tracksuit jacket, keeping the trousers on over her leotard, and began a solo warm-up run around the room. She was alone, which meant she was safe.

"Hey!" Rachael ran up beside her. "How many laps are we doing?"

Priya's heart sank. She was no longer alone, which meant she was no longer safe. "Um, five?"

"Let's do it." Rachael grinned. "So, where were you this morning?"

Priya had no idea which truth was going to come out of her mouth. Telling her dad how bad his cooking was? Crying in the loo? Avoiding seeing Dan? Anything but the last, please. "My dad made poached eggs," she said quickly, feeling a wave of relief that she hadn't said anything worse. "I mean – my dad tried and failed to make poached eggs. It made us late."

Rachael laughed. "Are they as obsessed with your diet as my parents are? I swear it's impossible to get through a meal without my mum labelling every single protein on my plate."

"Yes," cried Priya. "And is it just me, or does it make your food taste worse? Even if I'm excited to eat something, my appetite fades the second my dad proudly points out he's used complex carbs."

"A hundred per cent," agreed Rachael. "I used to love beans until my parents shoved them into every meal I eat."

"Me too! And ever since Olaf sent round the diet recommendations sheet, they keep trying to make me eat m—"

"Mackerel!" Rachael finished her sentence. "It's the actual worst."

"I know!" agreed Priya. "It's so..."

"Fishy?"

"Yes," Priya laughed, as Rachael grinned at her in total understanding. She'd never really spoken to Rachael about anything but gymnastics before, and she was starting to wonder why. It felt good to speak to someone who understood things about her life that nobody else could.

"Listen up!" called out Olaf. The room instantly fell silent and they all gathered around the six-foot-three Scandinavian. Olaf was in his fifties but his biceps still bulged impressively as he crossed his arms and set his ice blue eyes on his gymnasts. "I've got big news. As you all know, it's the Junior Nationals on the 30th of June. And there's been a last-minute decision to include a round for a team floor routine. So I've entered us in.

You'll all still be doing your individual events, but the team event gives our club an extra chance at getting more points and the prize money could pay for new equipment. We'll do the routine we've been working on in practice, but we have less than a month to go. So, I'm going to need extra effort from you all, okay? No missing practice, no turning up late." Priya could have sworn he was looking straight at her when he said this. "But we've got a real chance, so let's go for it!"

There was an excited buzz as Olaf finished speaking and Rachael turned to Priya, her eyes shining. "This is so fun! I love team events. Don't you?"

Priya shook her head slowly. "I don't know. It's a lot of pressure. At least in an individual event, if I make a mistake, the only person I'm letting down is myself. Well, and Olaf. And my parents. But...a team event sounds stressful."

Rachael laughed. "As if you need to worry about making mistakes! You're the only one of us that can do a perfect double somersault beam dismount."

"Yeah, but I'm also the only one who messed up my split jump and fell right off at Nationals."

"Two years ago!" cried Rachael. "You're so hard on yourself, Priya."

"What's this?" demanded Olaf, walking up to them. "Are you practising or just having a nice little chat?"

"A nice little chat," said Priya, cringing at herself as she spoke. "Sorry."

Rachael gave her a weird look while Olaf shook his head. "Rachael – go join Kieran and James. I want you to practise synchronized handstands. Priya, go and join Dan. You're going to practise handsprings together."

"Alone? Just us two?!"

Olaf nodded as Rachael walked off to follow his instructions. "Yes. You're both my strongest so I want you at the front for the group routine, okay?"

Priya gulped. She'd never been asked to practise in pairs with Dan before. She'd barely ever *spoken* to Dan alone before! He'd said normal things – "Hey, how's it going?", "Are you entering into the Worlds?" and once, "Nice backflip!" – but Priya had never engaged in an actual *conversation* with him. She'd only ever smiled, nodded, and whispered: "Good", "Yes" and "Thanks." One-word answers only. The thought of being alone with him was terrifying – let alone being alone with him WHILST WEARING THE BANGLE.

Priya stared at the laminated wooden floorboards. She couldn't bring herself to move.

"Priya? Is there a reason you're not moving?"

Priya's eyes met Olaf's in absolute panic. Oh no. She tried to swallow it, but the stubborn syllable spurted out. "Yes."

"Well?" he demanded.

"I don't want to," she whispered.

"Don't want to what?" Olaf's voice was so loud that everyone around them fell quiet.

"Work with Dan," said Priya, as quietly as she could. She stared at the ground, praying that nobody could hear her.

"What's that?" asked Olaf. "Speak up, Shah!"

"I don't want to work with Dan today," whispered Priya, three per cent louder than last time. Please let it be enough.

Olaf frowned. "Teenagers," he muttered. "How many times do I have to tell you? Leave your drama off the mats. Dan! Come over. You and Priya are practising your flips together."

Priya closed her eyes. She could feel Dan slowly coming closer towards her. When he was right by her, she knew she had to open her eyes. She slowly lifted her head.

"Hey," he said, running a hand through his dark black hair. "Did you, uh, just say you didn't want to work with me?"

Priya looked down and finally understood what people said when they talked about wanting the ground to swallow them up. "Yes."

"Are you upset with me?" asked Dan awkwardly. "Have I... done something?"

"No!" cried Priya, looking up again. His face – his perfect smooth symmetrical face – was crumpled in concern. And it was all her fault. She tried to think of the best way to answer his question. She knew one syllable wouldn't be enough – but which version of the truth would the bangle let her say? She tried to think quickly. "Of course not!" That was true. What else? "It's, um...I'm not exactly having the best day. And by that, I mean I am actually having the worst day. Ever."

Wow. She'd never said so much to Dan in her life. It was just unfortunate that the one time she was having a proper conversation with him, she was rejecting him.

Dan's face relaxed good-naturedly. "I've had my fair share of those. Do you...want to talk about it?"

Priya stared at him in total amazement. This was the first time today someone hadn't asked her a black and white question. He'd given her the *option* to answer him. She didn't have to tell the truth – she could just opt out. She felt her heart flutter happily; this was exactly why she (and everyone else) liked Dan so much. Not only was he insanely cute – probably the cutest boy on the whole team – but he was *kind.* "I really, really don't," she said, with genuine gratitude, realizing that for once, she was actually happy to tell the truth.

Dan shrugged. "Okay. What do you say we just focus on our flips today?"

Priya had never been so into Dan Zhang as she was right this second – and last summer, she'd dreamt about him fourteen nights in a row. She beamed as she replied: "Great." It seemed she was back to one-word answers – and it really did feel great.

They launched straight into the practice and Priya was instantly reminded of why she loved gymnastics so much, no matter how stressful it could be sometimes. All the worries in her mind disappeared as she focused entirely on making sure her body did what it did best – bounce, whirl and glide through the air. There was no space for anything but the present moment, and seeing as Dan Zhang was currently flipping alongside her in absolute synchronicity, the present moment was *exactly* where Priya wanted to be.

Chapter 6

Priya jolted upright at the sound of her alarm. Time for yet another day of school. Another day of life-ruining honesty. She looked down at her wrist. The bangle was still there, looking incongruously innocent, with its shiny gold and sparkling gemstones. She'd spent hours last night trying to get it off – she'd slathered her hands in soap and tried to slide it off, she'd used her dad's pliers to try and break it, and she'd googled "how do you get a cursed bangle off your wrist?" dozens of times. But it seemed she was the only person in the history of the internet who was dealing with this precise problem. Because the only things that had come up online were normal people stuck in normal bangles – bangles that eventually came off with soap and pliers.

In an act of desperation, Priya had even tried to sneak into Pinkie's room to see if the treasure chest that Ba had left her had magic powers too. It didn't. All Priya had found inside were weird collections of broken wires and screws, and a blaring alarm that went off when she'd tried to open the bottom drawer. It turned out that Pinkie had rigged up an alarm system to the chest because she kept her private diaries in there, and when she'd stormed in on Priya, Priya hadn't even been able to lie her way out of it. Thanks to the bangle, she'd been forced to admit that yes, she had been snooping, and yes, she had deliberately ignored the *DO NOT OPEN* sign on the chest. Pinkie had forced her to do her chores for a week in exchange for not telling their parents what she'd done.

"Priya?" Her mum's head popped around the door. Without make-up, her face was lined with exhaustion. "Are you up? Can you help me make sure Pinkie's ready? I need to make a quick call."

"Okay," said Priya. A spark of hope suddenly flared up inside her. What if she was back to normal today and the truth-telling curse had gone? "Mum, ask me a question!"

"I just did."

Priya rolled her eyes in frustration. She was about to ask her mum again, and then she realized that she didn't *need* to respond to a question. She could just try and lie straight-out. She smiled brightly at her mum. "Also, Mum, I just wanted to say that you don't look great today." She gasped and her hand flew to her mouth. "OH NO! I'm sorry! I didn't mean to say that."

"Charming," her mum replied, looking offended. "I'll be sure to come to you the next time I need an ego boost."

Priya slumped back into bed, her sudden hope completely dead. She'd meant to tell her mum she looked great today, and yet somehow, she'd ended up adding in the word "don't". This whole situation made absolutely no sense, and it was so *unfair*. She couldn't bear the thought of another day like this. She needed a way out. "Mum?"

Her mum turned around and raised an eyebrow. "Yes? Do you want to tell me how old I look too?"

"No! I *really* don't want to tell you that." She paused, and then added quickly, "Also, please don't ask me if I think you look old." She thought carefully about what she wanted to say. She felt sick to the core about going to school, but maybe, if she phrased things correctly, she could get out of this horrible nightmare. At least for a day.

She tried to make her face look sick as she thought about what words to use. She needed to just be really general about not feeling great – that was *definitely* true. "Mum, I...don't feel good right now. Can I miss school today? Please?"

Her mum frowned as she approached Priya's bed. She sat on the edge and placed the back of her hand against her forehead. "That's not like you. What's wrong? You don't have a temperature."

"I just feel really not okay," said Priya slowly, trying to gauge what the bangle would let her say. "I know I would definitely feel *so* much better if I could stay home today."

"You look fine to me. And you're not at all warm."

"I'm just...generally bad." Priya didn't know how to explain that her main symptom was obsessive honesty. And if she admitted to her mum that her secondary symptoms were anxiety and stress, she might get a day at home, but she'd also make her mum worry. Priya didn't want to do that to her, not when she was so stressed already. "Please, Mum!"

Her mum shook her head. "Sorry, Priya. Feeling 'generally bad' is not a reason to stay home. I'm going to need something specific – otherwise you're going to school."

"I think I don't have a cold," said Priya desperately. She groaned – yet again the word "don't" had made its way into her sentence – and tried once more. "I'm not contagious. Oh my god!" She buried her head inside the duvet in frustration.

"Wonderful," said her mum, standing up. "See you downstairs."

An hour later, after her mum had dropped her off, Priya stood outside the doors to the classroom trying to psych herself up. She was grateful she didn't have morning gymnastics practice that day – their schedule changed all the time, and for once, it was in her favour – but there was no getting out of school. Still, maybe it would be okay. There was at least a ten per cent chance she could get through the whole day without Katie, Angela, Sami, Mei or a teacher asking her a personal question. Okay, maybe one per cent. But it would be fine. So long as she spent every spare minute hiding in her new favourite toilet cubicle.

"Priya!" cried Sami, putting an arm around her shoulders. "How's it going, girl?"

"Not great." Priya sighed unhappily. Her chances had just gone from one per cent to zero.

"Why are you standing outside the classroom?" asked Mei, materializing by her side.

"I...don't want to go inside," said Priya honestly. She prayed she could get away with leaving it there.

"Tell me about it. Double maths is a brutal way to start the day," agreed Sami.

Mei looked directly at Priya with a slight frown. "Are you *sure* it's just maths? Or is there another reason you don't want to go in?"

Priya fleetingly shut her eyes. "I'm...scared of what could happen," she said reluctantly. "Scared of the unknown."

"Wow, that's pretty existential for eight forty-five a.m.," commented Mei.

"But, brutally honest," added Sami. "After all, how many of us can truly say we're at peace with the idea of the unknown? Who among us has not shaken in fear at the sight of a spontaneous French vocabulary test? Or felt a pang of anxiety as we walk onto the stage of Heartland Secondary School for Girls?"

Mei rolled her eyes at Priya. "And the dramatic monologue has begun."

Priya smiled gratefully. Her secret was safe. For now.

"There she is." Priya swung round at the sound of the sharp voice behind her. Katie. "Loo lunch girl. Have you got my essay?"

Priya stared at Katie in confusion. What was she doing? Katie never approached her in front of Sami or Mei! They'd find out what she was doing! But then she noticed that Katie was grinning widely. She'd done this on purpose. She *wanted* Sami and Mei to find out. This must be her way of trying to create more drama between them after Priya had accidentally revealed that she'd been avoiding Sami and Mei yesterday. Priya knew how conniving Katie was, but this was a whole new low.

"Well?" demanded Katie, looking from Priya to Sami and Mei. "I need my essay."

Priya quickly looked down at her bag to avoid her friends' gazes. "Um, yes. Here." She handed Katie an essay titled: *Why Anne Boleyn is the most sympathetic of Henry VIII's wives*. It had been surprisingly cathartic – she'd taken a secret pleasure in having "Katie" herald the most manipulative (and okay, probably the coolest) of the Tudor king's wives, even writing about how much they had in common. The comparison made sense; she could *definitely* imagine Anne Boleyn blackmailing her ladies-in-waiting to write an essay for her.

"Thanks," said Katie, pushing past her to get into the classroom. She glanced back. "Oh, and I'll come find you tomorrow for my maths. Tha-anks."

Priya flushed red as Katie left. She couldn't believe that had just happened. And it wasn't even the bangle's fault! She tried to swiftly follow Katie into the classroom, but Mei laid a gentle hand on her arm, stopping her. "Priya, why are you doing Katie's homework? And...why didn't you tell us?"

Priya bit her lip in panic. She wished desperately that she could lie her way out of this. But she knew there was no way. Because in about two seconds, three if she was lucky, she was going to have to reveal—

"I was embarrassed to tell you both," burst out Priya against her will. "She asked me to, and I just couldn't say no. I know I should be stronger, but...she's Katie Wong."

Sami nodded sympathetically. "An incredibly well-dressed tyrant. I wouldn't have been able to say no either."

Priya's mouth dropped open. "Really?"

"Pri, Katie's kind of terrifying," said Mei. "Anyone would be intimidated by her."

"I thought she'd chosen me because I was the only one who couldn't stand up to her," admitted Priya quietly.

"Um, she chose you because you're super smart!" said Sami.

"This isn't your fault," said Mei gently. "Katie's bullying you, Priya."

"She's not!" said Priya. "Well, not properly. I mean, it's not like she'd *hurt* me if I didn't do it. She just, sort of, threatens to tell on me if I don't do her work."

Mei's face tensed. "How long has this been going on?"

"Only the last few months," said Priya. "I don't know what changed. She never used to even acknowledge me."

Sami nodded wisely. "The silver lining of unpopularity."

"Wait, this has been happening for *months*?" asked Mei.

"Yes, but it's normally just maths," said Priya hurriedly. "Which is super easy. It's only this week she wanted her history homework too, because she saw me – uh, I mean..." She squeezed her eyes shut, trying to think of something to say that was true but not *embarrassingly* true. "She saw me eating my lunch in the loo and threatened to tell everyone." Embarrassingly true it was.

"Why were you eating your – oh, never mind," said Mei. "The point is that this *is* bullying, Pri. And it's not okay. I wish you'd told us earlier. We could have been there for you."

"Totally," agreed Sami. "And we could have used it to blackmail her into inviting us to her party."

Mei shot Sami a look before turning back to Priya. "What Sami *means* is that you didn't need to go through this alone. And Katie can't get away with this."

Sami nodded furiously. "Yes. We need to do something!

A takedown. A coup."

"But she said if I stopped, she would tell Mrs Lufthausen I'm the one who's been copying *her* this whole time," said Priya, suddenly realizing she wasn't clenching against the truth so much. It was kind of a relief to just tell her friends what was going on.

"Ah," said Sami. "On second thoughts, maybe best to carry on as you are."

"Mrs Lufthausen isn't going to believe her," interjected Mei. She paused. "Actually, she might. She kind of hates you, Priya. I think she sees you falling asleep in her lessons as a personal insult on her teaching skills."

"I might fall asleep a lot, but I still get nines!"

Mei shrugged. "I think that makes it worse...you're a good student *and* you fall asleep on her. That's not exactly a good ego boost for Mrs L."

"Great." Priya sighed. "Guess I'm going to keep on doing Katie's homework. Though it's not so bad really. I made her write about how much she relates to Anne Boleyn. The one that got beheaded."

Sami snorted with laughter. "I can't wait to see her face when she reads that."

Mei grinned. "Good for you. But it's not fair you have to do all this work alone, on top of everything else you do." She paused. "Look, why don't we split the work with you? Until we come up with a plan to make Katie stop."

"I couldn't ask you to do that," said Priya. "It's too much!"

"Well, luckily, you don't have to ask," said Sami. "Because we've offered. Well, Mei has."

"Uh, you're helping too," said Mei.

Sami rolled her eyes. "Fine. I guess it's only fair. All for one and one for all!"

"We're not the Three Musketeers," retorted Mei. "Stop trying to make that happen."

"But it's perfect; we're a trio too!" pointed out Sami. "I'm totally going to make it happen – just you wait."

Priya looked from Sami's bright shining green eyes to Mei's resolute dark ones. She felt like her heart was going to break. She was *so* lucky to have friends like these. "Thank you," she blurted out uncharacteristically. "You're the best friends ever. I love you."

"And we love you too," replied Sami calmly. "Even if you do eat your lunch in the loos when you could be having spag bol with us, and you've spent months doing Katie Wong's homework without telling us – not to *mention* how you have written an essay comparing said-tyrant to a woman accused of sixteenth century witchcraft. There is only one Priya Shah and we are beyond thrilled that she hangs out with us."

Mei pointed to Sami. "What she said."

For once, there was no danger of Priya falling asleep in math. She was so scared of Mrs Lufthausen asking her a question that she was doing everything in her power to avoid being picked on. She diligently wrote down everything on the board and quietly did the exercises the teacher set.

Until Mrs Lufthausen asked for a volunteer to come to the board to work out an equation. Nobody responded, and Mrs Lufthausen's eyes scanned the room, before settling on the one person who was avidly praying she wouldn't get picked. "Priya. Would you like to come up and do this?"

Priya felt the panic rising in her. Please could she say "yes", not "no"? Please. She'd do *anything* to just have the bangle's truth curse disappear for this one moment. She tried to clamp her mouth shut, but the harder she tried, the more she felt the words gain power. "No!"

Mrs Lufthausen's face dropped in absolute shock.

"Uh, I mean, no *thank you*?" added Priya, hoping the politeness would diminish her rudeness.

"Excuse me?" spluttered Mrs Lufthausen.

Priya felt her heart pounding. She had to do something. There *had* to be a way to fix this. "I'm sorry," she said desperately. "I meant, um, I'd rather not. But I'm also happy to not – I mean, oh no, happy is a lie – um, I can do the equation! I will do the equation if I have to."

"Yes, you *do* have to," cried Mrs Lufthausen. "Because I am your teacher and I am telling you to! Is that clear?"

"It is now."

"And it wasn't before?" demanded Mrs Lufthausen.

"Well, it's just that it was a question before," said Priya, looking down miserably at the desk, wishing she was anywhere but there. "You asked if I'd like to do the equation, so, um, I answered honestly. I'm sorry. I'm really sorry. I would have just done it if you'd told me to." She could feel the heat of her friends' questioning looks on either side of her, but she couldn't bring herself to face them. It was too much. All of it.

"I cannot BELIEVE you think it's appropriate to speak to a teacher in this way!" cried Mrs Lufthausen. "I am shocked. And I am going to have to ask you to leave the room this instant."

"Shall I do the equation first?" asked Priya hopefully.

"No, you shall not," thundered Mrs Lufthausen. "I'll come and speak to you later."

Priya slowly stood, her face burning as she picked up her bag. She refused to look at any of the stunned faces around her – nobody had ever seen Priya Shah talk like that to a teacher before, and she knew they'd all be dying to find out what was going on. Instead, she kept her gaze resolutely on the anxious faces on her New Balances.

Priya left the room and found herself alone in the hallway for the second time that week. When it had happened the first time, she'd thought her life was terrible. But she hadn't even known the meaning of the word terrible back then. This was so much worse, and at the rate things were going, they would be ten times worse next week. If Priya didn't come up with a plan ASAP, it looked like the bangle was going to get her expelled.

Chapter 7

Priya curled up in her toilet cubicle, her arms hugging her knees, with yet another sad sandwich for lunch. Mrs Pringle had remembered her comments about the shepherd's pie and rewarded her with more leftovers. Although at least this time it was a vegan sandwich, so there was less chance of getting salmonella. She glumly pulled off the cellophane and forced herself to eat the limp lettuce and thin layer of hummus. It tasted as bad as it looked. But at least she'd managed to grab it before Sami and Mei had seen her. She'd been avoiding them since maths.

She glanced down at the bangle on her wrist in frustration. She still didn't have a plan. But what she did have was plenty of anger – and all of it was directed at the bangle. If she was really honest, some of it was also directed at the person who'd given her the bangle. She knew her life hadn't been perfect pre-bangle, but at least back then she'd been able to eat her lunch in the canteen with her friends and get through maths without insulting her teacher. So *why* had Ba given it to her? Had she known this would happen? Why would she have wanted Priya to go through this? It made no sense at all. Priya dropped her head into her hands. She wished Ba had been able to explain more before she died. But all she'd said was that the bangle would help her when she felt lonely. And that didn't help at all, because so far, the bangle had been making Priya feel lonelier than ever.

"Hello? Priya?"

Priya jolted upright. Oh no. Someone had found her again. She really needed to get herself a new cubicle.

"We know you're in there."

She strained as she tried to place the voice. Was it Sami and Mei or was it Katie? At this point, she didn't know what would be worse.

"Your bag's on the floor again." Mei.

Priya looked down at her bag and sighed. She'd better make sure her new cubicle had a hook to hang her bag on.

"We just want to talk to you," said Sami. "That's it! A harmless, loving conversation. Nothing scary."

"Saying something isn't scary makes it sound way scarier," remarked Mei. "We're trying to get her to come out, not stay in there for even longer."

"Uh, that's what I was trying to do," said Sami. "If you

think you can do it better than me, then *adelante, amiga*."

"You know I do French not Spanish," grumbled Mei. "Priya. Can you just come out? Please."

"I'd rather not," whispered Priya, dreading the questions she knew would come next.

"But *why*?" asked Sami.

"Because I'm kind of going through something," she said, desperately trying to find a way to phrase the truth without scaring her friends. "Something complicated."

"So, tell us!" cried Sami. "That's the whole point of having friends."

"She's right," agreed Mei. "We can help you. You just need to tell us what's going on."

Priya stayed silent. She knew they had a point, but she couldn't just tell them something like this. They wouldn't believe her. They'd think she was crazy. They might stop hanging out with her.

"Priya, what's going *on*?" Sami and Mei's frustrated voices asked her in unison.

This was it. The direct question Priya had been fearing this whole time. But now it was here, it wasn't as bad as she'd thought. She felt kind of...relieved. She took a deep breath and it all burst out of her. "I can't stop telling the truth! I'm wearing Ba's bangle and I think it's, like, magic and it's put a curse on me where I have to be honest the whole time."

There was silence from behind the cubicle door.

"Uh, hello?" asked Priya. Her heart was thudding. She was so scared her friends would judge her. But at the same time, she also felt...kind of amazing. She'd just told them everything! She was free!

Nobody said anything.

Priya stood up and unlocked the door cautiously. "Hello?" Both Sami and Mei were standing in front of her, their faces flat with disappointment.

"Whatever," said Mei, crossing her arms. "All we wanted was to help you. You didn't have to make up some dumb story."

"And if you did, you could have at least asked me for some dramatic guidance." Sami sniffed, flicking her long hair behind her shoulder. "You know I love magic realism."

"No!" exclaimed Priya urgently. "It's all *true!*"

"Uh, sure," said Mei, tucking her shoulder-length hair behind her ears to display her silver hoops. "And my earrings are magically making me sarcastic right now."

Priya creased her face up in frustration. "How can you not believe me? I've spent this whole time trying to hide it from you both, and now I tell you the truth, you think I'm lying! This is ridiculous. Why does nobody listen to me when I'm being honest?"

Sami turned to Mei, her brows creased in doubt. "I've never heard Priya say so much in one go. And you know she's not good at acting. I don't think she could fake that much desperation. Do you think...?"

"No, I do not think she's telling the truth!" said Mei. "Come on. I'm not a baby who believes in magic; I'm thirteen years old."

"Okay, ask me anything," said Priya, with a sudden surge of inspiration. "Something embarrassing I would never normally admit. And you'll see."

Sami and Mei exchanged a look, then slowly grinned at each other. Priya gulped. This was scary, but if it was what it took to get her friends to trust her, it would be worth it.

"All right," said Mei. "How about you tell us how you *really* feel about—"

"Dan Zhang," finished Sami triumphantly.

Priya paled. "What?"

Mei nodded. "Yup. Dan *Zhang*. The boy you always surname every time you reference him, which is every single time you talk about gymnastics. Do you, or do you not, like him?"

"And we mean *like* like," clarified Sami.

Priya felt a blush creeping up her cheeks. Again. She hadn't ever wanted to tell Sami and Mei about her crush on Dan because, well, she knew nothing would ever happen. It was crazy of her to think that someone like Dan would like someone like her. So, there was no point talking about it. It was just embarrassing.

But now she didn't have a choice. "I like him so much it physically hurts every single time I look at him. Even when

I look at him in my dreams. Which I do most nights." She clamped her hand over her mouth in horror. She hadn't thought she'd go into *that* level of detail.

Sami's eyebrows shot up. "Oh my god! You *dream* about him!"

Mei gasped. "Wow. I can't believe you told us that – you're always so...private. Every time we've asked you about him before, you've just gone bright red and said the only thing you like about him is his backflips."

"I lied," admitted Priya. "I mean, his backflips are amazing. But so is he. It's why I always surname him – he's too special for me to just use his first name."

"I'm dying at how cute you are right now," squealed Sami. "Priya with a crush is the best! Oh my actual god – you *have* to invite Dan to my bat mitzvah. Sorry, Dan Zhang – I forget he gets celeb status. Can you imagine? You'd have a date to my BM!" Suddenly, her mouth fell open in panic. "Wait – *I* don't have a date for my BM! Who am I going to ask?"

"You don't need one; it's not 1999," retorted Mei, before observing Priya closely. "Why did you just tell us all of that? When you've always denied it before?"

"Because the bangle made me," explained Priya, lifting up her right arm. She pulled her shirtsleeve back so her friends could see the shiny offender, in all its gold glory. "See?"

"Whoah, that is fancy," commented Sami. "How are you allowed to wear diamonds and rubies to school?"

"Because my parents haven't noticed. And even if they had, I can't take it off. It's stuck." She showed her friends by attempting to remove it again. As always, it remained firmly in place. "It's here to stay."

"Oh my god." Sami breathed out dramatically. "That's so strange. And it totally explains why you were so weird with Mrs Lufthausen! I mean, it is undeniable that you told her the truth. The entire truth. Even when it was way too much truth."

"I'm still not convinced," said Mei. "I think you're going to have to tell us the whole story. From the beginning."

"Agreed," said Sami. "But..." She looked around the bathroom in distaste. "Can we maybe do it somewhere else? As much as I love the dramatic incongruity of having this chat in the first-floor girls' bathrooms, it doesn't smell so good."

Priya nodded eagerly. "Yes, please! I'm starving! Can we go to the canteen? And can you maybe get some pasta for me from Mrs Pringle, please?"

"Uh, why can't you get it yourself?" asked Mei.

Priya pointed to the bangle. "It made me tell her how gross the shepherd's pie looked. She's been giving me salmonella sandwiches ever since."

Sami's eyes widened. "You said that to Mrs Pringle's *face*? This is some serious magic we're dealing with here."

Ten minutes later, Priya slurped up the last bit of her spaghetti bolognese as her friends stared at her open-mouthed.

"How are you eating so casually when you're stuck in a truth curse?" asked Sami.

Priya shrugged. "I've been in it for two days already. I'm hungry."

"She's going to need her strength," said Mei grimly. "Getting that bangle off is not going to be an easy task."

Sami nodded. "Getting it off. That's what we need to do. Not...ask Priya all the questions we've always wanted to ask her?"

Priya looked worried. It had crossed her mind that knowing about the bangle would give her friends huge power over her – they could take advantage of it to ask her anything at all. But Sami and Mei wouldn't do that – would they?

"Obviously we would never do that," said Mei firmly. "That's the kind of thing Katie and Angela would do – not real friends like us."

Priya felt her shoulders relax. She should have known that she could trust Sami and Mei. Mei carried on speaking: "We need to focus on helping Priya get out of the bangle."

"Right!" said Sami. "By...?"

"There's nothing you can do," said Priya, using the back of her hand to wipe tomato sauce from her mouth. "I've already tried taking it off. It's magic, remember?"

"I still can't believe your grandma said it came from an

Indian princess," said Mei. "It's so fantasy movie." Her eyes lit up. "Do you think we need to track the princess down and find out the historical secret to unlocking it? You know how good I was at getting us out of the escape room that time – I feel like we could do this."

"No," said Priya firmly. "The princess died centuries ago. And I tried to google the legend, but nothing came up. For all we know, Ba made it up."

"Or the legend died with the princess and you're the only one who knows!" said Sami, her eyes sparking. "It's so romantic!" Then she saw Priya's face. "By romantic, I obviously mean inconvenient and unfair."

"If the princess story is real, I wish I could have gotten a different piece of her magical jewellery," said Priya. "Like one that can turn things to gold. Instead, I get the power to tell the truth. Lucky me."

"Yeah, it's not exactly the superpower I would have chosen," agreed Sami.

"Well, we need to focus on getting it off," said Mei. "If we can't do it a magic way, we're going to have to get it off a practical way."

Sami nodded. "You're right. Let me help." She gestured to Priya to bring her wrist towards her. "Wow, it's *really*—"

"Ow!" yelled Priya, as Sami tugged at the bangle.

Sami released the bangle apologetically. "Sorry, I thought if I just used a bit of force I could slide it off your wrist..."

Priya shot her a dark look as she nursed her arm. "I already tried that. Obviously. But my hand's too wide."

"What about with these?" Mei triumphantly held up a bunch of butter sachets.

"Ooh, nice!" said Sami. "We'll slide it off with those!"

"Uh, I don't know," said Priya doubtfully. "I already tried it with soap."

"Butter is way more slippery," said Sami authoritatively. "And there's no harm in trying. At the very worst, you'll have delicious hands."

The second Priya reluctantly placed her hands in Mei's, Mei began slathering them in copious amounts of butter.

"Gross," cried Priya. "And you know you just need to do my right hand, not my left one?"

"We're covering all bases," said Mei, rubbing the butter in.

"Let me help," said Sami, opening even more sachets. "How's that? Bit more pressure or less?"

"Ooh, that's kind of nice with more pressure!"

Mei rolled her eyes. "We're not in a spa. That's enough massaging. Time to try and slide it off."

Sami nodded seriously, as she placed her hand next to Mei's on top of the bangle. "Yup. On the count of three? One...two..."

Priya looked from one friend to the other in abject terror as they prepared to yank the bangle down her wrist. She had a feeling this wasn't going to be—

"OW!" cried Priya. She pulled her arm – with the bangle still firmly on it – out of her friends' clutches, cradling it to her chest. "Seriously? You're going to take my entire hand off. And what happened to waiting till three?"

"WHAT is going on here?" The girls looked up in shock to see Mrs Lufthausen standing over them. She inhaled sharply as she looked at the buttery mess on the table, Priya's arms, and the sparkly gold bangle. "Wasting food. Wearing inappropriate jewellery to school. And making a mess of school property. This. Calls. For. Detention."

"But we were helping her *remove* the inappropriate jewellery," explained Sami. "It's stuck."

"I said *detention*," bellowed Mrs Lufthausen. "All three of you. Come and see me in form time this afternoon. And I want that bracelet gone from your wrist by then, Priya Shah. Or I'll be calling your parents."

Chapter 8

Priya, Sami and Mei had tried absolutely everything to get the bangle off – soapy water, a rubber band trick they saw online, even a saw from the DT workshop (though Priya hadn't let them actually *touch* the bangle with its serrated edges; she wasn't that desperate. Yet) – and it was officially time for their detention.

Priya looked glumly at her friends as they walked down the corridor towards Mrs Lufthausen's office. "She's going to call my parents. They'll ask me what's happening, and then I'm going to have to tell them everything. Every. Thing."

"Look on the bright side," said Mei. "They probably won't believe you."

"Or maybe they will and then they can help you," suggested Sami. "Like if the secret has been passed down for generations and Ba told your mum how to reverse the spell."

"This isn't a Pixar movie," said Priya gloomily. "There is no way my mum knows anything – she's seen the bangle in my room millions of times and has never said anything except 'make sure you don't lose that; it's valuable'. She's going to lose her mind if she finds out about this."

"She won't be the only one." Mei gestured to the end of the corridor where Mrs Lufthausen was standing, waiting for them. "I have no idea how we're going to get out of this."

Priya gulped. "Oh god. What if I'm rude to her? What if she gives me an after-school detention? I'll have to miss gymnastics practice." She swallowed sharply. "My parents will *kill* me if that happens."

Sami winked at her. "Leave it to me. I've just had an idea." Mei and Priya glanced at each other nervously, but Sami simply shook her long red hair and cleared her throat. "Don't worry. I'm the best actress in our year. I've got this – trust me." Mei and Priya looked even more nervous.

"So?" demanded Mrs Lufthausen. "Is the mess cleared up? And the bracelet removed?"

"We cleaned everything up, of course," said Sami, her eyes widening in faux innocence. "But I'm afraid we have to admit that Priya's still wearing the bangle." She picked up Priya's limp arm and showed the teacher said bangle. "You see, it's not just a *normal* bangle."

"Sami," whispered Mei, as Priya's face contorted in panic. "What are you doing?!"

Sami carried on, unperturbed. "It's a *religious* bangle."

Mrs Lufthausen looked tense. "Religious?"

"Uh huh," said Sami. "It's a Hindu tradition that when a girl comes of age, she wears a golden bangle. Or, you know, gold-plated if you can't afford the real thing."

"And why is this the first I'm hearing of this?" asked Mrs Lufthausen uncomfortably. "You know that any exceptions to the school dress code need to be detailed in a letter from your parents to notify us staff."

"It's true," said Sami, bowing her head apologetically. "It's just...it's a bit culturally *sensitive.*"

Mrs Lufthausen tensed even more. "In what way?"

"Let me just check that Priya's okay with me talking about it," said Sami. She turned to Priya and whispered in her ear. Priya swallowed a smile, then nodded.

Sami turned back to a scowling Mrs Lufthausen. "It's about *periods,*" she continued loudly. "Girls are only given their gold bangles after menstruating." She practically shouted the word "menstruating". "And Priya's parents are Indian. They don't like to talk openly about periods. That's why they haven't spoken to you about it."

"All right, all right," said Mrs Lufthausen quickly. Her face suggested she didn't like to talk openly about periods either. "Fine. Just...keep it underneath your uniform, Priya."

Priya nodded hurriedly, and looked humbly down at the ground, hoping that a lack of eye contact would stop her least favourite teacher from asking her any questions. "Yes. Of course. I will."

"Thanks so much, Mrs Lufthausen," chirped Sami. "You're the best. Have a lovely afternoon!"

"Wait!" Mrs Lufthausen raised a hand. "You all still have detention. PE cupboards. Now."

In detention, Priya gave Sami yet another admiring look. "I still can't believe you managed to get us out of that. You're a genius."

Sami folded a lacrosse bib with a flourish. "Why, thank you. It's not that hard really – most teachers can't handle talking about menstruation. So, naturally, I reference it in every single excuse I invent. Mr Carter still hasn't noticed my menstrual cycle is so synced up with our swimming lessons that it only lasts seven days not twenty-eight."

Mei wrinkled her nose as she picked up a sweat-stained sports shirt. "Shame the fake menstrual tradition you invented didn't get us out of detention too."

"I have no problem tidying up sweaty sportswear if it means my parents don't get called in," said Priya. She looked anxiously at her watch. "Although I hope it doesn't make me late for gymnastics. Again."

"Oooh, late for Dan Zhang," said Sami. "What are we going to call you? Priyang? Diya? Pandang?"

"Uh, none of them! This is why I didn't want to tell you guys!" Priya covered her face with a lacrosse bib in embarrassment. Until she inhaled the sweaty scent and gagged, quickly lowering the bib. "Ew, they really need to wash these."

Mei had paused mid-folding and was staring at her. "Uh, Priya?"

"Yes?"

"You're about to go to gymnastics. With Dan. With the bangle on. And...we're not going to be there to lie for you."

Priya bit her bottom lip. "Um, yes."

Sami's eyes widened. "Oh no. This is not going to go well."

Priya shifted uncomfortably. "It might be okay. You never know. I saw him yesterday, and..."

"What happened?" asked Mei. "The whole truth, please."

"Well, normally, I never actually speak to him. Even though he's so friendly and fun and gets on with everyone, I always avoid him."

"Naturally," said Mei drily.

"But yesterday, Coach put us in a pair together..."

Sami shrieked. "Oh my god!"

"But then I kind of told him – via Olaf – that I didn't want to work with him," said Priya in a small voice. "And then he asked me why. And I said I didn't want to tell him."

"You said you didn't want to work with him?!" cried Sami. "He's going to think you're crazy! Or that you hate him! Or both!"

"He might not," said Priya. "We did our backflips in perfect synchronicity." She smiled shyly at the memory. "It was kind of amazing..."

"Oh my god, you guys are communicating through movement, not words," cried Sami. "That's so beautiful!" She paused. "But, um, maybe it would be good to use words too?"

"Yeah." Priya sighed. "So long as my words aren't totally mortifying."

Mei cocked her head thoughtfully. "There has to be a way around this. A loophole. Or a trick."

"Uh, we've tried everything," said Sami. "Unless Priya's ready to try the saw again?"

Priya shook her head quickly. "Priya's definitely not ready to try the saw again. And I already tried some loopholes. Like only answering yes or no – but depending on the question, the bangle won't always let me. And I've tried to only tell part of the truth, like when I told my mum I didn't feel good enough to go to school this morning. But you can guess how that went, seeing as I'm here right now."

Mei frowned, and then her eyes lit up. "I know what we can try! Writing!" Sami and Priya stared at her blankly. Mei rolled her eyes. "I'll show you; I need a pen and I need paper."

Sami rummaged around her bag and pulled out a notepad and pen. "Got it!"

"What are you going to do?" asked Priya. "Because I don't think it's going to work. We've tried everything, remember?"

"Not this," said Mei. "Right, Priya. I'm going to ask you a question. And you're going to respond by writing instead of speaking, okay? And you're going to lie."

"Oh my god," burst out Sami. "You're a genius!"

"Let's try it first," said Mei, putting the notepad on a pile of bibs in front of Priya. "Okay, Priya, what do you think of that soft rock playlist I sent you last week?"

Priya flushed. "Uh…"

Mei laughed. "I know you hated it, don't worry. So, maybe try writing down the opposite?"

Priya hesitated for a moment, then picked up the pen. She slowly started to write, leaning on the bibs. The letter "I" appeared on the page as normal. But as she started to write the word "loved", the pen began jerking around the page. She got as far as "I" but the pen wouldn't let her write an "o" next to it. Instead it somehow turned into an "h". Before she knew it, she'd written: *I hated it.* Stricken, she stared up at her friends. They were staring back at her in shock.

"That was creepy as hell," announced Mei.

"Are you sure you weren't faking that?" asked Sami. "I mean…it's a pen. You're a person. You can make it do what you want."

"I tried!" protested Priya. "I broke out into a sweat – look! I have actual sweat patches!"

"Maybe we should try again," suggested Mei. "As…extra proof."

"Okay," said Sami. "I've got a question: who's your favourite – me or Mei?"

Mei and Priya both gasped at the same time. Priya's heart thudded, but before she could think, she found herself saying: "I don't have one; I love both of you the exact same."

Sami clutched Mei and Priya's wrists. "That is the cutest thing ever, especially because we know the bangle means it's one hundred per cent true! Musketeers for ever!"

Mei freed her wrist from Sami's grasp. "Yes, it's cute, but you weren't meant to ask Priya questions like that, remember? We're not here to take advantage of her situation."

"But I knew she'd answer the way she did," protested Sami. "You're not mad, are you, Priya?"

She shook her head. "It's okay. I'm more relieved than mad."

"Either way, can we please get back to giving Priya questions to practise written lying?" asked Mei.

"Okay, I've got an easier one," said Sami. "Do you like detention? Remember to lie."

Priya started writing and the word flowed right out of her pen: *Yes.*

Mei and Sami looked at each other in delight.

"It worked!" cried Sami. "You lied!"

Priya felt blood rushing to her cheeks in embarrassment. "I think it's maybe *not* a lie. Because I kind of do like detention... Hanging out with you guys is fun. If it wasn't for detention, we'd have to be in form time working right now, but instead I get to fold bibs and chat with you both."

Mei smiled at her. "I hear you. Though I'd much rather do it somewhere that doesn't smell of feet."

Sami looked confused. "So – that was the truth? Try another lie."

Priya picked up the notepad and started to write: *You aren't my...* But as she tried to write *best friends*, the pen started to jerk out of control. She used all her strength to control it, but the pen refused to do what she wanted. Before she knew it, the pen had manically scribbled out the word "aren't". She cried out in alarm as the pen then forced her hand to write the rest of the sentence: *You are my best friends*.

Sami and Mei stared at Priya, the pen, and then each other. "I can't tell if that's the sweetest thing I've ever seen, or the scariest," said Mei finally.

"Seconded," agreed Sami. "That was like something out of *The Exorcist*. If I didn't know it was real, I'd be telling you to go for a career in film, Pri. You'd be guaranteed an Oscar for that."

Priya bit her lip. "Gymnastics tonight isn't going to go well, is it?"

"You never know," said Sami brightly. "Maybe telling Dan the truth is what you need to get him to ask you out. And be your date to my batty M."

Priya laughed nervously, trying to hide the anxiety she felt every time Sami mentioned her bat mitzvah.

"Batty M sounds terrible," declared Mei. "And Priya, we can come with you, if you want? To gymnastics? And try to lie for you?"

"But we have tickets to watch the new Marvel movie!" protested Sami. She caught Mei's eye then changed her tone. "I mean, sure. I am more than happy to try to help. Obviously."

"Thanks." Priya smiled sadly, wishing she could watch movies after school with her best friends, instead of going to gymnastics and facing her crush whilst stuck in a truth curse. "But I think this is something I have to do on my own."

Chapter 9

Priya tried to slip into practice without anyone noticing that she was late; Mrs Lufthausen hadn't let them leave until every single bib was folded. But she'd barely done a single star jump before she heard her name being called by Olaf. His tone did not sound positive.

"Priya!"

She reluctantly turned around to see Olaf standing there with his hands on his hips, glaring. "Nice of you to show up for practice."

"Sorry. It was my teacher. She—"

"I don't want any excuses," he snapped. "Every time you're late, it's someone else's fault. If you wanted this badly enough, you'd be here on time. You know how important it is that we get this team routine perfect."

Priya stayed silent. It was *true* that it was always someone else's fault. It wasn't like she'd wanted Mrs Lufthausen to give her detention. But...maybe what Olaf said was also true, and she didn't want this badly enough.

"Do you want this badly enough, Priya?" demanded Olaf. Priya's heart sank – now that Olaf had framed it as a question, she guessed they were all about to find out. "Because if you want that spot on the Olympics team, you know you have to give it one hundred and ten per cent. Nothing else can come first. Not your friends, your family, your schoolwork. So, tell me, do you want it enough?"

Priya could feel the word on the tip of her tongue. She tried as hard as she could to keep it there – so hard she was practically sweating. But the harder she tried, the stronger the urge to speak became. And then it flew out of her mouth as fast as Dan Zhang on the vault.

"No."

Olaf gaped at her. Rachael fell over mid star jump. The entire room fell quiet and turned to stare at Priya. She felt her cheeks grow red.

"Excuse me?" asked Olaf.

"I'm sorry," whispered Priya, with tears in her eyes. Olaf was going to kick her off the team – she knew it. His number one rule was "no disrespect" and she'd just been seriously disrespectful. She couldn't believe she'd just thrown away *everything* she'd worked so hard for with a single word. "I don't mean that I don't want it at all. I love gymnastics – you know I do. But I don't want it if it means giving up my entire life. I'm so tired. I miss my friends. It's too much."

Olaf turned angrily to the rest of the group. "Did I say you could stop? Thirty burpees – now!" He turned back to Priya and gestured for her to come over to the corner of the room. "Okay, Priya. I get it. You've been working too hard lately. You need a break."

"I...do?" This was not what Priya had expected.

He nodded. "I should have noticed. You're not yourself. I think you need to have a bit of time off to relax."

"Relax?" echoed Priya. She had no idea what was happening right now.

"Yes. When's the last time you had a Friday night off?"

"Christmas," said Priya automatically. She smiled as she remembered how she'd gone to get pizza with Sami and Mei on the last day of school. "It was really, really good."

Olaf looked guilty. "From now on, you have Fridays off. See your friends. Do your homework. Sleep. Whatever you need to do. Okay?"

Priya nodded mutely. This felt like a dream. Then she remembered the competition. "Wait, but, what about training? Don't I need it for the Nationals?"

"You'll be okay. There's still plenty of time left. I'll make sure we do individual practice on Friday nights, so you don't miss out on the team training."

Priya frowned. The individual event was the one with the

prize money – which meant it was the one she had to do well in. She'd have to make sure she practised extra hard alone now if she was going to miss out on these sessions. But it would be worth it to have Friday nights off!

"To be honest," continued Olaf, "your biggest issue right now is your rigidity. There's not enough lightness in your movements. Maybe a bit of rest will help with that." He nodded decisively. "From now on, what you need is less training, more relaxing. How does that sound?"

Priya gave Olaf the look she normally reserved for a giant Oreo milkshake. "That. Sounds. Incredible. Thank you so much."

Olaf scowled awkwardly. "Well, you still have to finish practice today. Go on. Burpees."

Priya left the gymnasium beaming. She hadn't even minded doing endless burpees. If anything, they'd helped her get even more height in the jumps for her individual routine and Olaf said he was thinking of putting her at the top of the pyramid for the finale of the team routine! It was a major honour. But none of it could beat the fact that from now on, she had Fridays off. For once, she was going to be able to join Sami and Mei, and do normal Friday night things. Like act out Greek plays and eat pizza in bed.

"Hey, Priya, wait up!" It was Dan Zhang.

"Heeeeeey," said Priya in a weirdly drawn-out way. Why was she speaking like that?! It wasn't even the bangle's fault! "Sorry, um, I mean, how...are you?"

"Good, thanks. I just wanted to say – I thought it was amazing you were so honest with Coach back there. Sorry for overhearing, I just, uh...thought it was really cool. I'd never have the courage to tell him I didn't want to sacrifice my whole life for gymnastics."

Priya stared at him in amazement. He was *complimenting* her! With adjectives! He thought what she'd done was *cool*! That it was *amazing*!

Dan coughed loudly.

Priya suddenly remembered to speak. "Thanks!" Then she realized what he'd just said. "Wait – do *you* feel that way too?"

"Of course. I just wish I could do what you did and tell Coach..." He looked at her curiously. "What made you do it? You're normally so...polite and stuff."

"What made me do it?" Priya choked.

"Yeah!"

She panicked. Her eyes widened as she tried to think of something true to say that wasn't the word "magic". She lifted up her arm quickly before it blurted out of her. "This."

"Your...arm?"

"No. The bangle."

"Oh." Dan leaned towards her to look. "It's...very shiny."

"It was my grandma's," explained Priya, trying to give away

as little detail as possible. "She died. Last year. And left it to me."

"That makes so much sense," said Dan. Priya raised an eyebrow – it did? "The memory of your grandma inspired you to be honest. Wow, Priya, you're really brave."

Priya felt a whole wave of feelings wash over her – sadness at how much she missed her grandma, confusion at whether she was behind the bangle's truth curse or not, gratitude to Dan for being so wonderfully Dan, and...maybe a little bit of pride in herself for being brave. She smiled cautiously. "Thanks, Dan."

"Also..." Dan's face turned into an awkward frown. "Um, about the other day...and you not wanting to work with me... I know I said we could forget about it, but..."

The smile fell off Priya's face. Oh no. She couldn't have this chat with Dan – if he asked a single question, she'd be forced to tell the truth – a truth that would make her die of absolute shame. "I'm sorry," she said quickly, grabbing her bag. "I have to— I mean, I don't *have* to. But I'm going. I need to— Oh my god, it's a turn of phrase! Ahem. Sorry. I am leaving. Now."

"Wait!" Dan ran a hand through his thick black hair. "Have I, uh, done something wrong? Because I know we never normally chat that much, so I was kind of, uh, surprised you didn't want to work with me."

Priya squeezed her eyes shut. She turned around slowly to

face Dan. She had no idea how she was going to survive this conversation. "No. You haven't done anything wrong at all."

The frown eased slightly off his face, but it wasn't fully gone. "Okay, good to know. But is there...something else? Like, a reason you didn't want to work with me specifically?"

Oh no. Priya really didn't want to answer this question. But the "yes" was already creeping up her throat. She tried to swallow it down and make it go away. There was no way she could say the word "yes". She couldn't. She forced it down and used the remaining energy she had post-burpees to keep the word inside her. "YES!" Priya's hand closed on top of her mouth and she looked at Dan in horror. She hadn't just said yes – she'd *shouted* it. She had no idea what to do. But she knew one thing – she needed to get out of there right now. The next thing Dan was going to ask her was what exactly the reason was – and there was no way she could tell him. She grabbed her bag and ran away as fast as she could.

Priya sat in her room feeling sick with regret and frustration. She'd been feeling amazing at practice – Friday nights off was the best news she'd had all year – but that chat with Dan had ruined everything. She'd come back home and gone straight to her laptop to try and find another solution to getting the bangle off. She'd started googling local jewellers who could help her take the bangle off and had even started filling in an online form to book an appointment. Until she'd reached a list where she had to tick a box for her specific problem. "Magic bangle" was not on there. And "broken clasp" didn't quite explain the full extent of her issue. In that moment she'd accepted there was no way she could go to an ordinary jeweller; if they couldn't remove the bangle, they'd end up calling her parents, or taking her to a science lab, or even worse. There was still no solution in sight.

The only good news was that when she'd got home, her parents were too busy dealing with the mess Pinkie had made with her latest experiment (it turned out that you couldn't microwave bath salts) to ask Priya how her day had been. Priya was relieved – she really didn't want to tell anyone the truth about what had just happened. Except...she sat up straight as she realized that actually, she *did*.

She wanted to tell Sami and Mei. Normally she kept everything to herself. But it had felt so good to tell her best friends about the bangle earlier. She'd felt so much lighter. And less alone. So why not do it again? They already knew about the bangle *and* how much she liked Dan, so why not tell them about the humiliating update? Especially when she got to lead with the news that she'd be able to make the next sleepover! For once, it wouldn't just be Sami and Mei hanging out on weekends, sending her selfies, while she looked sadly at them during her breaks at practice, wishing she could be there and secretly worrying they'd stop being her friend one day. It would be all three of them. Together.

Priya picked up her phone before she could stop herself and pressed "call all" on their group chat. Mei picked up first, her face filling the phone screen, instantly making Priya feel marginally better. "How did it go?! What did you say?"

"I'm here," cried Sami, her face red. "Oh my god, I can't... breathe. I had...to...run upstairs. Privacy."

Priya gave them a small smile. "It was...mixed. But mainly bad."

"I'm sitting down," said Mei. "I'm ready."

"Wait..." said Sami, panting. "I'm not. Water." She gulped down a whole pint glass as her friends watched, with raised eyebrows.

"How can you fit that much inside you?" asked Mei.

"I have strong lungs," replied Sami.

Mei shook her head. "You really need to work on your biology."

Priya interrupted them. "So...Olaf asked me if I wanted gymnastics badly enough and I said no."

Sami and Mei gasped.

"Did he kick you off the team?" asked Mei. "Are you okay?!"

"I'm actually more than okay." Priya grinned, despite everything. "Because, guess what? He said it must be because I was too tired, and he's giving me Fridays off. To relax!"

Sami squealed in excitement. "SLEEPOVERS!!!"

"Wait, this is amazing!" cried Mei. "Why do you look so sad? You said it was bad?"

Priya nodded, her face falling. "I wanted to share the good stuff first. The bad stuff is..."

"It's about Dan, isn't it?" Mei gripped the phone tightly, bringing it closer to her face. "Tell us."

"Oh my god, wait, I need more water." Sami gulped down more. "Okay. I'm sufficiently hydrated. Hit me."

"He asked me if there was a reason I didn't want to work with him before," said Priya. "And I tried so hard to not say it, to the point where I was using every ounce of my strength to keep it inside of me, but then I *shouted* out the word 'yes'! It was horrific."

"No!" shrieked Sami.

"And then I ran away. Without saying a single thing."

"Oh my god," said Sami. Her face was pale. "He's going to think you're—"

"Insane," finished Priya. "Completely and utterly insane."

Mei frowned. "Wait. You tried really hard to not say yes and then you shouted it?"

"Exactly."

"So, the yes came out more intensely than you planned?"

Priya's face fell even more. "Yes. Thanks for rubbing it in."

Mei beamed at them both. "I think I've got it!"

"Got what?" asked Sami. "Why are you smiling? Did you not just hear what she said? She's ruined things with Dan Zhang."

Priya's face drooped all the way into her hands. "I've ruined things with Dan Zhang!"

"Not for long," said Mei, still grinning widely. "I have a plan. But first, I'm going to need you to tell me absolutely *everything* that happened. In detail. Word for word."

Priya lifted her head out of her hands and squinted at Mei. "Seriously? You want me to relive my humiliation in detail?"

"Yup." Mei nodded, grabbing a notebook. "I'll be taking notes."

"Feel free to do voices," said Sami. "What? If you're going to relive it, you may as well make it as realistic as possible."

Chapter 10

Priya couldn't wait for the bell to ring. She'd somehow got through the whole day with minimal drama – mainly thanks to Sami and Mei following her everywhere and making sure she didn't end up telling Mrs Lufthausen that the school sports equipment smelled so bad it had almost made them pass out – and in precisely two minutes, she'd be free to speak to Sami and Mei alone. And there was *a lot* to speak about.

Mei hadn't been able to explain her idea much the night before – Priya's mum had barged into her room just after Priya had finished her one-woman re-enactment of gymnastics practice, demanding to know why she was talking to two people she'd already spent the entire day with – so they'd decided to save it for the sleepover tonight. Priya grinned to herself. She knew a sleepover wasn't that exciting compared to whatever Katie and Angela did at the weekend, but for her, it was huge. She finally got to be normal, chat to her friends till dawn (or until they fell asleep – whichever came first), eat non-complex carbs – oh, and try to break a magic truth curse.

The bell rang and the class erupted.

"We're free!" cheered Sami. "Let's go!"

Ms Carlyle sighed. "You're not prisoners. We are trying to educate you, so you have more freedom in your futures."

But nobody replied to their teacher – they were too busy packing their things and running out the door.

"My mum's in the car park," said Mei. "She's brought spring rolls."

Priya put a hand on her heart. "This is already the best Friday night I've ever had."

"Wait till you see the stash I've got for our midnight feast," declared Sami. "Stolen from the treat cupboard."

"You have a treat cupboard?" exclaimed Priya. "I hope you both know just how lucky you are."

"Lucky to have you coming to the sleepover," said Mei, linking her arm through Priya's. "If I have to spend another Friday night alone with Sami, I'm going to go crazy. What?! You made me sit through an hour-long monologue last time!"

"It was a work of art," clarified Sami. "You're lucky you got a preview."

Mei rolled her eyes. "Come on. The quicker we get back

to mine, the quicker I can explain my plan. And I have *a lot* to explain."

Later, in Mei's bedroom, after *a lot* of food, Priya leaned back against Mei's padded headboard groaning. "I can't believe I ate so much. I feel sick."

Sami wiped cheese grease from her mouth with the back of her hand. "I can't believe you beat my record. I don't know whether to be jealous or proud."

"I hope you didn't forget to save space for dessert," said Mei, pointing to a pile of chocolates, sweets and macarons in the middle of the bed.

"Maybe it's a good thing I haven't been able to come to sleepovers until now," said Priya. "If I ate this much every week, I'd be too full to ever do a backflip."

Sami shrugged. "It might be worth it."

Mei cleared her throat. "Okay. Now we've finished the pizza, I think it's time we take a digestive pause while I explain my bangle theory."

"Oh my god, yes!" cried Sami. "Finally!"

Priya tried to sit up straight to listen, before realizing that her stomach would not allow that. She collapsed back against the bed. "Okay. I'm ready."

"Right," said Mei. She sat up and pulled out a notebook, flipping it open to a page filled with her neat round handwriting. "So, what we know so far is that it's impossible for you to lie when you're wearing the bangle, Pri. Even if you're writing. Or doing hand gestures. Or nodding. The bangle forces you to tell the truth with your entire body."

Priya nodded glumly. When Mei phrased it like that, the situation felt hopeless.

"And that sometimes the bangle forces you to shout out the truth," continued Mei. "Like with Dan."

Priya felt even worse. "Is this meant to be helpful? Because it would be great if we could skip to the helpful bit."

"Well, according to my research," Mei waved her notebook in the air, "the bangle forces you to shout when you try to resist the truth. So, the harder you try to fight it, the more you end up blurting it out."

Priya jerked upright, not even noticing the discomfort in her stomach. "Oh my god. You're right! Like with Mrs Lufthausen, when she asked me if I wanted to write the equation on the board. I was dreading the bangle making me say 'no', so I forced it down, and then I shouted it out." Her enthusiasm faltered. "And...with Dan."

"Whoah," said Sami. "This is Jedi-level stuff."

Priya chewed her lip. "But...I don't get how this is useful. I can stop resisting the truth, fine, and I can stop shouting. But I'll still end up *saying* the truth."

Mei's eyes twinkled. She turned over a page in her notebook. "Sure. Unless you take control of the situation.

Do the opposite of resisting the bangle. If you *choose* to tell the truth, then you get to do it the way you want to."

Sami and Priya looked at her blankly.

"I guess I'm just saying that if you pause before you answer, and you choose *which* truth to share and *how,* then you have some control over it," explained Mei. "Rather than being at the mercy of the bangle forcing you to share the most awkward truth in the most abrupt way."

Priya nodded slowly. "You're right. Sometimes when I don't know what the most true answer is, I pause, and then the bangle lets me say whatever feels right. There was a moment with Rachael at gymnastics where she asked me why I was late, and I was scared I'd overshare about my parents arguing, but in the end, I just said it was because of my dad's bad cooking. Which was also true. Or when I told my mum I was feeling bad. I was feeling a lot of things at the time – mainly huge levels of anxiety about being stuck in a cursed bangle – but I just shared one of them: that I didn't feel so good."

"Oh my god, we've found a loophole!" cried Sami. Mei raised an eyebrow. "Okay, Mei's found a loophole. Yay! Celebratory macaron, anyone?"

Priya shook her head quickly, looking queasily at the desserts, while Mei took a pistachio macaron. "Yes, please! That's why *I* stopped at five slices." She turned to Priya, hesitating. "So, um, please don't feel you have to answer this. But do you want to talk about your parents arguing?"

Priya froze. She hadn't meant to reveal that. But as she looked at her friends – the compassionate expression on Mei's face, the relaxed ease on Sami's – she realized that maybe it was okay for them to know. "I...guess I could," she said slowly. "They...do argue a lot."

"I hear you," said Sami, munching casually on her macaron. "My parents used to argue non-stop before their divorce. Sometimes it was so intense I couldn't even concentrate on learning my lines for *The Hunger Games*."

"Really?!" Priya gasped. She couldn't believe Sami could relate. "My parents do that too! The other day it was so loud I could barely sleep."

"That sounds exhausting," said Mei, with concern. "I had no idea things were so bad at home."

"They're not—" Priya choked. The others looked at her in alarm, but she shook her head as she coughed. "Don't worry, it's just the bangle. I...okay, fine, I guess things *are* bad at home, but I hate how that sounds. I don't know. It's why I never told you both before. I didn't want you to, well, judge me."

"Why would we judge you?" asked Sami in confusion. "Do you judge me for having divorced parents?"

"Of course not!" said Priya. "Never! I just...my mum always says there are some things you should only share with family. Not friends. You know, 'blood is thicker than water', 'don't air your dirty laundry in public'. All that stuff. It just...made me feel I couldn't share this with you both."

Mei looked down at the leftover pizza for a weirdly long time before speaking. "I'm sorry, Priya. I didn't mean to be judgy when I said things sound bad at home. It was just my way of trying to say that I'm sorry they argue so much. And that I care."

Priya looked at her friend in surprise. "Thanks, Mei. That's nice of you to say."

"And I *totally* relate to it all," said Sami. "So, you can call me *whenever* you need to rant about them. I still remember how stressful everything was before my parents divorced." She shuddered. "The fights. The tension. It would have made a great thriller."

Priya frowned. "But you never said anything. I had no idea it was like that for you!"

"I suppose the worst parts were before I met you," reflected Sami. "I used to tell Mei though, when we were in primary school. By the time we met you, they'd already decided to divorce, so things had calmed down."

"I just assumed your parents had a super amicable divorce and never argued," admitted Priya.

"Uh, no way," clarified Sami. "It was hell! I was *thrilled* when they finally divorced. And they're so much better now. My mum loves dating, and my dad loves taking care of his plants. It's perfect."

"My parents argue loads too," added Mei. "Especially when my mum tries to cook dinner. My dad can't handle how much of a mess she leaves the kitchen in."

Priya laughed. "Same! Except it's my dad who can't cook, and my mum who gets stressed. But – do they argue every night? Till really late? And about money?"

Mei shook her head gently. "No. Only once in a while. They seem kind of happy otherwise."

Priya looked sad. "I don't remember the last time my parents were happy. Sometimes I wish they'd get a divorce already!" She breathed in sharply. "I can't believe I just said that out loud."

"It's okay," said Sami, taking her hand. "I used to wish my parents would divorce all the time too, it's not that weird. It's actually kind of sensible – what's the point in people being together when they're totally incompatible?"

"But everyone knows that kids aren't supposed to want their parents to divorce," whispered Priya. "They're meant to be devastated about it."

"I'd be really sad if my parents said they were divorcing," said Mei. "But that's because they seem happy together. And I don't think there's a 'meant to be' or 'supposed to be' in situations like this. It's personal."

Priya nodded slowly. "Yeah. But I don't think they'll ever split up anyway – apparently Indians don't 'do' divorce. Or at least that's what my parents say."

"Tell me about it," agreed Mei. "The list of things Asians don't 'do' is my parents' favourite dinner topic. Like getting nose piercings or studying art at university. Everything is taboo if you're Chinese."

"Jews don't 'do' a whole bunch of things too," added Sami. "Like recite Lady Macbeth at their bat mitzvahs, apparently. Or cartwheel in synagogue."

"Right," said Mei, raising an eyebrow. "Because that's totally the same thing."

"The point is that it sucks being a teenager – or almost-teenager – when your parents are in charge and make terrible life choices all the time," concluded Sami. "It's going to be way better when we're adults."

"I hope so," said Priya. She glanced at the bangle. "And I *really* hope I'm not still wearing this by then."

"You'll be fine," said Mei confidently. "Look how well you just navigated this honest conversation about your parents without blurting out anything that would make you feel embarrassed."

"But that's because I chose to share with you guys," said Priya. "I mean, not initially, but then it felt right. And it helps so much to know you can both relate, on some level."

"Totally," confirmed Sami. "Now how about we carry on talking about super personal things so you can keep practising being honest without being weird?"

Priya looked at her in alarm. "Uh, if we're going to do that, I think I'm going to need some more sustenance. Pass me the macarons, please."

Chapter 11

The next morning, Priya said goodbye to her friends feeling surprisingly light and free, considering she'd just shared things with them that she'd never thought she would.

Her mum was waiting for her in the driveway. "Morning, *beta*. You look happy! I'm guessing you had a nice time?"

Priya nodded happily. "The BEST!"

Her mum put the car into gear and drove off, turning to face Priya. "So, what did you do? I want to hear everything."

Priya smiled. She loved it when it was just the two of them – her mum actually had time to ask her about her life. "We ate so much! Mei's mum let us eat whatever we wanted. And I slept *so* well. I don't remember the last time I woke up feeling this relaxed."

Her mum looked mildly offended. "The only reason *I* don't let you eat whatever you want is because I care about your health."

"I know, Mum," said Priya quickly. "I didn't mean that."

"Hmph. And why did you sleep so much better sharing a bed with Mei than you do at home?"

"Oh, Sami took the bed. I slept on the floor in a sleeping bag."

"And that's more comfortable than your bedroom at home?!"

"No..."

"So, why did you sleep better there than on the expensive foam mattress I bought you after Olaf practically forced me to?" demanded her mum.

Priya bit her bottom lip. She really didn't want to answer this, but she knew she had to tell the truth in her own way before the bangle did it for her. "I guess it was...more peaceful at Mei's house."

Her mum turned to face her as they stopped at traffic lights. "Do you not find our house peaceful?"

Priya sighed inwardly. The only thing her mum disliked more than mess, strong smells and refined sugar was anything she perceived as criticism. And Priya knew she'd definitely perceive her next comment as criticism. "Um...not exactly."

"Why not?!"

Priya turned to look out of the window. They were almost at the gym. She wished they were already there so she didn't have to do this. But she knew the more she resisted, the worse it would be. So she forced herself to answer her mum's

question as gently as she could. "Well...maybe because...
I guess...sometimes...well, often...you and Dad argue."

Her mum's cheeks flushed. "You...can hear us argue?"

Priya nodded apologetically. "It's kind of hard not to."

Her mum pulled up outside the gym and turned to face
Priya. She looked as awkward as Priya did whenever she had
to speak to Katie. Priya really hoped she wasn't making her
mum feel the way Katie Wong made her feel.

"I'm sorry, Priya. I had no idea you could hear us argue.
Does it...bother you?"

Priya nodded silently.

"Oh, Priya," said her mum. "Why didn't you tell me
before?"

Priya looked up. Her mum's eyes were wide with concern.
"I don't know...I didn't want to upset you."

"You're my daughter – you're supposed to upset me!" cried
her mum. "I mean, it's not upsetting me. It's just – oh, Priya,
I want to know how you are. How you *really* are."

"Okay," whispered Priya. She couldn't believe she was
having this conversation with her mum. And she couldn't
believe that she felt okay about it – actually *more* than okay.

"And, um..." Her mum bit her lip awkwardly. "About your
dad and I arguing...there's just a lot going on."

"I know," said Priya quickly. "You don't have to explain.
I know there's money problems. It's why my prize money is
so important. I'm practising lots for my individual event,

so hopefully that will help things if I win. And I know that Dad gets everything wrong. And you're tired from work. And Pinkie can be a lot sometimes. And that my schedule is super intense. Sorry."

Her mum was taken aback. "Well, yes. But none of that is your fault, Priya, you don't need to apologize. And none of those are things you should be worrying about. They're our responsibility, not yours." She paused, then looked into Priya's eyes. "You do know we're so proud of you?"

For a moment, Priya felt her heart grow warm. Her parents were proud of her for being herself. And they always would be.

But then her mum continued. "How can we not be with your gold medals and perfect grades! I always say I wouldn't know what to do without you and I mean it! We don't want to make things hard for you with our, well, problems..."

Priya felt her heart sink, as the familiar hum of pressure coursed through her veins again. The anxiety would always be there – how could it not be when there were so many expectations on her? – but at least her mum knew more about how she felt.

Her mum's brow furrowed. "Do you know if it affects Pinkie too?"

Priya shook her head emphatically. "She can sleep through *anything*."

"But...emotionally?" asked her mum.

Priya shrugged. "I think she's fine."

Her mum nodded. "Okay, well, I'll speak to her properly about it anyway. And..." Her mum hesitated. "I'm sorry it's been hard, Priya. But I'm really glad you told me. I'll make sure me and your dad work things out."

"Really?" Priya wanted to believe her mum, *desperately*, but she knew it couldn't be that simple. If it was, surely her parents would have done it years ago. "You think you can?"

Her mum nodded confidently. "Yes, of course, *beta*. We're just a bit stressed because things are so much more expensive these days, and your dad obviously earns less now he's part-time. But we're just adjusting. And we...we both love each other."

Priya's eyes widened in hope. Maybe things really would start to get better. "You do?"

"Of course, darling! Honestly, we'll sort everything out. It will all be fine. Don't you worry about a *thing*."

Priya's face lit up. "Okay. Cool!"

"Good." Her mum's face relaxed into a smile. "Right. You still have half an hour before practice. How about we go get milkshakes?"

Priya's mouth dropped open. "Actual milkshakes? Or wait, do you mean fresh juices?"

"I mean milkshakes," said her mum. "One won't kill you."

Priya walked into the gymnasium feeling rejuvenated by the rush of sugar and cream. She could do this. All she had to do was remember Mei's rules. She pulled out her phone to double-check them.

Priya's rules for navigating the bangle of truth:

1. *Speak your truth in as casual a way as possible before the bangle makes you do it in a very uncasual way.*
2. *When you really don't want to tell the truth, DON'T resist it! Relax!*
3. *If all else fails, call Sami and Mei to come and lie for you.*

She slipped her phone back into her pocket, grinning. It was very un-her to want to share about her life, but she couldn't *wait* to tell Sami and Mei about the chat she'd just had with her mum. And all over a milkshake! It was something she'd never thought would happen. But her uptight mum had consumed refined sugar, promised she'd work things out with her dad, and admitted that Pinkie's wobbly faces were not a good addition to Priya's New Balances. She hadn't instantly handed over her credit card to buy a new pair, but she had at least validated Priya's frustration towards her younger sister. She knew things weren't Pinkie's fault, not really, but knowing that didn't fix her trainers. And it felt good to have her mum acknowledge it for once.

"Hey! You look lost in thought."

Priya looked up, startled. She relaxed into a smile as she saw Rachael's face beaming at her from beneath her tight braids. "Yeah. I was just reliving the Oreo milkshake I shared with my mum earlier."

Rachael's mouth dropped open. "No! I'm so jealous."

"And that's after the seven pizza slices and mound of macarons I ate last night."

"Wow!" said Rachael. "I just ate chicken and rice. It was jollof, which is my favourite. But still. Oh look, there's Dan. Hey!"

Priya's stomach lurched. She knew she'd have to face Dan – that was why Sami and Mei had helped her come up with her three rules – but that didn't make it any easier.

He walked up to them and nodded. "Hey."

"Priya was just telling me she's been eating the best food." Rachael sighed. "I have major envy."

"Oh, really?" Dan turned to look at her. He was always smiling – but there was absolutely no trace of a smile on his face right now. "So, your Friday night off was everything you wanted it to be then?"

Priya nodded. "Yes. Thanks."

"Cool."

"Tell him what you ate," urged Rachael. "I want him to be as jealous as I am right now."

"Um...pizza. Macarons." Priya flushed as she looked down,

avoiding Dan's gaze. All she could think of was the last time she'd seen him and the hurt look on his face as she'd practically run away.

"Nice," said Dan. And judging by his monosyllabic vibes right now, he was remembering the exact same thing.

"Oh-kay," said Rachael. "Shall we go warm up? Olaf wants us to go through the whole routine today."

Dan and Priya nodded in response, but neither of them moved. Rachael shook her head and walked off. "I'll be by the bars."

Priya forced herself to say something. She needed to get over her fear of talking to Dan and make things better. Before the bangle made things worse. She looked over at the beam and tried to imagine she was psyching herself up for a back handspring. Deep breaths, strong core and self-belief. She could do this. "Um..." She shifted awkwardly, as Dan looked at her expectantly. She tried to summon up the strength she needed for a back handspring. "Um, I...just wanted to say sorry. For being weird. The other day."

"It's cool." Dan shrugged. "I won't ask what's going on. I'm getting the sense you don't want to talk about it."

Priya's face tensed. "I'm really sorry. I've had a lot going on. But...things are starting to make a bit more sense. I think."

"Okay. Do you...want to talk sometime?"

Priya bit her lip and tried to think back to the rules. She knew Dan meant talking about her weirdness and potential issue with him, but he hadn't *technically* said that. She nodded slowly. "Yes! I would love to talk sometime – how about over a milkshake?"

Dan's face lit up. "Yeah. That sounds great! How about the Monday after next? We don't have practice that afternoon."

Priya beamed back at him. "Great! I'll let Rachael and the others know!"

Dan nodded slowly, still smiling. "Sure. The others."

Just then Olaf clapped loudly. "Everyone, come on over! I have an announcement. The Teen Olympics scout will be at the Nationals all day on the 30th of June, so I want everyone to be on top form. Even if your chances don't look that high this year, the scout could remember you for next year. Of course, some of you have a very strong chance." He looked directly at Priya and she felt her blood tingle. It would be amazing to be picked for the new Teen Olympics team – she couldn't think of anything more exciting than training with the best gymnasts in the country! And getting to travel all over the world doing what she loved best. Her family would be *so* proud of her.

Although, it would also mean she'd be even more unavailable for everything else in her life... She didn't imagine the Olympics gave people Friday nights off for sleepovers. But she didn't need to think about that yet.

"And so, I want to give the person with the strongest chance the best opportunity to impress the scout," continued

Olaf. "Priya – I want you to be at the top of the pyramid in the team event. The finale will be you jumping up and landing in splits. What do you say?"

"Yes!" burst out Priya, not even needing the bangle to tell the wholehearted truth about this. "Thank you so much! I can't wait!"

"Good," said Olaf. "But just don't mess this up for us, all right? No more coming in late. I want full commitment from you."

Priya nodded as the others grinned and came over to congratulate her. "You're going to be amazing," said Rachael. "Well done!"

"Definitely," said Dan, smiling gently at her. "And Olaf wants me at the bottom, launching you up, so I'll make sure I get you up to the top. Promise."

Priya's mouth dropped open. Not only was she going to be at the top of the pyramid, but Dan was going to get her up there! She caught sight of the bangle flashing and grinned at it widely. This had to be Ba's doing. She whispered a silent "thank you", and imagined she could see Ba giving her a wink back.

Chapter 12

"Who even is Priya Shah?" cried Sami. "Asking out cute boys, drinking milkshakes with her mum and telling everyone how she feels?! This is the best weekend update ever! I spent the rest of mine binge-watching Netflix. Although I did wow my entire drama group on Sunday with my rendition of Hamlet if Hamlet had been a woman."

"Uh, you forgot the fact that she's going to be jumping from her crush's hands onto the top of an actual human pyramid, *and g*etting a spot on the Olympics team," added Mei. "Even Hamlet would be impressed by that."

Priya rolled her eyes. "Let's not get carried away – the Teen Olympics is super competitive. I might not get onto the team. And I didn't ask Dan out! It was just the bangle, and me trying to find a loophole. It's not a big deal."

"It totally is and you know it," declared Sami. She rolled

over on the grass and pulled up her shirt. "Oh, this sun is heaven. I'm going to get the perfect bat mitzvah tan."

"And your priority is a tanned tummy?" asked Mei.

"I'm thinking of wearing a crop top with statement trousers," said Sami, rolling over onto her side to look at her. "On that note, when are we going BM shopping?"

Priya's stomach lurched. As much as she was sharing the truth lately, she still hadn't told Sami about the date of Nationals being the exact same date as her BM. And she really, really didn't want to have that conversation. "Um, isn't it time to go back in soon? It's almost two."

"Since when do we go in *before* the bell goes?" asked Sami. "And it's quarter to. How about this weekend? I need to get an outfit, stat."

"Fine," said Mei. "But only if you promise not to take over the entire store's changing room again by doing a live 'movie montage' and connecting your phone to their speakers. I don't think I can survive the humiliation.";

"Humiliation? That was an award-winning performance! The staff loved it."

"If by loved, you mean tolerated," corrected Mei.

Sami shrugged breezily. "Tomayto, tomahto. Anyway. Priya, you coming?"

Priya froze. "Am I coming...where?"

"Shopping! On Saturday."

Priya breathed out in relief. She'd gotten away with it

again. "I might be able to after practice. I'll ask my mum."

"Perfect." Sami beamed. "We can discuss at our next Friday night sleepover. And we can go shopping for both your outfits too! I'm thinking we can colour coordinate – how do you guys feel about tangerine and turquoise for a colour scheme?"

Mei turned to Priya. "I'm going to leave this to the truth bangle."

"Um…" Priya bit her bottom lip. "I can't say I'm the biggest fan."

"Hey, look at you telling the truth so diplomatically!" said Mei. "Good progress."

"What do you mean?" demanded Sami. "It's the perfect colour scheme – it's all over TikTok right now. Summer shades, guys."

Priya laughed at the expression on Mei's face. "Let's just say, I'm not sure we could pull it off as well as you. And you're the bat mitzvah girl. You've got to stand out – you don't want us detracting attention from you."

Sami sat bolt upright. "Oh my god, you're right. Maybe you guys can wear neutrals? Pastels?"

"Or maybe, just a thought, we can wear whatever we want and you do the same?" suggested Mei.

Priya's face clouded over. She'd got so caught up in the conversation that she'd forgotten she wouldn't be there. "I'm going to head in. I need to pee."

"So long as you're not going to hide out in the far-right loo of the first-floor girls' bathrooms again," said Mei. "Because if you do, we know exactly where to find you."

Priya laughed nervously. That had been exactly what she was going to do. "See you in maths!"

Priya flushed the loo and left the cubicle. She was washing her hands when she heard two sets of boots stomping towards her. She groaned inwardly.

"Loo lunch girl," said Katie with a smirk. Angela crossed her arms as she stood at Katie's side. "How was the cubicle today? We could set you up a little table in there."

"Actually, I ate outside," said Priya. She pressed the button on the hand-dryer hoping it would drown out any more questions.

But Katie ignored the sound, and walked right up to her, leaning into her ear. "So, where's my maths homework?"

Priya's heart stopped. Oh god – had she forgotten to do it? Then she relaxed as she remembered the Three Musketeers and their deal. "Uh...I think Sami has it."

"Sami?" Angela frowned and came to stand on Priya's other side. "What's she got to do with it?"

"She did it this time," explained Priya. "To help me out."

Katie's mouth dropped open. "Uh, I never said you could do that. *You* do my homework for me – not Sami, not anyone else. How does that sound?"

Priya forced herself to breathe. She could do this. She could tell the truth in a careful, controlled way before the bangle did it for her. "It doesn't sound...very fair."

"Excuse *me*?"

"It's just...I have a lot of work to do myself. And gymnastics practice. And Sami and Mei are happy to help."

Katie turned to stare at Angela. "Am I hallucinating or is she saying she's too busy to do my homework?"

Angela shook her head slowly. "She said it. What are we going to do to her?"

"Exactly what I said I'd do," said Katie, crossing her arms. "I'm going to tell Mrs Lufthausen you're the one who copies me. You're not exactly in her best books right now, Shah – how do you think she's going to react to that? Suspend you maybe? Or flat-out expel you?"

Priya paused as she really thought about it. It was true that Mrs Lufthausen wasn't her greatest fan, but...she was also a smart woman. "To be honest," said Priya, cautiously speaking her truth. "I don't actually think she's going to believe you."

"What?" Katie momentarily lost her composure. "Of course she will!"

"No, she won't," said Priya, her voice slowly becoming more confident. "It's true she hates me, but she's not an idiot. All she has to do is look at our grades in exams – you might get nines all year because I do your homework for you, but I bet your exams tell another story. And even if you've somehow cheated in your exams too, then Mrs Lufthausen will probably just set us an assignment to do right there on the spot, and it will prove which one of us has actually done the work."

Katie stared at Priya in silence, her face setting in cold anger. Priya felt her confidence fade away. She couldn't believe she'd just said all that to Katie! There was no way she would have ever done that if it wasn't for the bangle! And now Katie was going to...oh god, what *was* Katie going to do?

"Whatever," said Katie, turning to Angela. "I've got better things to do than deal with loo lunch girl." She gave Priya one last look. "And I don't need you to do my homework any more anyway. Your Anne Boleyn essay only got a six. Mr Long said it 'lacked self-awareness'. So, thanks for nothing." Katie stalked out of the bathroom with Angela in tow – the latter glancing back to give Priya a menacing look.

Priya let out a deep sigh of relief without even realizing she'd been holding her breath. But she'd done it. She, Priya Shah, had just stood up to the scariest girls in school – and it was all thanks to the bangle. She looked down at the innocuous band of gold on her wrist and thought back to Ba and the legend she used to tell her. Priya had no idea if the bangle really had belonged to the princess or not, but now she was sure that Ba had known about its powers. She'd done her classic Ba thing of foreseeing the future and had figured out that the bangle would be able to help Priya do what she couldn't do alone: stand up for herself.

Chapter 13

Priya sat at the dinner table nervously reaching for another roti. She looked around and couldn't believe her eyes. Pinkie was eating her spinach shak with no complaints, her dad was putting dahl on her mum's plate, and her mum was *smiling* at him in response. This was unheard of in the Shah household – a normal family dinner with no drama. Yet.

"This shak is really nice," said Priya, and her mum beamed. "It tastes exactly like Ba's." The smile dropped off her mum's face and Priya realized her mistake. Her parents had never specifically said she couldn't speak about Ba, but it was clear that it was yet another unspoken rule in their household.

Her mum coughed uncomfortably. "I'm glad you're enjoying it. So, um, how was everyone's day?"

"Eventful," said Pinkie, spooning more yoghurt into her bowl. "Miles ate a dead slug, Ms Cromer cried when I pointed out her diagram was wrong, and my volcano exploded so much that Miles got bicarbonate of soda in his hair."

"That does sound eventful," replied their mum faintly.

"Poor Miles," remarked their dad. "He did not have a good day."

"He cheered up when I told him I liked him," said Pinkie, spooning more rice into her mouth.

"What?!" cried Priya. "You told him you *liked* him. Like, *liked* him?"

"What's the big deal?" asked Pinkie.

"She's ten years old," whispered their dad to himself. "Ten!"

Their mum cleared her throat awkwardly. "Pinkie, do you think you might be too young to be telling boys you like them?"

"No. And it's not like we kissed or anything."

Priya's mouth dropped open. "How is this happening?"

"I have no idea," muttered her father. "And I really wish it wasn't."

"Right, well, how was your day, Priya?" asked her mum. "Did *you* tell anyone you liked them?"

Priya choked on her roti. "No!" Thank god her mum's question was so specific. She hoped that was the end of this topic of discussion.

But Pinkie grinned at her. "She *wishes* she did though! A certain Da—"

"Pinkie!" Priya shrieked. "Stop it!"

Their dad sighed loudly. "I thought I'd have at least another six years before I had to deal with this."

Priya took a deep breath. "Moving on. My day was...pretty good, thanks. Gymnastics was fun – I'm practising being at the top of the human pyramid in the team event, which is cool. And I..." She tried to think of another way to say "stood up to a bully". "... Fixed a difficult situation. And I sunbathed with Sami and Mei."

"I hope you were wearing sunscreen," commented her mum. "But well done on the pyramid, honey."

"Great news, Pri!" said her dad. "I can't wait to come and see you. What day is it again?"

"Darling, you know you get all the emails about Priya's training now," her mum said, tapping his hand lightly. "All the info will be in there. Forward it to me when you check."

"There's no rush," said Priya quickly, her stomach heavy with the reminder that her competition was the same day as Sami's BM. Her parents would find out at some point – though ever since her dad took over gymnastics admin from her mum, it was mainly on Priya to keep them updated about anything important because he never checked his inbox – but she wasn't ready to deal with the reality of it right now.

"You should invite Sami and Mei over soon," said her mum suddenly. "You're always going to theirs, but we hardly see them here. What do you think?"

Priya choked for the second time. "Sorry. Um – what do I think? I guess I...think that I could technically invite them over, yes. But there's no need. I can just go to theirs."

"It's not fair to always go over to theirs without inviting them back," persisted her mum. "Why don't you want them here?"

"It's not because of my cooking, is it?" asked her dad anxiously. "We can order in."

Priya froze helplessly, trying to think of an appropriate truth to say. But before she could, Pinkie answered for her: "She doesn't want them over because you'll both argue loads and it will be embarrassing."

Priya's mouth dropped open. Her parents turned to each other in obvious discomfort. Pinkie carried on eating, nonplussed.

"Uh, is that true, Priya?" asked her mum.

Priya squeezed her eyes shut. "Um. Yes."

There was a silence so long that Priya slowly opened her eyes again to check everyone was still alive. Her dad looked right at her, with a strange smile. "You don't need to worry about that any more. We promise."

"I know you don't *want* to argue in front of them," said Priya hesitantly. "But what if..."

Her mum shook her head firmly. "No – it won't happen. Look at us now – aren't we all having a lovely family dinner?"

"I guess so..."

"Exactly." Her mum beamed. "Your dad and I have sorted everything out, and there'll be no more arguments. We'll host Sami and Mei here this Friday night."

"Perfect – that gives me four days to tidy up." Her dad grinned. He reached over and took her mum's hand. Priya stared in shock as her mum didn't flinch – instead she *squeezed* his hand back.

"Uh, wow, okay," said Priya. "I guess, if you really have sorted things out, then that would be...nice. Thanks."

Later that evening, Priya pushed opened Pinkie's door. Her younger sister was sitting on her bed intently playing a video game. When Priya walked in, she threw the console into the air and cheered loudly. "Wooohooo! I won!"

"Uh, congratulations?" said Priya.

"Thanks. That'll show Miles who's best!"

Priya sat on the edge of the bright bed, ignoring the fact that her little sister seemed to be more confident with boys than she was, and got straight to the point. "Pinkie – what do you think of Mum and Dad? They seemed happy tonight, didn't they?"

"*Seemed.*"

"What do you mean?"

"They're just putting it on for us."

Priya frowned. "What? No, they're not! Things are changing.

Didn't you see Dad take Mum's hand? And she *let* him. They didn't argue – not even when Dad burned the roti."

"Exactly. They put on a good show for us."

Priya stared at her sister in dismay. "But – why do you think it's a show?"

"Because you told Mum their arguing was bothering you. She asked me about it too. And now they're trying to pretend things are okay."

Priya thought back to her chat with her mum over milkshake. But the change couldn't just be because of that one conversation – the affection between her parents had been real. She'd *seen* it. "What did you tell Mum?"

"That it's annoying but I'm good at blocking it out. It doesn't bother me as much as it does you. I know it stops you sleeping and stuff."

"How do you know that?!"

Pinkie looked at her like she was stupid. "We live in the same house? The walls aren't exactly thick. I can hear you singing Taylor Swift songs to yourself in the mornings."

Priya blinked. She hadn't realized her sister was so perceptive. She'd always assumed that Pinkie was less sensitive than her and didn't notice what went on. But that clearly wasn't true. She saw it all – she just had her own coping mechanisms. "Oh," said Priya. "I'm...sorry. But even if my chat with Mum did inspire her and Dad to talk things through, that doesn't mean they were being fake at dinner."

She nodded, more certain now. Pinkie was only ten – what did she know? "Their affection was real. They're doing what they said and working things out, and, guess what? It's working."

Pinkie shrugged, turning back to her video game. "Maybe. Who knows?"

"Me!" said Priya. "Trust me."

"Fine," said Pinkie. "Also, I heard you asking Mum about doing something for Ba's death anniversary. I know she shut you down, but I think it's a really cool idea."

"Thanks," said Priya, surprised again by her younger sister. "I just wanted to do something to keep remembering her and talking about her. But—"

"The parents won't," finished Pinkie. "Yup. Annoying. I'm here if ever you want to talk about her though. I miss her all the time."

"Me too," said Priya softly. "Thanks, Pinkie. Also..." She tried to summon up her backflips energy before asking the question that was on her mind – and had been ever since dinner. She took a deep breath. "Um, what did you tell Miles when you said you liked him?"

"That I liked him."

"In those words?"

"Yep, all three of them: I, like, you."

"And...it went well?"

Pinkie didn't move her eyes from the screen as she replied.

"Yeah. He said he likes me too and then he let me borrow his space pen – it's seriously cool."

Priya smiled.

"You should tell Dan you like him," continued her sister. "He's been single for a few months and he's ready to date now. But there's interest from other girls. So, you should act soon."

Priya's mouth dropped. "What? How do you know all this?!"

Pinkie turned to face her older sister with a sympathetic look. "It took me two minutes on his socials. How do you *not* know all this?"

Chapter 14

Sami swallowed a crunchy avocado roll, sighing in satisfaction. "This has seriously raised the stakes of the Friday night sleepover. Sushi is the height of sophistication, and I'm officially addicted."

"I think you have to eat the raw fish ones to call yourself a sushi addict," said Mei. "You've only eaten the vegetarian ones."

"So? It's better for the environment. I'm saving the world while you gobble up all the salmon," declared Sami.

"Well, unlike my dad's attempt at dinner, it's actually edible," said Priya, holding up a rice roll with her chopsticks.

"It's really nice to see your parents again," said Mei, reaching for a prawn tempura. "It's been so long since we've been over."

"Totally," agreed Sami. "I forget how clean your house

always is. And how good it smells. Shame about the lack of desserts though."

Priya grinned. "Don't worry – I persuaded my dad to sneak us in some chocolate." She mock-bowed as her friends cheered, then hesitated. "Also. There's something I want to say. In the spirit of honesty."

"Is this tofu roll not tofu?" shrieked Sami. "I knew it tasted fishy. And I'm sorry, but raw seafood just sounds gross!"

"It says tofu on the packaging," said Mei as Sami sighed in relief.

Priya chewed her bottom lip. "I'm just going to be brave and share the truth with you both, which is that, um, your not coming over for a while was deliberate. As in, I avoided inviting you over." She took a deep breath. "Because...I was scared my parents would argue in front of you. And I was embarrassed."

Mei nodded calmly. "I had a feeling that's why you never invited us over. Especially once you told us about the arguing."

"Totally," said Sami. "It was obvious something was up."

"But – why did you never say anything?" asked Priya in amazement.

"I just figured you'd tell us if you wanted to," said Mei.

Priya sat still, taken aback. All this time she'd felt she was hiding things from her friends so they wouldn't judge her, yet they'd kind of known all along – and they didn't mind at all. They *cared.*

Sami swallowed a cucumber maki. "Also, you know it's not a problem if they did break out in a massive fight. I'm practically immune to arguing after my parents' divorce. And it's always good inspo for my acting to see other people's emotions in action."

"Good to know." Priya smiled. "But...I think it might not even *be* a problem any more. They haven't argued for days. And they're being *nice* to each other. I saw my dad hold my mum's hand – and she *let* him."

"Whoah," said Sami. "My parents never did that when they were on their way out. Maybe they're going to fix things?"

"That's exactly what I thought!" agreed Priya. "I think things are finally looking up!"

"Mazel tov," cheered Sami.

"Seconded," said Mei. "That's so good to hear, Pri. But just so you know, if anything changes again, we're here to talk."

Priya nodded, trying to ignore the discomfort in her stomach – she wouldn't need to talk to Mei; things would be fine. "Thanks. But I think it's all going well. Even if Pinkie doesn't agree."

"She doesn't?" asked Mei.

"She thinks they're faking it for our sake," replied Priya. "But what does she know? She's ten years old."

"Well, *I* firmly believe there is a strong chance that the Shah household could be argument-free by my bat mitzvah," affirmed Sami.

Mei rolled her eyes again. "Can you not use your BM as a marker of time? It's not like Christmas."

"It's going to be *better* than Christmas," clarified Sami. "And I love that you just said BM! Proud!"

Priya laughed and reached for more sushi. She loved this – sitting in the middle of her bedroom floor, eating takeaway sushi on top of a carpet of paper towels her mum had laid out, surrounded by her best friends. It had been so long since she'd had them both in her bedroom, but now, she couldn't remember what she'd ever been scared about. Things were finally changing – for the better.

"Let's do a toast," said Priya suddenly. She raised her salmon maki in the air. "To us. Friends for ever."

"The Three Musketeers," cried Sami, lifting her avocado maki up. "One for all and all for one!"

"Sure," said Mei. She pierced a sweet potato tempura with her chopsticks and held it up. "To us."

All three of them clashed their chopsticks together, laughing, before eating their food. Mei reached for her green tea, took a sip, and then stared into the cup for a weirdly long time. She didn't speak, and Sami and Priya looked at each other in confusion.

"Is it me, or is Mei giving off major serial killer vibes right now?" asked Sami.

"I feel like she's kind of giving the vibes to the tea," said Priya. "Is there something wrong with it?"

Mei cleared her throat, then finally looked up. "Sami. Priya. I have something I need to tell you both."

"Oh no!" Sami gasped. "Did I just eat salmon by mistake?"

Mei sighed. "No. Unsurprisingly, none of our truths are about your food consumption. Also, raw fish is delicious – you should try it."

"A truth?" asked Priya anxiously, as Sami shuddered. "Is it something serious?"

Mei took a deep breath and pushed her thick fringe behind her ears. "Look, I don't want to make a big deal out of this. I'm only telling you because Priya's been so honest lately, and well, it's made me realize I want to do the same."

"Is it something we've done wrong?" Priya's face was tense with worry. "Are you upset I told you I didn't like your new pencil case? I'm so sorry I didn't navigate the truth bangle better that time."

Sami gasped. "Oh my god – is it that you can't come to my BM? I can't believe it! This is the worst day of my entire life. I'll die without both my musketeers by my side!"

Priya felt her stomach lurch with guilt.

"Can you both just stop guessing?" demanded Mei. "It is neither of those things. I just wanted to say that, well, I've figured out I like girls. Only girls. Not boys. I'm, well, I'm a lesbian."

"Eeeeeeeeeeeee!" squealed Sami. "This is AMAZING! I am so proud of you!" She flung her arms around a squirming Mei.

"You are an inspiration to us all. I support you in every way, and I cannot *wait* to go to gay clubs with you."

Priya laughed as Mei swatted Sami off her. She turned to her best friend, her eyes shining. "Mei. That is so, so cool you've figured that out. I'm so happy for you. I love you so much."

"Me too," said Sami. "But we had better be the first people you've told. If you've told—"

"You're the first," interrupted Mei. "And it's not a big deal. I just wanted you both to know."

Priya leaned over and hugged her tightly. "I'm so glad you told us. Thanks for being honest, Mei. You know we're here if ever you need anything."

Sami wrapped her arms around them both, joining in the group hug. "Totally! But..." She pulled away to look sternly at Mei. "I have questions. And I'm going to need answers. I mean, if you consent to answering them. I respect your boundaries."

Mei exhaled dramatically. "Okay. Let's do this. So long as you know, I might not be answering all of them." She gave Priya a quick glance. "I'm kind of relieved I'm not the one stuck in the bangle right now."

Priya gave her a sympathetic smile as Sami sat up straight and launched into her questions. "So, first, when did you know? Secondly, have you told your parents? And most importantly, who do you fancy right now?"

Mei counted her answers off on her fingers as she replied.

"I've kind of always known but I only realized properly this year. I haven't told them yet because I'd rather wait until I'm seeing someone. And I fancy Sarah P. Is that enough?"

Sami shrieked. "Sarah P! You guys would be SO cute! I'm obsessed!"

"It's true, you would be." Priya grinned. "Although, I'm not so sure about her new perfume... I kind of truth-bangled her about it the other day."

"Oh yeah, the musky one," said Mei, nodding. "I feel like it brings out a different side to her."

Sami and Priya burst into laughter – they'd never seen Mei like this before, and it was officially adorable. Just then the door opened, saving a blushing Mei from total mortification.

Priya's dad stood in the doorway, looked at them in concern. "Is everything okay? I heard so much shrieking I thought someone might have had a wasabi related accident. That stuff is lethal – I once swallowed so much I cried for days."

"Things are very okay." Priya smiled. Suddenly, she frowned. "But is everything okay with you? And...Mum?"

Her dad nodded reassuringly. "More than okay. There's no need to worry, *beta*. Especially because...I've come with a delivery!" He revealed a bag overflowing with chocolates as the girls cheered. "Who wants dessert?!"

An hour later, Sami, Mei and Priya were lying flat on Priya's bed. "Why are my eyes so much bigger than my stomach?" groaned Sami. "I always eat too much."

"At least you don't have to do three hours of gymnastics tomorrow," moaned Priya. "I'm going to die."

"You both need to learn to save room for dessert," said Mei, shrugging. "I'm fine."

Priya rolled over to face her. "Can I just say, I'm so proud of you for telling us about your sexuality earlier. You're a million times braver than I am."

"You like girls too?!" cried Sami. "Oh my god, am I the only basic hetero one?"

"I don't *think* so," said Priya slowly. "I haven't really thought about it. All I do know is that I like D—"

"Dan Zhang," her friends chorused together. "We get it."

Priya blushed. "Right. Anyway, what I was *trying* to say is that I've needed a magic bangle to help me tell the truth. Whereas you just did it solo, Mei."

"I don't know," said Mei thoughtfully. "You're pretty brave for handling everything you're going through. It takes guts. And I feel like you're making it work. I mean, as bad as it is for you having a truth bangle stuck round your wrist for ever, it's been kind of inspiring too."

"Totally," agreed Sami. "Personally, I feel like it's helped bring us even closer together! And okay, yes, it's got you into some *seriously* humiliating situations, Priya, often with the guy you fancy."

"Thanks for the reminder," said Priya drily.

"*But* it's also got you Friday night sleepovers with us," continued Sami, undeterred. "And it's helping your parents' marriage. Not to *mention* what it's done with Katie Wong. I bet she'll never bother you again."

"Plus, it inspired me to sign up for LGBTQ+ club at school," said Mei. "I'm going to start on Wednesday..."

Priya squeezed her arm. "That's amazing."

Sami clapped her hands together. "I *love* that for you!"

Mei smiled. "Thanks. I'm excited. It's fun to start owning my sexuality. And who knows, maybe one day Sarah P will come to LGBTQ+ club and we'll have the meet-cute of my dreams."

"I'm not sure you can have a meet-cute with someone who's been in the same form as you for two years," pointed out Sami.

Mei shrugged airily. "Details." Then she turned to Sami. "Hey, you're the only one who hasn't shared a secret. Who's your crush?"

Sami sat upright. "Oh my god. I don't have one. What's wrong with me? I haven't fancied anyone since that boy in the year above played the Peeta to my Katniss!"

"That doesn't mean there's anything wrong with you," said Priya firmly. "You don't need a crush – to be honest, life is probably simpler without one."

"True," acknowledged Sami. "I'm free to follow my own dreams and prioritize myself."

"As if you'd ever stop doing that even if you liked someone!" said Mei.

"Maybe you don't *have* any secrets from us," said Priya. "You are pretty open already."

Sami bit her bottom lip. "Um, that is not technically fully true. There is *one* thing I've never told you."

Priya and Mei sat upright. "Tell us!"

"So, you know I'm a sophisticated young woman?" said Sami. "And my maturity is a big part of my personality?"

Mei stifled a giggle. "Um, yes?"

"Well, I am not actually as grown-up as I may seem." Sami took a deep breath with her eyes squeezed shut, before exhaling and opening her eyes wide. "I still sleep with Dolly. Every night. Except sleepovers – she's more of a homebody."

"Dolly being...?" asked Priya.

"My doll, obviously! I've had her since I was five, I love her and I'm sorry, but I will sleep with her till my dying days." Sami paused. "Just so long as nobody finds out."

Mei grinned. "Well, your secret's safe with me. I wish you and Dolly the best for your future together. You sound like a great couple. Maybe you can bring her to LGBTQ+ club too."

"Totally," agreed Priya. "I can't wait to meet her." She shrieked as Sami threw a pillow at her and Mei. "Okay, okay.

I promise I'll keep your secret! Besides, it's not a big deal. I still have Teddy – look he's over there."

Mei raised an eyebrow as she turned to look at the stuffed bear with a missing button eye. "Teddy the teddy bear? And Dolly the dolly? You guys really went for the obvious, huh?"

"We were little," said Sami defensively. "The creative part of our brains hadn't fully developed. Why – what did you name your toys?"

"I had three stuffed monkeys," said Mei. "Called—"

"Monkey, Chimp and Gorilla?" asked Sami.

"Aristotle, Socrates and Plato," corrected Mei. "I was into ancient philosophy."

Chapter 15

Olaf clapped his hands together. "Warm-up over! Partner up, please. Same ones as last time. I want you all to work on your routines for the team event."

Priya turned to Dan with a nervous smile. "I guess that means we're together? We probably need to practise my final jump."

Dan smiled back. "Definitely – I've been putting in extra practice to make sure I get you right to the top of that pyramid."

"Cool." Priya blushed.

"So, uh, how was your Friday night off?"

"Really good, thanks," she replied, realizing that for once, it was true. "My friends came over for a sleepover. We ate sushi and overdosed on chocolate."

"What, while we were slaving away in here?!" Dan shook

his head ruefully. "I really should follow your lead and ask Coach for more time off..."

Priya grinned. "I can give you tips if you want. I've had a fair bit of practice in being honest lately."

"That's really cool," said Dan. "I think it takes courage to speak the truth – I wish I was better at it." Suddenly, he flushed. "Sorry, that was pretty heavy chat. And anyway, we should probably start practising before Coach loses it."

"You're right," said Priya, following him to a free spot on the mats. "But, um..." She looked away as Dan turned to face her. "I don't think what you said was heavy. I agree, actually. It's hard to be honest. I'm not always brave enough to tell the truth, but I wish I was."

Dan hesitated, shifting awkwardly. "I know you don't want to talk about it, but is that why you've been weird with me? Because there's something about me that's been hard for you to be honest about?"

Priya felt blood rush to her cheeks. It was happening. He'd asked her directly. After all this time trying to avoid this very situation, she was in it. And her heart was pounding so fast she felt like she was about to pass out. "Um. Yes?"

"What...is it?" Dan's face reddened. He looked nervous. But not as nervous as Priya.

She tried to remember Sami and Mei's advice. She needed to breathe. Not resist the truth. Try and think of a good way to say it. Maybe there was a subtle way to say it without *saying* it? But then she thought of Pinkie. Her direct honesty. Her courage. Could Priya be more like her and *choose* to say the truth, instead of trying to skirt around it?

Before she knew it, Priya – who was staring fixedly at the bright blue gym mats and completely avoiding Dan's eyes – said the three words that she'd never, ever thought she'd say out loud. "I...like...you."

And then she squeezed her eyes shut. She couldn't believe this. Her heart was thudding as adrenaline seeped through her entire body. She'd just said that she liked Dan Zhang. OUT LOUD. What had she done?! What was Dan thinking? What would he—

"You like me?" He repeated her words. "Like...*like* me?"

And now she had to clarify it?! Priya kept her eyes tightly closed as she confirmed: "Yes."

"But – if you like me, why didn't you want to partner with me?" asked Dan. "And you kept running away from me. I thought you really *didn't* like me."

Priya opened her eyes hesitantly. Dan's (beautiful) face was crumpled in confusion. She gulped. "Um. I guess because I was scared I'd tell you that I like you."

Suddenly Dan laughed out loud, revealing his neat white teeth. Priya stared at him and his perfect mouth (he'd definitely had braces) in horror. She'd imagined this situation millions of times in her head, each time watching it play out in a slightly different way. But not once had it occurred to her that Dan Zhang would humiliate her by *laughing.* She spun around to run away, hot tears threatening to spill out of her eyes.

But something stopped her.

Dan.

He was holding her arm.

"Sorry for laughing, Priya." His expression was serious now. "It's just..." He coughed awkwardly. Then swallowed. Loudly. "I've liked you for ages too. And I was scared to tell *you.* That's kind of why I just said that thing about how it takes courage to speak the truth. I guess I don't have as much as you do."

Priya slowly lifted her eyes. Dan's dark hair was flopping into his eyes. He was smiling tentatively. He looked as cute as usual – but he was also *telling her he liked her back.* Priya felt her stomach somersault inside her like it was competing for gold at Nationals. The tears in her eyes dried up and she felt a giant grin spread slowly across her face. She opened her mouth to speak in delight – she had so much she wanted to say. But only one word came out. "Oh."

"Yeah." Dan grinned back at her. "Oh."

"Um..." Priya tried to think of something else to say but it was impossible. Her mind was exploding. She couldn't even focus properly – she just had Dan's words playing on repeat in her head: "I've liked you for ages too." *For ages!* Priya grinned even wider, knowing she must look crazy, but she was too excited to do anything about it. The only thing she wanted to do was video-call Sami and Mei and tell them every single detail of this conversation – and then scream out loud for half an hour. This was officially the best moment of her entire life. Ever.

"So, how about we go for milkshakes together on Monday?" said Dan finally. "Without the others?"

"Yes, please," blurted out Priya. She cleared her throat. "I mean, sure. Sounds cool."

"Great." Dan beamed. "I mean, cool."

"Shah! Zhang! Why haven't you done a single flip?!" Olaf shouted at them from across the gymnasium. "Move it!"

"Sorry, Coach, we were talking," said Priya.

Olaf raised his eyes to the ceiling. "Dear god. Teenagers. And what exactly is so important that you need to talk about it when you should be moving?!"

Priya laughed and caught Dan's eye. "Um. Our feelings?"

"Feelings?! Priya Shah – if you want to keep your place on the top of the pyramid, you'll put your feelings to the side and MOVE! We've got a competition to train for!"

Priya and Dan grinned at each other, then they both spoke in unison: "Yes, Coach!"

"Uh, Sami, are you okay?" Priya leaned into the phone screen to look at her sobbing friend. "Mei – why is she crying?"

Mei shrugged. "Don't ask me. I thought she'd be happy for you."

Sami lifted her head so quickly that her red hair flew into the air like a huge halo around her. "I *am* happy for you," she wailed. "It's why I'm weeping, obviously! I just can't believe this is happening. I'm so proud of you, Priya. You've just really come out of your shell and I feel like you've blossomed and been so brave. I mean, you *told a boy you like him.* Do you know how major this is?!"

"I'm pretty sure she does," remarked Mei. "Seeing as she's the one who did it."

"I just can't believe you have an actual date," said Sami. "You're the first one of us musketeers. I don't think any of us saw it coming."

"Thanks," said Priya drily. "But – to be honest – I don't think I saw it coming either. I never thought I'd be able to do something like that. Let alone have Dan say it back to me."

"It is amazing," agreed Mei. "Seriously, Priya. You were so brave. I'm proud."

"Thanks, guys, but...it wasn't me, not really. It was the bangle. I only said it because Dan asked me flat out."

"Yes, because you said things to lead him there," said Sami. "I'm sorry, but you can't give the bangle *all* the credit. You said more words to Dan than you've said in your life, and you barely even tried to resist the bangle!"

"She's right," said Mei. "And you can't deny it because you

just gave us an entire play-by-play of the situation. We were basically there."

"Maybe," said Priya. She hesitated, then asked: "Do you think that Ba knew the bangle would help me do things like this?"

"If so, your Ba is a total legend," declared Sami. "She's basically the reason you've got a date."

"I feel like she knew the bangle would help you open up," said Mei thoughtfully. "To *everyone* in your life. I've loved hearing more about you ever since you got the bangle."

"I've kind of loved telling you," said Priya slowly. "I think it's why Ba said the bangle would help me to not feel lonely. You know how she said something about how we feel lonely when we can't be honest with people."

"That's so true," said Mei softly. "I feel way less lonely now you both know I like girls."

Priya smiled warmly at her best friend. "I'm so glad you shared it with us."

"And I never feel lonely when I'm with you both because I know I can tell you *anything*," said Sami. "Musketeers for life!"

Mei rolled her eyes and Priya laughed as Sami flexed her biceps in what was apparently the musketeers' new signature pose.

Then Priya bit her lip. "Can I tell you both something crazy? When Dan asked me flat-out what was going on, I was trying to think of a way to fudge the truth again. But what changed my mind was *Pinkie*. She told some boy she liked him the other day and he gave her a pen. She made it sound so simple that I kind of thought...why not do the same?"

"You're taking dating advice from your ten-year-old sister?" asked Mei.

"She does sound wise," pointed out Sami. "Maybe you should ask her for some tips too, Mei. On how to ask out Sarah P."

Mei flushed. "Sami! I don't need to ask her out. I'm happy liking her from afar. It's safer that way. Besides, I don't even know if she likes girls."

"Hasn't Priya inspired you?" persisted Sami. "She's going for milkshakes with Dan *next week* – wouldn't you like to have a milkshake with Sarah P.?"

"She's lactose intolerant," said Mei. "So no."

Sami sighed. "You're so literal."

"As much as I'm loving this," said Priya, "I have to go and journal about everything that just happened before I forget the exact wording. It needs to be documented."

"Couldn't agree more," said Sami. "It's a shame you didn't know in advance or you could have secretly recorded it. Or even better, filmed it."

"Yeah, I feel like that would raise some serious consent issues," said Mei. "But journaling sounds like a great idea. Enjoy it, Priya. You deserve this."

Priya smiled widely at her best friends as she waved

goodbye to them, watching the bangle gleam on the screen. She couldn't remember the last time she'd ever felt this happy. She was so grateful to her grandma for giving her the bangle. For the first time in her life, it felt like things were going exactly the way she wanted them to – and it felt better than she could have ever dreamt.

Chapter 16

Priya stared out of the window, smiling to herself. She'd barely stopped smiling since her chat with Dan – even when her mum had made her clean the bathrooms (while Pinkie got the easy job of vacuuming the hallways) and she'd found an enormous, slimy hairball in the drain. She hadn't even minded when Pinkie had accidentally emptied the vacuum out on top of Priya's trainers. Or when her dad had ruined the dhal by putting in so much chilli that everyone's eyes started leaking. Because Priya had a date with Dan Zhang.

And – to top it all off – he had texted her that *very morning*.

Have a good day ☺ *Looking forward to our milkshake later!*

It was the best text she'd ever received. She'd already copied it out into her journal – emoji and all – and now she was reliving it for the fiftieth time in her mind. She even liked the punctuation. It was so Dan to put an exclamation mark – he was so enthusiastic and cheerful. And the smiley face looked just like his. She couldn't wait to see him later. To see his big smile, his sparkling eyes, his—

"Priya Shah!"

Priya jolted in her seat and turned to face the front of the room. Mrs Lufthausen was standing there, both hands on her thick knit trousers (Priya had never seen knit trousers before, and hoped she never would again), glaring directly at Priya. "Don't tell me you're daydreaming *again*."

Priya gulped. "I'm sorry, Mrs Lufthausen."

"What exactly is more interesting than my algebra lesson? Hm? What is it that you're thinking about when you're *clearly* not thinking about quadratics?"

Oh no. Priya tried to think rationally. Slowly. She didn't want to just panic and blurt out— "Dan Zhang." Too late.

Priya's eyes widened in terror – and serious regret. What had she just DONE?! She could hear Sami gasping in shock to her left and Mei groaning in quiet sympathy to her right. She glanced down at her wrist in mortification. She knew that Ba's bangle had done so much to help her, but did it really have to keep getting her in trouble with Mrs L as well?

"Dan Zhang?" Mrs Lufthausen practically spat out his name. "Who is that?"

Priya's cheeks flooded. "He's the boy I have a date with tonight."

Mrs Lufthausen started spluttering. "A date! In my – I mean – what – I can't *believe*—"

"Priya Shah has a date?!" Katie raised a perfectly threaded eyebrow as she turned to Angela. "Who even is Dan Zhang?"

"I think he goes to Heartland Boys," said Angela, pulling out her phone to check. "Year above."

At this, Mrs Lufthausen practically exploded. "Girls! This is a maths lesson not a gossiping session in the car park!"

"As if we'd ever hang out in a car park," said Katie, under her breath to Angela. "What century was she born in?"

"Put your phones away NOW," demanded Mrs Lufthausen. "This is unacceptable, Priya. I cannot believe you had the audacity to talk about your...your *date* in my maths lesson. I'm giving you detention. Tonight. After school."

Priya's face fell in dismay as Sami let out an audible wail. "Oh, not tonight! Mrs L, please – you can't make her miss the date!"

"It is Mrs Lufthausen and you will stay silent unless you want to join her, Samantha," thundered their teacher. She looked around the room to check everyone else was sitting meekly and then let out a sharp cry as her eyes landed on Katie. "WHAT do you think you're doing?"

Katie – who had been looking at Angela's phone under the desk – dropped it in alarm. "Nothing."

Mrs Lufthausen picked up the phone from the floor. Priya could see a zoomed-in photo of Dan Zhang on the screen, taken straight from the teen UK Gymnasts webpage. His name was written underneath in capital letters. Mrs Lufthausen pursed her lips together, staring at Katie in fury. "How dare you directly disobey me! You will be joining Priya in detention. Tonight."

"Me too?" asked Angela eagerly. "It's my phone."

"Not you," snapped Mrs Lufthausen. "This isn't a party. But I'm confiscating your phone." She slipped the mobile into her pocket, ignoring Angela's hurt cry. "And if ANYONE dares to say the name 'Dan Zhang' in this classroom ever again, they will have detention for the rest of the term. Understood?"

The entire class nodded in perfect silence, looking down at their work to hide from Mrs Lufthausen's wrath. But Priya could practically hear Sami and Mei's horror reverberating on either side of her. Not only would she have to miss her date with Dan tonight, but she had detention *with Katie.* There was no way this was going to end well.

At the end of the school day, when everyone was going home, Priya made her way to her first ever after-school detention. Things really had changed for her since the bangle came into her life. She just wished it was all dates and sleepovers, rather than detentions. Olaf was going to be livid when he found out she was missing practice today, and she had no idea how her parents would react when the school called to tell them about her after-school detention. But none of that was as terrifying as what she was about to do.

The two people she was most scared of – Mrs Lufthausen and Katie Wong – were waiting for her inside the maths classroom. She took a deep breath and turned around to get one last supportive look from Sami and Mei, who were watching from the end of the corridor. But the expressions on their faces suggested they were even more worried than she was. When they realized she was looking, they forced their faces into bright smiles and waved thumbs-ups at her.

"You've got this!" Sami whispered loudly. "Go, girl!"

"It'll be fine," mouthed Mei, before turning to Sami and quietly adding, "Thank god I'm not wearing the truth bangle right now."

Priya – who'd heard everything – sighed loudly. She agreed with Mei that this was not going to be fine, but unfortunately, she had no choice. If she did, she'd be on her way to have a milkshake with Dan right this second. Instead, she pushed open the door.

"There you are. I thought you were going to bunk detention. Which would be pretty badass of you. And also, totally out of character." Katie was sitting on a chair with her boots on the table, chewing gum. There was no Mrs Lufthausen in sight.

Priya looked around in confusion. "Where's Mrs Lufthausen?"

Katie rolled her eyes and gestured for Priya to take a seat. "Could you make it any more obvious you're an after-school detention virgin?" She flicked her hair over her shoulder, making Priya wince with envy – she wished her hair was as long, thick and glossy as Katie's. But sadly, hers was of average length, average thickness and less than average gloss. Katie rummaged in her bag for a small gold compact mirror and continued talking. "Mrs Lufthausen hates staying late because she needs to get back to her cats or kids or whatever, so she leaves us here. The caretaker comes in twice to check we stay the whole hour. But otherwise, we're free."

Priya's mouth dropped open. "Seriously?! We get to do detention alone?"

Katie nodded into her mirror, looking at Priya in the reflection. She put on another layer of rose-tinted lip balm, then pressed her lips together and snapped the mirror shut. "Yup. An hour away from the world, and all we have to do is a bunch of maths questions."

"Wow," said Priya, taken aback. "I had no idea detention was so easy." Then she realized that Katie was being, well not *nice,* but...not mean. She sat up straight, suddenly wary. "So, um, I'm guessing you want me to do your maths questions for you?"

Katie shrugged. "No need. The answers are on the internet. She always takes the exercises straight from the exact same teachers' website. And I've paid for a subscription."

Priya was impressed. "That's so...clever of you."

"You don't need to look surprised – I do have a brain," retorted Katie. Priya exhaled in relief – Katie was still being Katie and order was restored. She'd started to feel like detention was a parallel universe where Katie was a normal person instead of a bully. "So, tell me about this boy. Dan Zhang."

Priya's shoulders immediately tensed up again – that was not the kind of question a bully asked. Unless they wanted to use the intel to take you down. Was that what Katie was doing? "Um, why?" she asked nervously, hoping the bangle wouldn't interpret Katie's order as a question. She really didn't want to overshare about her crush right now.

"Why not? We don't have anything better to do in here."

Priya hesitated. Katie had a point – but that didn't mean she was ready to tell her about Dan.

Katie rolled her eyes. "You don't need to look so suspicious – I just thought it would be something to talk about. It's not like we have much in common, so I thought boys and dating might be a place to start. I've already had two boyfriends, so..."

"I know," answered Priya, without thinking. "It's part of what makes you so cool." Her eyes widened in embarrassment at what she'd just said, but Katie laughed.

"Weird, but I guess it's true. It's not like anyone else in our year has much experience with dating – except Angela."

She sat up impatiently. "Anyway, come on. Get to the deets – how did you meet? How did you get him to go out with you? And have you kissed yet?"

"Um..." Priya's heart sank as she realized she no longer had a choice – the bangle was about to take over. "We met at gymnastics. I told him I liked him and he said it back. And we *definitely* haven't kissed yet. I haven't kissed anyone." She winced – why did the bangle need to add that bit?!

Katie sniffed. "Hm. Well it's no surprise you've never kissed anyone. But it's pretty cool you were so straight with him. No playing games – just serious confidence."

"Thank...you?" said Priya. It seemed like detention *was* turning into a parallel universe.

"So, you were meant to meet him tonight?"

Priya nodded. "We were going to hang out after gymnastics. But obviously now I'm missing gymnastics, I can't."

Katie frowned. "Why can't you just go find him after?"

Priya stared at her like she was crazy. "And what, just tell my parents that I had to skip gymnastics because of detention, but then I was free to meet a boy for milkshakes afterwards? They'd kill me!"

Katie looked away, a weird expression on her face. But then she shook her head. "So, what did he say when you cancelled?"

Priya found the truth gushing out of her. It had been on her mind ever since she'd texted Dan that morning straight after maths, and even though she'd already triple analysed his response with Sami and Mei, she still felt anxious about it. "I explained I had to cancel because I had detention, and he said it was fine and we could reschedule. But he didn't do a *single* emoji or exclamation mark, and I feel like he's upset. What if he doesn't like me any more?"

Katie shook her head. "He's disappointed with the situation – not with you. Don't worry, it'll probably make him like you more."

Priya looked doubtful. "It will?"

"Totally – it creates mystery. And boys *love* mystery." Katie said it so authoritatively that Priya couldn't help nodding.

"Okay. I can do mystery."

"I'm not so sure you can, but...detention isn't a bad start. I have to say – I was pretty surprised you were so direct with Mrs L. I always thought you were a total goody two-shoes."

"Oh, I am," replied Priya instantly. She closed her eyes shut, wishing she was better at controlling the truth bangle.

But Katie just laughed. Again. "You're funnier than I thought too," she said, and it seemed like she was saying it as...a *compliment.* "Were you always this honest about everything?"

Priya blinked. She really had no idea what was happening right now. "Uh, I really, *really* wasn't this honest before," she admitted. "It's...a new thing."

"Well, I'm into it." Katie reached into her bag. "I've got some snacks somewhere...here!" She pulled a bag of crisps out of her bag. "Salt and vinegar?"

"I thought we weren't allowed to eat in the classroom."

"It's detention," replied Katie. "Nothing we're doing is allowed. Here. Catch. And I've got a spare Diet Coke if you want."

"Uh, okay," said Priya, catching the bag of crisps as Katie threw them at her. "Thank...you?"

"Do you always say 'thank you' like it's a question?" asked Katie. "Because it's kind of annoying."

"No, I'm just scared of you." Priya clamped her hand over her mouth. Oh no. Katie was going to think she was a total loser! She'd...wait, was Katie laughing *again?* And was it just Priya, or was Katie *smiling* at her right now?!

"I love it," declared Katie. "Honesty is the new black."

"It...is?" asked Priya, still trying to figure out WHAT was happening right now.

"Totally," said Katie. "It's hilarious. In a good way. Like you."

"Thank you?" Priya winced as she realized what she'd just said.

But Katie cackled loudly. "I asked for that. Right – YouTube or TikTok? We have at least forty minutes left before we need to copy out our answers, which means we can watch at least forty TikToks. Ready? You can sit closer to me, you know – I'm not going to bite."

Priya smiled weakly and moved her seat closer to Katie's, wishing that Sami or Mei was there to tell her that this was *not* a figment of her imagination – she was officially watching TikToks with Katie Wong in the maths classroom. Whilst eating her crisps.

"I know a good one with a dancing goat," she said tentatively. "If you want to see it?"

Chapter 17

"Pri!" Sami ran up to Priya in the locker room the next morning. "There you are! Thank god. Mei – I found her. And I can confirm she is still alive."

Priya smiled up at Sami and Mei, who was right behind her. "Hey! How's it going?"

"Did she just *how's it going?* us?" cried Sami, aghast. "When she's the one who had detention with Katie Wong and only messaged us with a THUMBS-UP emoji afterwards?"

Mei shook her head. "We expected voice notes. Detailed ones."

Priya laughed apologetically. "Sorry. I had masses of work to do when I got home. *And* I had to explain my after-school detention to my parents. I managed to get around the bangle curse and tell them it was for talking in class. Thank god they don't know it was for *talking about Dan Zhang.*"

Mei winced. "How did they take it?"

"My mum went on a mini-rant about how expensive gymnastics is and that I need to take it seriously. But then I think she felt bad, because she told me I shouldn't worry about money, and even if I don't win the prize money in my individual, they'll be okay. I don't fully believe her, but it was still nice to hear."

"I bet she remembered your last chat over the Oreo milkshake," said Sami, nodding sagely. "And the Mum Guilt kicked in."

"Probably," agreed Priya. "She made us quinoa bowls for dinner, even though it was my dad's turn to cook. He wasn't upset with me at all! Obviously, he pretended to be in front of my mum, but afterwards he told me he was glad to see me letting go and being a 'normal kid' – whatever that means."

"That's so good, Priya," said Mei. "I'm glad your parents are trying to see things from your point of view. Even though I have to say a quinoa bowl sounds like my idea of hell. They're just so grainy and—"

"Okay, why are we talking about quinoa when we haven't even *discussed* the Katie situation?!" interrupted Sami. "Details please!"

Priya pulled her blazer on as they left the locker room to walk to their English lesson. She bit her lip as she spoke. "Well, the thing is…"

"Did she attack you?" asked Sami. "Because if she did, I will KILL her."

"And I'll join in," said Mei darkly.

"No, it was nothing like that," said Priya. "The truth is that she was...well...kind of *nice* to me."

Sami and Mei stopped in their tracks.

"Excuse me?" asked Sami. "KW was NICE to you? Do you mean she ignored you like she used to before she realized you were smart enough to do her homework for her? Because I'm not sure I'd call that nice. I mean, is Katie even nice *to anyone* who isn't Angela?"

"She was to me," protested Priya. "I don't understand it either, but it happened."

"Priya, do you have Stockholm Syndrome?" asked Mei, looking concerned. "You know, the one where you develop fake positive feelings towards your kidnapper? Because an hour alone with Katie is probably the equivalent of a week with a normal kidnapper."

Priya rolled her eyes. "No! I'm not saying she's my new best friend or anything."

"Uh, you'd better not be!" said Sami hotly. "That's us and it always will be."

"I know," said Priya. "All I'm saying is that she was weirdly friendly. She asked me about Dan, gave me advice, then we ate crisps and watched TikToks. It was pretty chill."

"You watched TIKTOKS together?" cried Sami. "Oh my god

– which ones does Katie watch? Can you send me links?"

Mei frowned. "Priya, are you sure she doesn't have an ulterior motive? To...give you bad advice and steal Dan from you or something?"

"Oh my god, that is *so* the plot of a high school movie," said Sami. "Pri – you're going to need a makeover."

"Uh, offensive," said Priya. "But...I thought the same at first, Mei. Well, not the stealing Dan bit. The not trusting Katie bit. But her advice was kind of reassuring. She told me everything would be okay with Dan and maybe this would make him want me more."

"The whole mysterious girl thing," said Sami, nodding wisely.

"Yes!" said Priya. "That's exactly what Katie said!"

"Well, I'm not convinced," said Mei, crossing her arms. "I think you should be careful around her. Especially while you're still wearing the bangle."

Priya put her hand on her heart. "I solemnly swear I will be careful around Katie Wong. Okay? Now, can I please show you the last text that Dan sent me? It has two emojis in it."

"Obviously!" shrieked Sami. "How has it taken you so long to bring that up? I thought he was still being sad and not sending emojis after you stood him up. I mean, after you were forced to cancel your date because of detention."

"I sent him two sorry faces in a row and then he sent me this." Priya beamed, showing Sami and Mei her phone.

"*It's okay, we can do it another time, milkshake emoji, sunshine emoji,*" said Mei, reading the message aloud.

"He's obsessed with you," declared Sami.

Priya grinned. "I don't know. I'm just relieved he's not mad any more. Now I can stop freaking out about it and concentrate on my lessons again." She pushed open the English classroom door. "I'm so glad it's Ms Carlyle now. Finally, a normal teacher who isn't going to grill me into talking about my love life and then give me detention for it."

She followed Sami and Mei through the door, turning to Ms Carlyle's desk to say hello. But Ms Carlyle was not standing there. Mrs Lufthausen was.

"What's *she* doing here?!" asked Sami.

Mrs Lufthausen turned to face her with a glower. "*She* can hear you. And she is kindly covering for Ms Carlyle, who is off sick today. Any more questions?"

Priya quickly shook her head, and followed the others in sitting down in silence, before looking expectantly at their teacher.

"I'm not an English teacher, so I won't be discussing themes with you or whatever it is you normally do," said Mrs Lufthausen. "So, you can just continue your reading in silence. Books out. Come on."

Priya quickly dug into her bag to find her book. But it wasn't there. She rummaged further in panic, but to no avail. She turned to Mei, whispering, "I can't find my *Jane Eyre*!"

Mrs Lufthausen appeared in front of her. "I said *silence*, Priya."

Priya flushed. "Sorry, Mrs Lufthausen. I was just telling Mei I can't find my book."

"I think the person you should be telling is me." Mrs Lufthausen readjusted her glasses. "Well, you can work on your maths sums now, and do your reading this evening in detention instead. Let's hope your book turns up by then or you'll have to find one in the library."

Priya's eyes widened. "Detention?! But I already had detention yesterday."

"And today," said Mrs Lufthausen. "Let me get those sums for you."

"Is Priya getting detention just for forgetting her book?" asked Mei. "Because that's not fair."

"We'll speak to Ms Carlyle," burst out Sami. "She'd never give someone detention for that!"

Mrs Lufthausen turned to face the girls with a slow smile. "Oh no. Priya *already* has detention all week because of her behaviour in maths yesterday. Maths being my jurisdiction and not Ms Carlyle's."

Priya gasped. "All week?! But you only said one night!"

"Did I?" said Mrs Lufthausen, wrapping her beige cardigan tightly around her. "My mistake. I meant all week. You too, Katie."

Katie dropped her nail file and it clattered to the floor.

She looked up in surprise. "What's for me too?"

Priya swallowed her fury. This wasn't fair. There were less than two weeks left until the Nationals and now she'd miss training every night. They didn't even have many morning practices this week so she'd end up super behind! Olaf would freak out! Let alone her parents! She turned to Katie, who clearly hadn't been listening and looked confused.

"Detention," said Priya, trying to stop herself from shaking. "All. Week."

That evening, Priya stomped angrily around the empty maths classroom. "It's just so unfair!" she exclaimed. "Mrs Lufthausen can't do this!"

Katie shrugged as she focused on painting her nails. "She already has."

"But it's not fair!" repeated Priya, even though she knew she sounded exactly like her younger sister right now. "She's a total bully!" She paused as she realized she was saying this to someone who, up until very recently, had been bullying *her*. But Katie didn't bat an eyelid.

"She's in charge of us – she can do what she wants."

"Why aren't you more annoyed?"

"No point," said Katie, frowning in concentration as she painted the tips of her green nails hot pink. "You may as well accept it instead of stressing yourself out. It's not like we can change it." Priya raised her eyebrows – Katie sounded more like a zen monk than a bully. "Besides, I don't mind the peace and quiet. I mean, when you're not stomping around ranting."

Priya sat down sheepishly. "Sorry. It's just that I have a major gymnastics competition coming up. And now because of this detention situation, I have to miss evening practice all week, so I'll be behind, and my coach was *furious* when I told him. Not to mention how my parents will react." Priya paused. "Also, it means I don't get to…"

"Have your date with Dan Zhang?" asked Katie, looking up from her nails.

Priya nodded sadly. "Yup."

"How is he taking it?"

Priya smiled despite herself. "I texted him after English to tell him about the extra detentions and then he sent me a 'you can do it' gif! It was so cute – can I show you?"

"No, thanks," said Katie, back to her nails. "But clearly, I was right; he's more into you than ever now."

"I hope so. But it's still so unfair!" said Priya, indignant. "I was really looking forward to seeing him. And now I have extra work to do, *and* I'll have to do extra gymnastics practice alone at home – for the team event as well as the individual event. I don't even have the time to practise both properly!"

"Life is unfair," declared Katie, blowing lightly on her nails, looking like the main character of a movie. A movie with really good lighting.

Priya sighed, wishing she had main character energy. "Tell me about it. I just don't know why Mrs Lufthausen hates me so much."

"She's jealous. Obviously."

Priya's mouth dropped open. "Jealous of me? A twelve-year-old who hasn't got her period yet?" She winced – that was an overshare she really hadn't needed to say aloud.

Katie rolled her eyes. "Yes, precisely because of that."

"She hates her periods that much?"

"I'm not sure Mrs L still gets her periods. What I mean is, you have your life ahead of you. And youth is something Mrs L does *not* have. Plus, you're smart and basically an Olympic gymnast, and you have your two little musketeers who'd probably, like, murder for you. While she's just a miserable sadist."

Priya grinned – Sami would *love* that Katie referred to them as the musketeers. Then she absorbed what Katie had just said. "Huh, I never thought of that. But I guess it makes sense. Is that why Mrs Lufthausen gives you detention too? Because she's jealous of you being pretty and popular and terrifying?"

Katie let out a bark of laughter. "No. She gives me detention because I deliberately get into trouble all the time."

Priya frowned. "But...why would you do that?"

"Why not? That's my life motto." Katie screwed her nail polish closed and turned to Priya, her arms crossed expectantly.

"So, what other truths have you got to tell me today?"

"What do you mean?" asked Priya, confused.

"I want the next instalment of Priya's truths! So far, we have you telling Mrs L about Dan in the middle of class. Then yesterday, you told me you've never kissed a boy. And you just admitted you still haven't got your period."

Priya flushed. This was all true. Annoyingly true. She glanced at the bangle in trepidation.

"So, what else?" asked Katie. "Do you wear a bra?"

"The training kind," said Priya. She winced. "Wait – can we not play this game? I thought we could just watch more TikToks. I have some gymnastics ones I can show you?"

"I'll share too if you want," said Katie. "So you don't feel like it's just you."

"Really?"

Katie nodded. "Why not? I need a digi detox. And I told you yesterday – your honesty is funny. You should totally have your own TikTok."

"Uh, definitely not," said Priya in alarm. "No way. Never."

"Okay, chill. I was just saying, I reckon your honesty could go viral."

Priya shifted uncomfortably. She didn't disagree.

"Okay, so, secret spilling," said Katie, looking more alive than Priya had ever seen her. "Did you know that Angela is actually two years older than us? She got held back twice in Year Five."

Priya gasped loudly. "Seriously?! No wonder she's so strong!"

"I know – the PE teacher loves it," said Katie. "But we're not meant to know, so you can't tell anyone."

Priya nodded in disappointment. Now she'd never get to see Sami and Mei's faces when they discovered the real reason Angela Sutton was so lethal on a lacrosse pitch.

"Good," said Katie. "Okay, you do one. What about your musketeers? Do they have any secrets?"

"Yes!" Priya's eyes widened as she realized what she'd just blurted out. She needed to be careful – this conversation was going into bangle disaster territory. It was one thing admitting her own truths, but her friends' secrets weren't hers to tell. She spoke slowly. "Um. I mean. We all do. So, yeah, just the normal amount."

Katie's eyes lit up. "Tell me more about them. Sami wants to be an actor, right?"

"More than anything," said Priya, relieved that Katie's questions were moving onto safer territory. "She says it's part of her identity. That and being a sophisticated woman."

Katie laughed. "I love the way you phrase things – you're so funny, Priya. Seriously, you should think about my TikTok idea – you'd kill it on there."

Priya felt a flush of warmth run through her at the compliment. She had *never* imagined Katie saying something so nice to her before, and...it felt kind of great. She smiled back. "Yeah, Sami's having her bat mitzvah soon and she says it's the next step to womanhood."

Katie laughed again. "Oh my god, womanhood at thirteen – it's so ironic, I love it."

Priya continued, emboldened. "I know. She still sleeps with her doll though."

"No way!" cried Katie, giggling. "What's it called?"

"Dolly," said Priya. She felt a twinge of guilt in her stomach – maybe she shouldn't have said that... It was fine, she could just play it down. It wasn't exactly a big deal. "But, um, I still have a teddy called Teddy. So, I can't exactly talk."

Katie howled. "Dolly the dolly and Teddy the teddy. You guys are too much."

Priya joined in the laughter. "I know – so original."

"What about Mei?" asked Katie. "What does she have? Beary the bear?"

Priya smiled politely – Katie wasn't so great at the jokes. "No, she named hers after philosophers."

"Of course. The alternative option for the alternative girl. Does Mei always wear all-black?"

"She doesn't believe in other colours," explained Priya. "She thinks black is the truest colour there is."

Katie laughed again. Priya beamed – she couldn't believe she was making Katie laugh this much! "So, Mei is out now, right? She goes to LGBTQ+ club, doesn't she?"

Priya nodded proudly. "Yep! She's the best."

"Does Mei like anyone?"

"Sarah P." Priya slapped her hand to her mouth, growing bright red. She couldn't believe she'd just said that. That was too much. Way too much. Mei would KILL her if she ever found out. Priya turned to Katie in panic. "Wait. Please don't tell anyone I said that. I really shouldn't have. Nobody can find out."

Katie raised her eyebrows. "Do you really think anyone I know cares who Mei likes?"

"I don't know. But please don't tell anyone."

"Okay, your secret's safe with me," said Katie. "Or Mei's."

Priya's shoulders relaxed in relief. "Thank you so much. I would die if she found out I'd told you that."

"Honestly, I don't think I even know Mei's surname," said Katie. "This is really not that interesting to me. I just thought it would make a change from the TikToks – and, you know, you're funny when you talk about people."

Priya smiled. "Thanks. And it's Mei Chen." She hesitated. "But, um, maybe it's best to not tell anyone about Sami's doll either. Not that it's a huge deal."

Katie shrugged. "Sure. Now..." She picked up her nail polishes. "Which colour do you want? I've got purple, green or pink."

Chapter 18

Priya rushed towards Ms Carlyle's classroom, exhausted from the solo gymnastics practice she'd just done at lunch. She hated not being able to hang out with Sami and Mei, but she couldn't let her chance at gold slip just because Mrs Lufthausen had detained her for the week. The only problem was that it had taken Priya the whole of lunch to get her individual routine in shape. By the time she'd been ready to start practising her part of the team routine, the bell had gone for class, and she'd had to run out of the PE hall all the way to the humanities block.

She made it to the classroom just in time, slipping into her usual seat between Sami and Mei seconds before Ms Carlyle appeared.

"Sorry I haven't been able to hang out again today," whispered Priya. "The extra gymnastics practice is killing me."

"I know, we've barely seen you all week," replied Mei, her voice just as low, so as not to attract Ms Carlyle's attention. "How did your parents handle the news about the all-week detention?"

Priya sighed at the memory. She wished she'd been able to lie to her parents about having so many after-school detentions. They'd both been so shocked when she'd told them. Even her dad had said he was upset with her. It was so unfair though, because they assumed she'd done something terrible to justify a week's worth of detentions, when the truth was that Mrs Lufthausen had completely overreacted. But when Priya had tried to share Katie's theory about Mrs L being jealous of her youth, her mum had snapped at her to not be so judgemental of menopausal women. Apparently they faced enough problems as it was.

"Not great," she said quietly. "They didn't even get angry this time, they were just disappointed."

Both Sami and Mei winced in sympathy. "The worst," said Sami. Then she noticed Priya's nails. "Oh my god, these are amazing," she whispered appreciatively. "Dark green looks cool on you – very edgy."

"Thanks," Priya whispered back. "Katie did them for me in detention yesterday."

Mei's mouth dropped open and she forgot to be quiet. "*Katie* did your nails? I'm sorry – did Angela give you a head massage too?"

"Girls, quiet please!" said Ms Carlyle, frowning at Mei. "I want you to finish reading chapter five in silence and then we'll discuss it once you're finished. Come along now."

Priya mouthed "sorry" at Sami and Mei, then opened up her book in relief. She'd finally found *Jane Eyre* in Pinkie's room – where else? – wedged under the leg of her wonky table. Priya inspected her copy for any unwanted smiley faces or dissolved pages from one of Pinkie's failed science experiments, but it looked okay. She gingerly turned to chapter five and tried to concentrate, but her mind was elsewhere.

She knew that Sami and Mei were seriously confused by her changing relationship with Katie, and she got it. It was confusing her too and she was the one living it. Last night, Katie had been *messaging* Priya. She'd suggested they go out for bubble tea on Friday to celebrate surviving their week of detention. Priya had said yes before she'd fully clocked that it would mean skipping the sleepover at Sami's. And once she'd realized, she hadn't cancelled. She couldn't. It was like something out of a movie. After years of Katie Wong treating her like a total loser, now she wanted to be *Priya's friend*! There was no way Priya could resist. Especially because, if she was honest, she was enjoying hanging out with Katie too.

Obviously, Sami and Mei were still her best friends. They always would be. But it was fun spending time with somebody different. Katie was so brutal that it was refreshing, and even though her life was clearly perfect – what with her insanely wealthy parents, her swimming pool and the fact she'd already had two boyfriends when most people in their year hadn't even had their first kiss yet – she still had a "life sucks" attitude that kind of appealed to Priya, especially now that she was stuck in perpetual (okay, week-long) detention. Everything seemed so unfair right now, what with the bangle getting her in trouble, not being able to see Dan, and her parents and Olaf being upset with her. She knew that Sami and Mei were sympathetic, but they couldn't fully relate, because they weren't the ones stuck in detention every night. But Katie was. She got it.

Besides – Priya was allowed to have other friends. Of course, she was. She just had a feeling that Sami and Mei wouldn't approve of the new friendship she'd fallen into after just two detentions. And they *definitely* wouldn't approve of the fact she'd told said new friend their secrets... Priya felt a twinge of guilt in her stomach. She shook her head, trying to force the memory out of her mind. It was best not to think about it. It wasn't her fault anyway – it was all the bangle. Sami and Mei wouldn't be able to blame her if they ever found out. But just in case, it was best if they never did.

Priya spent the rest of the lesson focusing on Jane Eyre's impressions of her new – awful – boarding school and trying to answer as many of Ms Carlyle's questions about it as she could. She *really* couldn't afford to get in trouble with another teacher right now. As soon as the bell rang, she grabbed her bag and made an apologetic face at Sami and Mei.

"Sorry, girls, I have to run. Detention."

"Off to see your new best friend," sniffed Sami dramatically. "It's fine – we get it. Just don't forget us when you're busy going to house parties and wearing heels on weekends."

Priya laughed lightly. "As if I'd ever go to a party without you both! And you know I'm a trainers not heels kinda girl."

"Yeah, because heels are a patriarchal construction designed to hold women back, literally," said Mei, crossing her arms. "We'll accept you going to detention. But only because we know we'll get to hang with you properly on Friday at Sami's."

Priya gulped and tried to hide her feelings with a bright smile. It wasn't a question, so she didn't need to tell the truth. She quickly turned to leave the classroom.

"Wait!" Mei's clear voice stopped Priya in her tracks. "You *are* coming to the sleepover, right? After your detention?"

Priya froze. Her mind raced as she tried to think of a way out of this – maybe she *could* even go to the sleepover post bubble tea, post detention? But it would be so late by then that she'd have missed all the food, and that was the main *point* of the sleepover. Besides, what if Katie wanted to get food at the Boba Bar afterwards? "Um…" Priya desperately tried to think of a diplomatic answer but all she could think of were the old lies she would have been able to tell pre-bangle.

She panicked, and the truth rushed right out of her. "No. Sorry. I'm so sorry!"

"What?" cried Sami. "But why?! Oh my god, is it Dan? Are you blowing us off for a boy because that is *totally* against the girl code." She paused. "However, I may allow it if you tell us every single detail afterwards and let us live vicariously through you."

Priya looked up at her friends and forced herself to be brave. If she wasn't, the bangle would do it for her and by now, she knew exactly how that would turn out. "Um. It's Katie. She asked me to celebrate surviving our week in detention."

Mei stared at her. "You're choosing *her* over us? The bully who's made you do her homework for months and calls you 'loo lunch girl'?"

"She's not like that any more," said Priya defensively. "She knows my name. And she's...nice to me now. Besides, it's only one Friday. We can do it at mine again next Friday!"

"Seriously?" Sami's voice was strangled. "You're going to do a sleepover at Katie's instead of with us? The musketeers?"

Priya felt a pang in her chest. "It's not a sleepover – it's just going for bubble tea."

"To the cool Boba Bar where BOYS go?" Sami practically yelled. "Without us?! I thought we were all going to go there together one day. When we work up the courage."

Mei shook her head. "Katie paints your nails once – and now you prefer her to us? Seriously?"

"We have skills too!" said Sami. "Yes, okay, she has a really inventive take on a French manicure. But I can do a dramatic monologue like nobody else and Mei can, well, you know, say smart things."

"It's not like that," protested Priya. "Really. We've just bonded in our detentions, and it's mainly because of the bangle making me overshare. That's it. You're still my best friends. You always will be!"

"You share with her already?" asked Sami sadly. "You only just started sharing with us and we've been friends for two years. You've only spent two detentions with Katie."

"Whatever," said Mei. "Have fun at the Boba Bar."

That evening, Priya collapsed onto her bed in exhaustion. She'd spent yet another hour perfecting her individual routine, so hopefully Olaf wouldn't be too annoyed when she finally turned up to practice the next morning. It was plain bad luck that there hadn't been any morning practice on the schedule till Thursday, so Priya hadn't even seen the team since the last weekend. She felt bad just thinking about it. They would have all had to practise the routine without her and she was the one at the top of the pyramid – maybe Rachael would have stepped in for her?

She knew she really did need to try and practise her part of the team routine. But there were only so many spare hours in the day and obviously she had to prioritize the event that counted. The team event was fun and all, but it was the individual that came with prize money and a chance to get into the Teen Olympics. There was no point feeling bad about it. Everyone knew elite sports were competitive; her teammates were probably doing the exact same thing and prioritizing their individuals too.

Priya pulled her pillow close towards her and sank into its feathery softness. She couldn't remember the last time she'd been so tired. Detention with Katie had been fun – this time, they'd shared hilarious gossip about everyone in their year (well, Katie had. Priya had already accidentally shared the only gossip she knew) and Katie had told her she'd seen Ms Carlyle flirting with Mr Mendez, the geography teacher! But Priya still couldn't get the image of Sami and Mei's hurt faces out from the back of her mind. She'd never had a fight with them before – if that had even been a fight. In the past, Priya had never said anything that would upset them. She'd always, well, lied so that she could protect their feelings. But that obviously wasn't an option any more.

She looked at the bangle on her wrist with mixed feelings. How could this shiny bit of metal have changed her life so much? And did Ba know what was going on right now? Priya felt a surge of sorrow in her chest at the thought. She missed her grandma so much. She wished she was there to give her advice. She knew that Ba would have been so proud of her for telling Dan she liked him. And for opening up to Sami and Mei.

She grinned as she imagined Ba looking down at her from heaven like she'd promised, cheering and waving loudly as the musketeers shared their secrets and grew closer than ever. But then Priya's smile wavered as she imagined Ba watching her tell those secrets to Katie. Although that had only happened after the bangle had got her a week's detention, which got her into trouble with her parents *and* Olaf.

It was all so confusing. Had Ba known that the bangle would get Priya in trouble just as much as it would help her? Was there something that Priya was missing? She looked at the bangle desperately, wishing it would reveal all the answers. But – unsurprisingly – it didn't. She yanked it forcefully, hoping the clasp would suddenly spring open, but nothing happened. She sighed in frustration. It didn't make sense that the bangle was still there. She'd learned her lesson about the benefits of honesty. So why was the bangle refusing to budge, risking all the good it had done so far? At this rate, Priya would end up losing everything the bangle had helped her get. But the bangle just stayed clamped to her wrist, shining innocuously as it caught the lamplight.

She let the bangle slide back down her arm, then pulled out her half-started essay on *Jane Eyre*. She'd thought about suggesting to Katie that they use detention to do their homework, but then she'd changed her mind – it would just make Katie go back to thinking of her as a goody two-shoes. Besides, it was so much more fun to just distract herself with gossip and Diet Coke. The only problem was that it meant Priya now had hours of work to do before she could go to sleep. And tomorrow morning she had to wake up early for gymnastics. But that meant she'd finally get to see Dan again! Priya couldn't help smiling. They'd rearranged their milkshake date for Saturday and she couldn't *wait*. She hoped Sami and Mei were normal with her again by then – she needed their help planning a date outfit. And she knew Sami would want to do a movie montage with all the different options. She'd probably already started making a playlist.

Just then a door slammed in the hallway, knocking the smile off Priya's face. She frowned and got up off the bed, sticking her head into the hallway. "Pinkie? Is that you?"

There was no reply, but she heard raised voices from her parents' bedroom. Her heart sunk. *Surely* they weren't fighting again? They couldn't be. But as Priya tiptoed closer to their bedroom, the sound of her mum's voice was unmistakeable.

"A speeding ticket, really? Couldn't you have been more careful? You know things are tight!"

"I was rushing to get Priya to gymnastics, and Pinkie to school, and then come back here and clean the house," ranted her dad. "I'm only one person – I can't do everything around here!"

"YOU do everything?!" Her mum's voice was furious. "I'm

the one who has to redo everything you do because you make such a mess of it all, as well as be the breadwinner."

"Well, why don't I just move out and leave you to do everything without me making it so much worse?" retorted her dad. "It's clearly what you want."

"Yes, and it's clearly impossible," her mum shot back. "We can't get divorced. We both agreed we don't want people knowing our business, and it's not fair on the girls. So we need to find a way to make this work – for their sake."

Priya turned away and padded sadly back to her bedroom. She'd heard enough. It was the same old story again – her parents were back to their constant arguing, and they weren't going to get a divorce. They were just going to stay trapped in this horrible cycle for ever. She felt a fat tear slide down her cheek. She'd really thought that things were changing. That her parents were fixing things in their relationship and that soon, they'd be a normal family. A family that didn't argue every night. A family that loved each other. A family that ate dinner together and laughed about things that went wrong.

But even though her parents were admittedly making the effort to have a semi-normal family dinner every night, it seemed like they were going upstairs to secretly argue afterwards. Pinkie had been right all along – they'd only ever been faking things for them. Priya felt a lump of disappointment settle in her stomach. She closed her bedroom door and looked at the unfinished essay on her bed.

She couldn't write it now. She felt too sad. She needed...
her friends.

She pulled out her phone and video-called Sami and Mei,
instantly feeling better. This was the answer. It was precisely
why Ba must have given her the bangle in the first place; so
she could get closer to her friends and know she wasn't alone.
If she couldn't get rid of the bangle, she may as well use it to
help her keep opening up to her friends. She smiled hopefully
at her phone screen as it rang, but her smile faded as neither
of them answered. She ended the call sadly. Then her phone
vibrated. There was a message from Sami:

*Sorry, can't speak. Hope detention with your new BF went
well.*

Then one from Mei:

Me either. See you tomorrow.

Priya felt a wave of emotions flood her body. She'd been
hoping they'd make her feel better. But they hadn't even put
emojis at the end of their texts. What if things didn't get
better between them all? It wasn't fair – she needed them.
How could Sami and Mei just abandon her because she'd
made a new friend?! They were clearly jealous that Katie – the
most popular and powerful girl in the whole year – liked her
and not them. But they didn't have to act like children about
it. She needed them – this was the first time she'd reached out
to them to ask for help in all the time she'd known them –
and they were ignoring her. It was pathetic and immature.

Well, fine. She'd speak to her new friend instead! She video-called Katie without even thinking.

"Hey, what's up?" Katie answered, her immaculate face taking up Priya's entire phone screen.

Priya looked into Katie's dark eyes, accentuated with black eyeliner. She didn't know where to start. She stared at Katie in silence and sighed. "Everything."

"Tell me about it. I can't wait till I'm old enough to do what I want."

"Me too," cried Priya. "I'm so over everything! School, parents, friends…just all of it."

"Join the club." Katie brought the phone closer to her face so Priya could see the pores on the end of her nose. "Hey, I just downloaded a new game. Let me send you a link and we can play it together. It's so addictive – you'll love it. I've been doing it for hours and I'm almost at level two."

Priya glanced at her homework. Playing for *hours* probably wasn't the best idea. She had a bit of free time in the morning she could use to finish the essay, but she really needed to do more tonight. Or at least practise a bit of the team routine… Then she heard her mum shouting at her dad. She looked back at the screen and Katie's expectant eyes. "Let's do it," she found herself saying. "I've got plenty of time."

Chapter 19

Priya pushed open the gymnasium doors, trying to ignore how fast her heart was beating as she walked in. She had no idea why she was so nervous – was it seeing Dan for the first time since they'd declared their mutual liking of each other? Or was it having to face Olaf after missing so many days of practice? Priya swallowed as she saw both Dan and Olaf turn to look at her. Maybe it was both.

Dan waved at her, with a smile as nervy as her own, but Priya barely had a chance to wave back before Olaf stormed over. He did not look pleased.

"Look who has finally come back, when there's hardly any time to go before the big competition!"

"I'm so sorry, Olaf," said Priya. "I told you – I had detention."

"I don't want to hear it! Just…go and show me why you're still on the team." Olaf clapped his hands together. "Everyone, we're going to take it from the top. The synchronized team routine. Get into place."

Priya's heart sank. "Could we start practising our individuals instead?" she asked hopefully.

Olaf's eyebrows practically shot up into his hair. "No, we cannot! We're behind on the team routine – so come on! And – go!"

Priya quickly rushed into position and took a deep breath as the music burst out through the speakers. It would be fine. She could do this – she always managed to figure things out when it came to being on the mat. Sometimes she wished it was that easy in all other areas of her life... She gave Rachael a little wave as she stood on the corner of the mat and waited for the beat that was her cue. As soon as she heard it, she let her body do what it did best, responding to the music as it tumbled and flipped across the mat, while her teammates' bodies did the exact same. Priya felt time slow down as her muscle memory took her exactly where she needed to be. Then she wobbled. She felt a pang of anxiety – she'd almost messed up that jump! She forced herself to keep going, but...why was Rachael already in the splits? Weren't they meant to be doing handstands first? Priya looked around and saw that the rest of her row was in the splits too. Oh no. She'd got the timings wrong. She quickly slid down to the floor, but by the time she was there, they'd all moved on. She felt her breath speed up in panic as she realized that she'd forgotten the next bit.

This wasn't good. She was going to get in so much—

"STOP!" Olaf's voice thundered out. "What is going on here?"

Nobody said anything but Priya's eyes lowered to the mats in shame. It was all her fault – she knew it was. Why hadn't she practised her part of the routine to the music? Then she'd be in sync with the others instead of all over the place.

"Priya," said Olaf as her stomach sank. "What was that?"

"The routine we practised," she answered quietly, glancing at the bangle.

"That was the exact opposite of the routine we practised," cried Olaf. "Your timings were all over the place – not to mention your technique. You *wobbled* in your landing for a tuck jump! I've not seen you do that since you were six!"

Priya flushed. She knew the entire team was looking at her. But she refused to lift her eyes – it was too humiliating.

"I know you've missed a lot of practice," continued Olaf. "But this just isn't good enough. I gave you time off thinking that it would help you. But it clearly hasn't. What's been going on?"

"I'm sorry," said Priya, trying to think of how best to answer him truthfully. "It's just...I haven't had time to practise the group routine. And I didn't sleep well last night. Maybe it's that?"

"Why didn't you sleep?"

Priya was focusing so hard on not bursting out the truth

about her parents arguing that she didn't realize what she was saying until it was too late: "I was up late playing video games."

Olaf stared at her. "What?"

"I'm so sorry," whispered Priya, her eyes widening. "I'm really sorry."

Just then Rachael leaned against the vault and it made a horribly loud creaking sound. Olaf frowned and suddenly noticed everyone was listening. "The rest of you – again! From the top!" He turned to Priya and gestured for her to follow him into the corner. "Homework, I would have understood," he said angrily. "Even crying over your love life or whatever it is that you teens do in you spare time. But video games? Do you even *care* about what we're doing here?"

"Of course, I do!" cried Priya. "I've been training my entire life for this! It's my chance to get onto the Teen Olympics team!"

"Not if you perform like that at the Nationals! You've missed so many sessions this week, Priya."

"That wasn't my fault! It was detention."

"Which I imagine was a punishment for something you did, am I right?"

Priya nodded slowly. She had technically been the one to be rude to Mrs Lufthausen, though she was blaming the bangle. In fact, given the way things were going right now, a part of her was starting to blame Ba too.

"And, so, you haven't found the time to practise your routines at home?" continued Olaf. "You know it's essential at this stage in your career, Priya."

"I have!" said Priya. "I know my individual routine inside out. It's just…" Her voice trailed off and Olaf's eyes enlarged in understanding.

"You've only worked on your routine and not the one for the team," said Olaf slowly. "Is that right?"

Priya felt her skin grow hot. "Yes," she admitted. "But it's because I don't care!" What?! She clamped her hand over her mouth. Oh no. This couldn't be happening. She'd meant to say it was *not* because she didn't care. But the bangle had twisted her words. And it wasn't even true – was it? She cared more about her own routine, of course she did, but she still cared about the team routine. Or maybe she used to… *Did* she still care? Priya felt her stomach churn as she realized she didn't know.

Olaf shook his head in disappointment. "You don't care about the team event because you're convinced you're already getting your gold in your individual event, is that it? And that's enough to get onto the Teen Olympics team and get your prize money, whereas the team event doesn't have any obvious benefits to you, does it?"

Priya still had her hand tight over her mouth, but she found herself nodding.

"I really thought you were starting to open up and enjoy

being part of the team," said Olaf, disappointed. "It's why I chose you to be at the top of the pyramid."

"I thought that's because I was the best at jumps?"

"You know you're my top gymnast," said Olaf. "But it's not just about skill. Being a team player is essential too. Which is why I need to know – is the team a priority for you, Priya? Or is it more of a priority for you to do well on your own?"

"On my own," whispered Priya, lowing her head. She knew it wasn't the answer the coach wanted, but it was the truth. Olaf was right – the individual events benefitted her in a way the team ones just didn't. "I'm sorry. I do still want the team to win gold though!"

"That might be the case," said Olaf, looking saddened. "But your attitude isn't going to help us get there. I'm sorry, Priya, but...I'm going to have to take you off the team event."

"What?!" cried Priya. "You can't! I'm your best gymnast, remember? I'm the one at the top of the pyramid! And you need five boys and five girls!" she continued in desperation. "They won't be able to do it without me!"

"Hayley can sub in. She's worked with us before and I know she's keen for more team work."

Priya stuttered. "But— I— What—"

"You can still do your individual event," said Olaf gently. "But our practices up till Nationals are going to focus on the team routine, so I'll have to ask you to not come to those any more."

"What?!" Priya stared at him, aghast.

"I'm sorry, Priya. We can discuss your future on the team after Nationals."

Priya felt tears prick her eyelids. She pleaded with Olaf, her watery eyes wide. "Please, Olaf. I'm sorry."

"I'm sorry too," he said, looking at her sympathetically. "But my mind's made up."

Priya sat numb in the changing room. She'd left the gymnasium straight after her conversation with Olaf – she couldn't bear the thought of crying in front of the others. The others. Oh no. She looked at the time on her phone. Practice was almost over. She needed to get out of there before anyone came in and—

"Priya?"

Priya gasped as the door opened and Dan walked in, his hand over his eyes. "I'm not looking. Sorry to come into the girls' changing rooms – I just wanted to talk to you."

"It's fine, I'm not changing," said Priya. She was already wearing her school uniform. Her leotard was crumpled up at the bottom of her bag where it could stay.

Dan gingerly lowered his hand and looked at her. "Are you okay?"

"No," said Priya, the tears threatening to come again. "It was horrible."

Dan sat down next to her and put his arm around her. Even in her misery, Priya felt a tiny part of her start freaking out in excitement: Dan was touching her! She couldn't wait to tell Sami and Mei! Then she remembered they weren't speaking to her, and her heart sank even lower.

"I'm sorry," said Dan. "Coach told us that Hayley's coming in for the team routine instead of you."

Priya sniffed. "Yep. I'm not allowed to do it any more. And he's asked me to stop coming to practices till Nationals."

"What?" Dan's voice was indignant. "That's so unfair! Just because you were brave enough to be honest about playing video games? We've all done it before but none of us have ever told the truth. I get that he's annoyed – but enough to stop you from coming to practice?!" He stood up suddenly, his black eyes flashing. "We'll revolt. We'll go on strike – refuse to compete unless he reinstates you! We'll get you back in, I promise."

Priya gave him a watery smile. "Thanks. That's sweet. But you know Olaf won't change his mind."

Dan frowns. "I just don't get why he's taken you off the team event for this? It doesn't make sense!"

Priya sighed. "It's not just because of the video games. He thinks...that I don't care about the team. That I'm only bothered about winning in the individual event."

Dan's face crumpled in confusion. "But that's ridiculous! Of course, you care about the team!" He looked at Priya for confirmation, but when she didn't say anything, a flash of doubt crossed his face. "It's not true, is it, Priya?"

She bit her bottom lip, knowing she had no choice but to answer him honestly. "It is true."

"What?!"

"It's not that I don't care *at all*, I just don't care *as much* as I do about my own event," she said. "I really want to be on the team. I really, really do."

Dan leaned back. "But – you care more about yourself and your event?"

"Yes," said Priya instantly, before she could think of a way to say the truth cleverly. She glanced at the bangle in frustration. "I mean, I care about the team, of course I do. But if I win the individual event, my career could be set up for life. All the sacrifices my parents have made would be worth it."

"Yeah, but...we've been on this team for years," said Dan. "You've been on it since you were six! I thought we were like a family."

"You did?" asked Priya in surprise. She'd always been so focused on her actual family that it had never occurred to her she might have a surrogate one at gymnastics.

"Of course. I'm kind of surprised that you don't. I mean, I know you don't often hang out with us after practice and stuff. But I still thought you were a team player."

Priya sat in helpless silence. She wanted to correct Dan and say she *was* a team player – but she wasn't sure it was true enough for the bangle to let her say it aloud. And she really didn't want the bangle to force her to shout that she *wasn't* a team player.

Dan shook his head. "Maybe...it's not a good idea for us to go for that milkshake any more. I'm going to be pretty busy with practices now till Nationals – Coach says he wants us to do extra practices so we can get Hayley up to speed. Which means I'll have even *less* free time."

Priya's face fell. She knew this was all her fault. "I'm so sorry. Maybe we can reschedule for after Nationals instead? Celebrate our wins?"

Dan shifted awkwardly. "Uh, maybe, yeah. I just...I'm starting to wonder if we do have as much in common as I thought."

"What do you mean?!"

"Being part of a team is really important to me," said Dan. "I care about it a lot. And...you don't. You just told me yourself."

"But..." Priya desperately tried to think of a way to fix things. "I do care! I still want you all to win!"

"I don't think that's going to happen now we need to practise with someone new," said Dan. "Especially this close to the competition." He stood up. "Look, I'd better go. I'm sorry, Priya. Good luck with your training. I'll...see you at Nationals."

Dan walked out of the changing room. The second the door swung shut, Priya burst into loud tears. She couldn't believe that had just happened. Dan didn't want to see her any more. Because she was a terrible person – she was selfish. Coach thought so and Dan clearly did too. Her heart thudded. She couldn't breathe. She needed to get out of there before anyone else came in. Priya grabbed her bag and ran out into the hallway. She crashed right into Rachael.

"Priya! Are you okay?"

"No!"

"Do you want to talk about it?" asked Rachael, her eyes wide with sympathy. "Is it about what happened with Olaf? I tried to create a distraction so he'd stop shouting at you earlier."

"That was on purpose?" Priya gulped. "Thanks. It's just – it's all so terrible."

"I bet it's not that bad."

"I'm banned from coming to practice and Dan doesn't want to go out with me any more."

Rachael's eyes widened. "Okay, that's pretty bad. I didn't even know you and Dan were going out! Let's sit down and you can tell me everything."

Just then Priya felt her phone vibrate. She pulled it out quickly in relief – it must be Sami and Mei answering the SOS she'd sent when she was alone in the changing room. Thank god. She needed them desperately. But the person calling her wasn't Sami or Mei. They hadn't even texted her back. It was Katie.

"Do you need to get that?" asked Rachael. "I can wait if you want – and we can talk afterwards? Get breakfast on our way to our schools?"

Priya looked up, flustered. "Sorry. Um, yes. I think I do need to get this." Priya gave Rachael an apologetic smile. "Thanks for your help." She grabbed her bag and turned away, pressing "answer" on her phone as she did so. "Katie. I am having the worst day *ever*."

Chapter 20

Priya walked into school laughing with Katie by her side. She took a sip of her vanilla latte and fluttered her eyes to the sky in exaggerated gratitude. "I feel so much better already. How did you know this was exactly what I needed?"

"I'm telepathic," said Katie, draining the last of her latte and dumping the cup in the bin. "And I always start my day with a latte, so I figured, why not get you one too? Especially after everything you told me earlier."

"You are the best," declared Priya. Then she bit her bottom lip, hesitating. "Can I ask you something I've wanted to ask for a while?"

"Go for it. So long as it's not something weird about asking me to help you practise kissing your pillow or something."

"No, thanks. I can kiss my pillow solo. I mean, not that I... okay... Anyway. I just wanted to ask...why are you spending so much time with me? You're usually hanging out with Angela."

"Exactly," said Katie. "I'm bored of her." Then she looked down at her chunky boots before adding, "Also...she's pretty busy at the moment. She's got *Hamilton* rehearsals, and she got on the lacrosse team earlier this term, so they always have practice, even on weekends. She's hardly ever free."

"Sounds like me and gymnastics," said Priya sadly. "Well, before this morning."

Katie shrugged. "Their loss. Dan's too. Who is he to judge you for prioritizing your career? Your life, your choices."

"Yeah!" Priya nodded, feeling empowered. "You're right. I'll win gold in my individual event, and then I'll be on the Teen Olympics team. I don't even *need* this team any more."

"Definitely," said Katie. "And maybe—"

Just then Priya caught sight of Sami and Mei at the other end of the corridor. She gasped and turned to Katie quickly. "Sorry, I have to go."

She rushed over to her friends and burst out in relief, "Finally! I've been trying to speak to you both for ages! I have so much I need to tell you. Where have you been? Can we talk? Please."

Sami looked her up and down, taking in the coffee cup and Katie's hovering presence by the lockers. She shook her head in exaggerated slow motion.

Priya turned to Mei, but she realized that Mei was facing away from her, staring avidly at the noticeboards. Priya tried to make eye contact with her, but Mei stubbornly angled her face away, turning more towards the display on sedimentary rocks.

"What's going on?" asked Priya. "You're not looking at me now? Just because I'm not coming to the sleepover tonight?"

"Sleepover?!" repeated Sami, incredulous. "That's the LEAST of our problems! I mean, we're meant to be your best friends, but then not only do you ditch us for someone who spent years bullying you – yes, Katie," she bellowed down the corridor, "I'm talking about YOU!" Sami turned back to glare at Priya. "But then you do the one thing we never, ever thought you would do – you betray the ultimate musketeers' code and you tell her our secrets!"

Priya felt her stomach sink. Surely she couldn't mean... She looked at Katie, who had crossed her arms defensively. Mei was still refusing to face her. "But...what do you mean?" she asked, her voice weak.

"You know exactly what she means!" Mei finally spun round. Her eyes were red and she'd clearly been crying.

"Mei, are you okay?" cried Priya. "What's happened?"

"As if you care," replied Mei. "It's all your fault." Then she started crying again.

Sami put a protective arm around Mei and glowered at Priya. "See? This *is* all your fault," she said. "I thought it was bad enough that you'd become so self-obsessed lately, only ever talking about yourself and never asking us how things were going. I mean, Mei came *out* to us, and did you ever ask her how LGBTQ+ club was going? And when was the last time you asked me about *Hamilton* rehearsals? Let alone my BM prep?! It isn't easy to learn a whole chunk of the Torah off by heart, Priya!"

Priya lowered her eyes in shame as she realized that Sami was right. She hadn't asked her friends anything for weeks – but it wasn't because she didn't care! She'd just had so much going on. It *wasn't* her fault. It was the bangle. She felt a wave of hot anger rise up in her. Why should she get the blame for everything when she was the one literally locked in a truth curse?! "That's not fair!" she said. "I've been busy. You both know *exactly* what's been going on."

"Yeah, we do," said Sami hotly. "What's going on is that you told *her*," she jerked her head wildly towards Katie, who was still watching everything from afar with a scornful expression on her face, "our secrets. Which is why Angela asked me how my *dolly* was at rehearsals, totally humiliating me in the middle of my rap solo. And..." Sami looked sympathetically at Mei. "It's why Sarah P turned up at LGBTQ+ club last night to tell Mei that she's sorry but she doesn't fancy girls. Even though Mei had *never told her she liked her*. Sarah only found out because of *you* and *her*." Sami pointed angrily at Priya then at Katie.

Priya's mouth dropped open in horror. This could not be happening. It was worse than she could have ever imagined.

Poor Mei – to have Sarah P find out like that and come up to her to reject her. It must have been mortifying. But it wasn't like Priya had done this on purpose. The bangle had forced her to tell Katie, and she'd begged Katie to keep it a secret! Katie had been the one who had broken her word and betrayed her.

Priya spun on her heels to face Katie in fury. "Is this true? Did you tell people their secrets? After you specifically promised you wouldn't?"

"I just told Angela. It's not that big a deal."

"Yes, it is!" protested Priya. "You *promised*."

"So did you," pointed out Katie. "It's the exact same thing. And it's not like I deliberately told Angela – it just slipped out when I was bored. She's the one who went and told Sarah P."

"Don't blame Angela – it's your fault," yelled Priya. "You've ruined everything!"

Katie stared at Priya and then shook her head. "Whatever. I don't have time for this juvenile behaviour. After everything I've done for you, seriously." She shook her head and stalked off. Priya could hear her stomping down the corridor.

Priya looked at Sami and Mei in desperation. "You have to believe me. Please. I didn't mean to do this – it was Katie."

Mei scoffed. "Are you kidding me, Priya? It was *you*. You're the one who shared things that weren't yours to share."

"But..." Priya quickly checked to make sure there was

nobody else in the corridor. "The bangle! You know I can't go against it when someone asks me a question!"

"Did you even try?" asked Mei.

"Did you?!" repeated Sami angrily. "Mei – poor kind Mei who spent hours trying to help you – figured out a way to control the bangle. And did you use the stuff she taught you – did you try to say, 'that's not my truth to share'? Or redirect the conversation? Or literally *anything* that might have resulted in you not sharing our deepest, darkest secrets with the school bully?"

Priya lowered her eyes to the ground. Sami and Mei were both right. She hadn't tried to work around the bangle. If she was honest, she'd shared details about them without even being prompted by the bangle. Like how she'd just offered Katie the information about Sami's doll, when Katie hadn't even asked! And yes, the bangle had made her say that Mei liked Sarah P – but Priya had been so caught up in the excitement of bonding with Katie that she hadn't tried to control the truth. She'd just let it slide right out of her. "No," she whispered, closing her eyes, as the enormity of what she'd done fully engulfed her. "I'm sorry."

Mei's eyes started tearing up again. "I can't believe this, Priya! I *trusted* you."

"Please don't hate me," begged Priya. "You guys are my best friends. I never meant to hurt you. And, I mean, maybe it's a good thing? That it's all out in the open with Sarah P?"

"That was my choice to make, not yours," said Mei.

"And maybe we're not your best friends any more," snapped Sami. "It's obvious that Katie is."

"She's not!" Priya looked frantically from one to the other. "Please. I need you both. I can't do this without you. Everything's...everything's gone wrong. Olaf kicked me off the team event and Dan doesn't want to date me any more."

"What?" Mei's eyes widened. Priya felt a wave of hope – there was still compassion in her eyes.

"Why, did you betray them by outing their secrets too?" demanded Sami, with infinitely less compassion in her eyes. "I bet whatever happened, you deserved it. Maybe it's karma for spilling our secrets."

"It was all because of the bangle," said Priya in frustration. She tried to yank it off her wrist, but it was still stuck. She winced as it scraped her skin. "I just wish everything would go back to how it used to be."

"It's too late for that," said Mei. "Way too late."

"Exactly," said Sami. "Don't bother coming to my bat mitzvah either. You're disinvited."

"But I'm free now!" said Priya. "In the morning, anyway!" She suddenly realized what she'd said and backtracked. "I mean, I...I want to come. Please."

Sami's mouth gaped open as realization dawned on her face. "You weren't free. Oh my god. All this time. It was gymnastics, wasn't it? You had a competition, didn't you? But now you're off the team, you're free *in the morning.* Even though everyone knows the beginning of a BM is the most boring part, and the only bit that matters is the afternoon party!" She wiped her eyes furiously, not even letting Priya try and reply. "I can't *believe* this! You're meant to be my best friend, and all this time, you've been *lying* to me? Even with the bangle?!"

"I'm so sorry," said Priya, for what felt like the hundredth time that morning. "I just didn't know what to do. It was a competition – it's not like I didn't *want* to come! I was meant to be doing the team event in the morning, but Olaf doesn't want me to do it any more. And I have my individual in the afternoon – it's my chance to get on the—"

"Teen Olympics team," chorused her friends.

"We get it." Sami spat out the words, mid-tears. "It's all you care about – not us."

"You could have told us the truth," said Mei softly. "You've never really been honest with us, have you, Priya? The bangle might have made you share certain things, but you've never actually opened up to us the way we have with you."

"That's not true," cried Priya. "I have! I do!" She turned to Sami, who was shaking angrily. "Please. Forgive me. I'm so sorry."

"The worst part," choked out Sami, "is that you managed to override the bangle when it came to keeping the secret about not making it to my bat mitzvah. But you didn't even *try* to override it when it came to telling Katie our secrets."

"But... I... It wasn't like that," whispered Priya. "Please."

"Let's go," said Mei. She put her arm in Sami's and the two of them walked away, both crying loudly.

Priya stood staring at their retreating backs in dismay. She felt her eyes overflow with tears until she was also crying loudly for the second time that day. But unlike Sami and Mei, she had absolutely nobody to cry with at all.

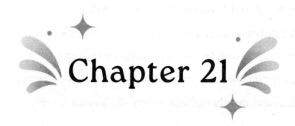

Chapter 21

The bell rang, signalling the end of the day for most of the school – and detention for Priya. She couldn't believe she still had to go and sit in the maths classroom with Katie after everything that had happened. Priya wasn't even sure how she'd managed to get through the day. Sami and Mei hadn't spoken to her once. They'd moved seats in French and in English, so that it was impossible for her to sit with them. Priya had been hurt, but not surprised. Why would they want to sit next to her after what she'd done? She'd tried to just focus on her schoolwork – with her gymnastics career, her friendships and her love life all in tatters, schoolwork was the only thing left in her life that was still going well. But then Ms Carlyle had asked for her *Jane Eyre* essay and Priya had realized she'd never finished it... She'd stayed up late playing dumb games with the traitor that was Katie Wong, and this morning, with all the drama, she'd been too distracted to get the essay done. So Ms Carlyle had punished her by giving her a demerit. For a normal student, it wasn't a big deal. But for Priya, who had a perfect record that was a source of pride for her parents, it was yet another failure to add to her growing list.

Priya stood outside the maths classroom, trying to muster up the courage to go inside. She had no idea what to say to Katie. She was beyond angry. But was she really brave enough to try and stand up to the only girl in their year who'd already had two boyfriends and had her birthday parties in nightclubs?

"Move." Priya looked up to see Katie. She'd put on green eyeliner, which made her look both more beautiful and more terrifying than ever. How could Priya have ever thought they were becoming friends? Katie was the scariest girl she knew, and right now she was glaring at Priya. "I can't get in unless you move, and if I can't get in, then I can't begin my hour of rest and relaxation. So...move."

Priya moved out of the way wordlessly. Katie pushed open the door and stomped straight to her usual seat, immediately popping open a can of Diet Coke. She kicked off her boots, crossed her legs and raised an eyebrow at Priya, who had followed her into the room but remained standing in the corner.

"I see you've elected to go with the silent treatment," said Katie. "Which is perfect for me. I can put my headphones in and we can go back to not acknowledging each other."

"Unless you want an essay from me," retorted Priya, her anger rising again. "Or to make fun of me, like you used to. Then I guess you'll need to acknowledge me."

"Oh, look, it speaks."

"I never should have trusted you." Priya shook her head bitterly. "The others were right all along. You're a bully *and* a liar. You just used me to get intel because you love gossip and drama. You even told me that to my face – why didn't I just *listen* to you? Then none of this would have ever happened."

"Because you liked the gossip and the drama too," replied Katie, her voice slicing through the tension in the air. "You liked the attention. Didn't you?"

"Fine, maybe a part of me did," said Priya, wincing at the truth forced out of her by the bangle. "But I'd never hurt someone's feelings like you did!"

Katie arched her eyebrow. "You literally did. You're the one who told me your little friends' secrets – I didn't make you."

Priya exhaled in frustration, wishing she could tell Katie that it was the bangle that had made her. Instead, she snapped at her. "Why are you *like* this?! Is your life really so miserable that you need to make everyone else's as bad?"

"Maybe it is. And what are you going to do about it?"

Priya scoffed. "Right – your life is so hard, being the most attractive, privileged girl in the entire year."

"As if you'd understand," said Katie, looking her up and down with coldness in her eyes. "How could you?"

"Because I'm not pretty or privileged?"

"Because you've never gone through anything hard in your life," corrected Katie, crossing her arms. "The biggest problem you've ever had is an argument with your friends."

Priya's mouth fell open. "Are you kidding me? My life is a complete mess! I've given everything to gymnastics but now my coach doesn't want me to go to team practices any more. My parents are already furious with me for getting a week's worth of detention, and now I'm going to have to tell them I'm banned from practice – they'll *kill* me. Not to mention that I've ruined things with the boy I have quite literally been obsessed with for as long as I can remember. And worst of all, my best friends in the world aren't speaking to me."

"Yeah, all of which happened in the last twenty-four hours," pointed out Katie. "It's a temporary blip in the perfection that is your life. It'll probably all blow over by the weekend."

"No, it won't," said Priya bitterly. "You don't know the half of it."

"Right," said Katie, "because things are hard for you outside of all this, are they? Like, at home?"

Priya knew this was her chance to try and override the bangle – she could feel the words rising up in her throat, and if she breathed slowly, she could find a way to order them that didn't give too much away. But right now, she didn't *care* about trying to control things. What was the point? Katie had already taken away her best friends; Priya no longer had anything to lose.

"Things at home have been bad for years," she said flatly, sliding down into the nearest chair. "My parents argue the entire time, but they refuse to divorce. My little sister has ADHD and accidentally ruins everything nice I own. I get that it's not really her fault, but sometimes, it seriously sucks. We have major money problems and I feel guilty that all my gymnastics training makes it worse. I can't sleep properly because I'm always so stressed. I literally *have* to win my competitions so we get the prize money, but it means I'm too exhausted to even do my schoolwork half the time, let alone when I had to do yours as well. And...I miss my grandma. She died last year."

Katie looked taken aback. There was a pause and then she raised an arched brow. "I don't think I've ever heard you say so much in one go."

"Well, there you go," replied Priya. "My life is officially miserable. Beat that."

Katie shrugged. "Fine. My dad walked out on me and my mum a few months ago, without even saying bye. It was hell, but what's worse is that my mum still isn't over it. She's depressed. Half the time she won't even shower or get out of bed. She just gives me her credit cards and tells me to buy whatever I like. I don't remember the last time we even ate a home-cooked meal. We – sorry, *I* – order in every night."

Priya stared at Katie, speechless. Katie Wong – the girl who had the most perfect life ever – was living a lie? "Oh my god," said Priya. "I...can't believe it. That sounds awful, Katie. I'm sorry. I had no idea..."

"There's nothing to be sorry for," said Katie. "I don't need your pity."

"I'm not pitying you!" replied Priya. "I just...I get what it feels like to live a lie." She looked down at the plastic floor. "Have you heard from your dad since?"

"He's been trying to call me lately, but there's *no way* I'm speaking to him after he abandoned us like that," said Katie, flicking invisible dirt from her nails. "Especially because, according to his Facebook page, I'm about to get a new half-sibling. Yay for me!"

Priya's mouth dropped. "Your dad's having a baby?"

"And there you have it – proof that my life is even more miserable than yours."

"That sounds hard," said Priya, unexpectedly understanding exactly why Katie loved being in detention so much – it sounded infinitely better than the loneliness of being at home with an unwell mother and a takeaway for company. In fact, a lot of things were making more sense now. Like why Katie was so cynical. And how the bullying had started a few months ago – around the same time her dad had left them. "Does it have anything to do with why you started getting me to do your maths homework?" asked Priya cautiously.

There was a long pause then Katie nodded. "My dad used to help me with it. We'd always do it together. But then he left. So, yeah. No more maths support."

Priya absorbed this in silence. This didn't excuse Katie's behaviour, but it did help to know there was a reason *why* she'd started forcing Priya into doing her homework for her. She shook her head and turned back to Katie. "Is there... anyone who can help? Like, family or...?"

Katie laughed darkly. "We're Chinese. Do you really think my mum has opened up to people about this? I'm banned from telling *anyone.* I probably shouldn't have even told you, but whatever – it's not like you count."

"My family's the same," said Priya, deciding to ignore Katie's last comment. "We have to keep everything a secret because they're terrified of the community – whoever that even is – judging them. Their favourite motto is *don't air your—*"

"*Dirty laundry in public*," finished Katie. "Don't look so surprised, all Asians do it. Mental health is taboo. Divorce is taboo. *Everything* is taboo."

"Mei says that too..." Priya looked down at the table as a sharp pang hit her chest. She already missed Mei so much.

"Well, it's true." Katie got out a biro and started doodling on the desk. "Anyway, whatever. I'll be out of here in five years. I can finally leave this all behind and go to art school. Somewhere really far away."

"But five years is a long time," said Priya. "You can't just hang out in detention until then."

"And why not?"

"Because you need support! And help! Does Angela know?"

Katie glared at her. "No and she's not going to find out. Is she?"

For a second, Priya foresaw herself getting revenge on Katie by telling the whole school her reality. But then she felt a wave of shame. She couldn't do that to her. "No," she finally replied. "But why can't you tell her? She's meant to be your best friend."

"Exactly. If she finds out what a mess my life is, she'll look at me the way you're looking at me – like I'm a tragedy. I don't want people to know. It's my private business."

Priya nodded slowly. She used to feel the exact same way. "I get it, but speaking to your friends really helps. You don't feel so alone, for a start."

"Thanks, but no, thanks. I'm fine as I am."

"Really?"

"Yes," snapped Katie. "I'm not the one who just lost her boyfriend, best friends and gymnastics team. You should be focusing on fixing your own life – not mine."

Priya's shoulders slumped as her reality hit her. Somehow, she really had ruined absolutely everything. Who was she to give advice to Katie? It wasn't like telling the truth had made her life any better – it had got her into a complete mess. "You're right. TikToks?"

Katie sighed. "Why not?"

Priya sat in her room with the DIY drawer emptied out across her bedside table. She picked up her dad's pliers, biting her bottom lip as she tried to use them one-handed – something she wouldn't have had to do if she was with Sami and Mei. She clamped them down on the bangle's clasp, using all her strength. But the bangle didn't even creak. She groaned in frustration. She angled the pliers onto the clasp once again, trying to be careful so she didn't— "Ow!" Priya cried out in pain as she accidentally jabbed the pliers into the side of her hand. They'd only left a tiny cut, but it felt like yet another sign that everything was against her. She flung the pliers away and collapsed onto her bed. There was no escaping the bangle's hold over her.

She let out an angry sob, hot tears sliding down her face. Everything was awful and she had no idea what to do about it. Then she gasped as it hit her: tears! What if they were the answer? She'd been crying on the day when the clasp had opened. So maybe she needed to cry for it to open up again? She quickly brought the bangle up to her wet cheeks, and rubbed her tears all over it. But nothing happened. No sudden *click*. She tried once more, desperate to open it up. It didn't work. The clasp refused to budge. Priya felt an urge to scream. She never really felt angry. If she did, she just swallowed it down, and would occasionally let herself cry with sadness instead. But this time, crying wasn't enough. She was furious. With life, with everyone around her, with herself and...with her grandma. *Why* had Ba left her the bangle and told her the truth would make her less lonely, when it had just done the exact opposite?!

Priya grabbed her pillow in anger. She pushed it against her face, opened her mouth wide and shouted deep into its thick memory foam so that nobody would hear her. She panted heavily with the release. It felt weirdly good to discharge all her pain and frustration and unhappiness into her bedding. So, she did it again. And then she started to pummel her fists into the other pillow and thump her feet on the bed at the same time. She was just so angry, and sad, and lonely and...well, *everything*. She probably looked like she was having some kind of exorcism, but it wasn't like anyone was there to see it. So, what did it matter?

"Um, you look like you're having an exorcism."

Priya froze mid pillow thump. She turned with dread to look at the doorway. Pinkie was standing there, looking at her older sister with the same fascination she showed her specimens in science experiments. "Pinkie! You can't just come into my room without knocking."

"In my defence, I thought you were dying," said Pinkie. "I figured that broke the 'no entry without knocking' rule."

"I am not dying," replied Priya crossly, wiping her wet tears onto her jumper sleeve. "I'm just...expressing my emotions."

"Into a pillow?"

"Yes," said Priya defensively. "You should try it."

"I'm all good, thanks," said Pinkie. She came and sat on the edge of Priya's bed. "So, what is it? Dan Zhang?"

Priya stared at her younger sister and then sighed. There was no point trying to manipulate the bangle – she had officially given up. It turned out that was the one upside of being at rock bottom: she couldn't go any lower. "Yes. And other stuff."

"Did you tell him you liked him?"

"Yes. He said it back. Then I ruined it, and now he doesn't want to see me again." Priya sniffed as the tears started to come back. "He won't see me again anyway, because Olaf has banned me from practice."

"Eeeek! Mum and Dad are going to lose their minds. They're already furious about your week-long detention."

"Thanks for reminding me," said Priya glumly. "They'll find out about gymnastics soon, but I'm trying to avoid it for as long as I can. Thank god that Dad never checks his emails. You were right, by the way – they're arguing again. They've been faking all the 'we're a happy family' stuff. They still hate each other and they're not going to divorce."

"Nothing new there," said Pinkie. "Are those the only reasons why you're so miserable?"

"Are they not enough?" Priya sighed again before her sister could reply. "But yes, there's more. Sami and Mei aren't speaking to me. I betrayed their trust."

"What did you do?"

"Spilt their secrets to the school bully. They'll probably never speak to me again."

"You've been busy," remarked Pinkie.

"Busy ruining my life," agreed Priya. It was kind of freeing to not have to hide from her little sister just how bad things were.

"So, what are you going to do about it?"

Priya stared at her in confusion. "What am I going to do? I'm going to sit here and scream into my pillow and pray that somehow it all gets better."

"Seriously? You don't have a game plan?"

Priya shook her head.

"Do you want one?" Pinkie fingered the bedspread, looking almost...shy. Priya had never seen her sister look shy before. She blinked. "Because I can help you if you want."

"Uh...thanks," said Priya. "But I'm fine. There's nothing you can do. I'm just going to...hide from the world. It's better that way."

"Okay," said Pinkie, shrugging. "Well, if you change your mind, I'm pretty good at experiments, so I could probably help you come up with a solution to this...mess."

"I'm not sure how I feel about you experimenting with my life," said Priya. "So, thanks but no, thanks." Then she sat up straight as an idea popped into her head. "Actually, there *is* something you can help me with. Can you lie for me?"

"Lie?"

"Yes. I'm doing this thing where I, uh, can't lie. Long story. But can you tell Mum I'm really sick so that I don't have to go to school tomorrow or gymnastics this weekend? Oh my god, maybe I can be so sick I don't have to go to school next week either! Oh, please, Pinkie – a week off school would be the *best* gift you could ever give me! I won't ever expect a birthday present again."

"Okay. I can probably get you a week off."

Priya's eyes lit up for the first time in days. "Seriously? Thank you!"

Pinkie grinned. "I'm going to tell Mum you're so sick that it's best nobody comes near you because it's super contagious. She's got a major presentation coming up, so she'll avoid you like the plague. And Dad won't ever notice, because, well, he's Dad."

Priya leaned across the bed and held her younger sister tightly. She couldn't remember the last time she'd spontaneously hugged her, but it felt good. "Thanks, Pinkie."

Pinkie patted her shoulder. "My pleasure."

Chapter 22

Priya wrapped the duvet around her and reached for more crisps. She'd claimed the big sofa in the living room as her new home, and a week into her fake illness, she had no desire to leave. Ever. Her parents had accepted Pinkie's lie that Priya had a madly contagious virus that had been going around the school, and the school nurse's advice was for anyone infected to stay home for at least a week. Priya had managed to get around all her parents' questions asking her how she felt. Because she did truly feel "awful", "terrible" and that "the only thing that will help is staying at home to recover". Which was why she was spending so much time on the sofa, watching really bad television, and eating all the snacks she wasn't usually allowed. Her mum was too busy preparing for her big presentation to say more than, "I hope you're doing all the extra work the school emailed over," and her dad had conceded that she'd had a lot going on lately, so it made sense her immune system was weak. She knew that she had to go back to school next Monday, and the gymnastics competition was only in two days, but Priya was in denial. All she wanted to do was hide away from her problems, and this sofa was the perfect place to do it.

"Priya?" Her dad hovered in the doorway with a worried smile. "Were the eggs okay?"

Priya glanced at her half-eaten plate of food. She breathed deeply and answered in a way that was both honest but not insulting – something she'd been able to practise regularly with all the "health-boosting" meals her dad kept bringing her. The only one that had been fully edible had been the slices of grapefruit. "They were definitely better than yesterday," she said finally. "Thank you."

Her dad looked at the plate and sighed. "I didn't realize how bad my cooking skills were until you started telling me recently. I wish I'd known earlier; I might have taken a course." He shook his head. "Anyway, how are you feeling? Any better?"

Priya shook her head morosely. The pain of losing Sami and Mei, not to mention Dan and the gymnastics team, was too much to bear. She had no idea how she'd survived for so long – and she had even less of an idea on how she'd survive the next few days, let alone the rest of her life. Things just didn't make sense any more. What was the point of watching a funny video if there was no Sami or Mei to send it to? And as much as she'd complained about all the time gymnastics took up in her life, she felt empty without it. She missed how calm and in control she felt on the mat. It was pretty much the only time Priya ever felt relaxed. But now, every time she tried to practise her individual routine to get ready for Nationals, waves of sadness and regret flooded over her. She couldn't help but think about how the team were doing. She hoped it was going well with Hayley. They deserved a gold – even if it was without her.

"You don't look any better," said her dad anxiously. "Do you need me to make you more hot water and turmeric? I can add ginger."

Priya shook her head rapidly. "No, thanks. I really don't need that. Just normal water is fine."

Her dad frowned. "Don't you have your big competition coming up soon? I hope you'll be well enough for it. Oh dear, I was meant to forward the details to your mum, wasn't I?"

Priya squirmed. "Um...kind of. It's...complicated."

"What do you mean?" asked her dad, confused. He pulled out his phone. "Let me check my emails from Olaf."

"No!" cried Priya. "Please don't do that."

"Why not?"

Priya's head fell into her hands. Not again. Would she ever be free of this bangle forcing her to ruin her life every ten seconds? She quickly tried to think of a way to twist the truth, but then she realized it would probably just come out later – it always did. With a sigh of resignation, she mumbled the truth through her hands. "Because he's banned me from the team event."

Her dad gasped. He steadied himself against the doorway with his hand. "I...I don't understand. Priya – what happened? Why?"

Priya felt tears prick her eyelids. "Dad, I really don't want to talk about it."

"Hey." Her dad came over, crouching down next to her. "You can tell me anything. It's okay. We'll handle it together. Whatever it is."

"I messed up!" she burst out. "I ruined everything. After all the things you and Mum have sacrificed for me, I've thrown it all away."

"Priya, you haven't ruined anything," said her dad. "No matter what's happened, it will be okay!"

"But I have," wailed Priya. "I'm jeopardizing my entire gymnastics career after everything you and Mum have spent on my training. I haven't even done any practice for my individual event this Saturday – I've been too sad – and now I'm probably going to lose out on the prize money, when I know we need it." She shook her head self-critically. "I'm sorry I've been so selfish. It isn't fair on you and Mum."

Her dad paled as the words spilled out of her. Finally, he laid his hand on her shoulder and looked into her eyes.

"Priya – you're not some kind of investment. You're our daughter. All we want is for you to be happy. Our money problems aren't your responsibility. You don't need to ever compete for money."

"But I thought we needed my prize money. How can we afford it otherwise?"

Her dad smiled sadly. "Oh, Priya. I'm sorry we've led you to believe that you have to earn money for us. You don't. Things aren't great for us financially, but I promise, we don't need you to win. We can still afford your gymnastics. It's okay."

"Really? Do you actually mean it?" asked Priya, her eyes wet.

"Of course," he said. "We only want you to do gymnastics if you enjoy it. Whether it's practices or competitions. It's about you having a good time, not earning for us. I promise."

Priya sat in silence, absorbing her dad's words. It had been *so* long since she'd just focused on the pure pleasure of gymnastics. But if her dad was right and they didn't need her prize money as much as she'd thought, then...maybe she *could* go back to just having fun with gymnastics. Like at the start of her career, when competitions had been a chance to keep improving and seeing all her friends. She didn't know when things had changed, but they really had.

"Now," said her dad firmly. "Tell me what's going on. Everything."

Priya bit her lip apprehensively. "Will you tell Mum?"

Her dad unconsciously copied Priya, biting his own lip. "I really should..."

"*Please* don't," begged Priya. "Please! It'll just stress her out. And then I'll feel even worse."

Her dad sighed. "All right. Fine. I won't tell her *yet*. Only because I don't want to worry her before her big presentation next week. But," he looked at Priya sternly, "once her presentation is over, we're telling her."

Priya nodded reluctantly. "Okay."

"Okay. So, why *exactly* did Olaf ban you from the team event?"

That evening, Priya curled up under her duvet in her actual bed. She felt so much better. She'd told her dad everything – well, not about the bangle. Or Sami and Mei. Or Dan Zhang. But she'd told him all about her conversation with Olaf, and he hadn't been angry! He'd told her that it made sense she'd told Olaf she cared more about winning her individual gold than the team one – she was just trying to please her parents. It was their fault, not hers. They'd put too much pressure on her, and they'd never do that again.

Priya had thrown her arms around her dad, temporarily forgetting she was meant to be infectious. It was just such a relief to hear that there wasn't any more pressure. It felt like a huge weight had disappeared from around her neck.

She didn't need to keep winning – she could just go back to enjoying it all and doing her best. She might still win – Priya knew she had a competitive side – but she didn't *have* to. She wasn't even sure she still wanted to do her individual at the Nationals. She'd finally told her dad the competition was that Saturday and he'd said she didn't need to go if she didn't want to. It was all her choice.

"Have you seen this?" The door burst open, revealing Pinkie in her Yoda nightgown, her hair looking wilder than ever. She was waving her phone in the air.

"Oh my god, I *told* you to knock!" said Priya. "You're so annoying."

Pinkie bounded onto the bed and waved her phone in Priya's face. "Look!"

Priya reluctantly pulled herself up onto her forearms and looked at her sister's phone screen. It was Dan's social media page. "Pinkie, why are you looking at this?"

"Because I started following him when you told me you liked him," said Pinkie impatiently. "Anyway – look! The new gymnast they found for the team event has sprained her ankle! They're a gymnast short for the Nationals!"

Priya stared at the screen. It was true. Hayley was injured and Dan had posted a shoutout for people in the gymnast community to spread the message. They needed a female gymnast ASAP. For the competition that Saturday. At eleven a.m.

"You can do it," encouraged Pinkie. "You can go and save the day and win the competition."

"No, 1 can't," said Priya, pushing the phone away. "I've done absolutely no practice for it at all! And Olaf won't allow it. He's already told me."

"I bet he will now he's this desperate!"

"The team won't want me there anyway," said Priya. "It's not going to happen, Pinkie. I'm not doing it."

Pinkie frowned. "But 1 thought you had an individual event there anyway?"

"I do, but Dad said I don't have to go if I don't want to. And I'm not sure I do. I'd have to see everyone again. It's probably best if I just opt out."

There was a pause, then Pinkie asked: "Are you scared?"

"N-yes!" shouted Priya. She groaned loudly as she glanced at the bangle. "Ugh! Fine, I'm scared!"

"Thought so. Scared that everyone hates you?"

Priya nodded reluctantly. "Pretty much."

"But this is the way to get them to like you again!" said Pinkie. "Trust me. You have to go to this competition and help win it for your friends. Imagine if you get back on the team, and Dan forgives you. That will solve half your problems, right?"

"I guess so... But they won't want me."

"Priya?" Her mum knocked on the door and gently prised it open. "Are you feeling be— Pinkie! What are you doing?

Your sister's contagious! Get off her bed."

"She's actually feeling better," said Pinkie confidently. "Aren't you?"

"*Marginally* better."

Her mum's eyes lit up. "Oh, thank goodness! You can go back to school tomorrow!"

"Not that much better," said Priya quickly, and it was true. Sami and Mei hadn't sent her a *single* message since she'd been off school. They hadn't even replied to any of the many voice notes she'd sent them apologizing. She was so anxious about how they were doing – were they being teased at school for their secrets? Was Mei feeling better? They'd never gone so long without speaking before and every time Priya thought about it – normally around once an hour – she felt sick with regret.

"Well, I suppose there's no point going back for just one day before the weekend," said her mum. "And it sounds like you'll be better for Sami's bat mitzvah on Saturday! I'm looking forward to it."

Priya froze. "What? What do you mean?"

"She invited all of us ages ago – Pinkie too," said her mum. "I've had my dress dry-cleaned."

"But we can't!" said Priya. "I..." She turned to look at Pinkie in panic. "I won't be well enough."

Her mum frowned. "You just said you were feeling better." Then her phone started vibrating. She looked at it anxiously.

"Oh, it's work. I have to get this. Pinkie – leave your sister to rest. I don't want you getting sick too." She walked away, closing the door behind her as she answered her phone.

Priya turned to Pinkie. "Sami specifically said she doesn't want me to go to her BM. I can't turn up – it'll just make her even more upset with me."

"You could tell Mum and Dad about your gymnastics competition," Pinkie suggested. "Then they'll insist that we have to skip the bat mitzvah and go to that instead."

"But Mum doesn't know I got banned from the team event. I can't deal with her finding out about that yet. And if she goes to Nationals, she'll *definitely* end up speaking to Olaf."

"Wait, let me think," said Pinkie, frowning. "This might work in our favour... If you just say you're still sick, then they'll go to the bat mitzvah with me and leave you here. And you can go to the gymnastics competition, win gold for your team, fix everything – and Mum and Dad will never know!"

"I'm not sure I will help them win gold after a whole week without practising," said Priya doubtfully.

"You were practising for ages before that – it'll be fine," said Pinkie impatiently.

Priya sat up, feeling marginally cheered. Then she paled again. "What if Sami's disinvite extended to Mum and Dad? They'll be so upset if they find out what I did!" Priya pulled the duvet up over her face, groaning loudly. "Why is this such a mess? What about I going to do?"

Pinkie patted Priya's duvet-covered head. "It's a good thing you have me. Are you ready to help me come up with a plan to fix your life?"

Priya slowly lowered the duvet to reveal her doubtful face. "Do I have a choice?"

Pinkie smiled cheerily. "Nope."

Chapter 23

Early the next morning, Priya sat on Pinkie's bed holding a notepad and pen while her younger sister stood by her desk pointing at her computer. Priya nodded furiously, taking notes as her sister finished explaining the plan in detail.

"And that", said Pinkie, "is how we are going to get you back on the gymnastics team and back in Dan Zhang's good books."

Priya stopped writing and looked up nervously. "Do you really think it's going to work?"

"Yes!" said Pinkie. "Of course, it will. You just need to call Rachael now and ask her to tell Olaf she's found someone to do the team event. Then when you turn up, he'll be mad. But he'll also be desperate enough to agree to it. You'll win. Dan will forgive you. And you'll get home before we're back from the bat mitzvah, so the parents won't know a thing. How does that sound?"

"It sounds good," admitted Priya. "Thanks, Pinkie." She'd had no idea her younger sister could be so *practical*. Priya thought her sister was always busy creating messes, but now she could see that she was pretty good at clearing them up too. And she was brave. She didn't spend all her time worrying about things like Priya did – she just did them. It was kind of refreshing. Priya never would have had the courage to come up with a plan like this if it wasn't for her younger sister.

"Go on then," said Pinkie impatiently. "Call Rachael."

"Do I have to?" asked Priya reluctantly.

"Well, it's either that or you call Dan," said Pinkie. "What would you rather?"

Priya's eyes widened in alarm. "I'll call Rachael."

"Great," said Pinkie. "I'll go downstairs and prepare Mum and Dad for tomorrow by telling them how gross and ill you are. Good luck!"

The door closed behind Pinkie, and Priya was left alone with her phone. She was scared to call Rachael. She didn't usually ring anyone on the team – they'd only ever message, if that. But she knew she had to be brave if she wanted to fix things. And that meant doing things that scared her. She took a deep breath and picked up her phone.

"Priya?" Rachael picked up after a few moments, but she sounded confused. She probably had no idea why Priya was suddenly calling her. "Is everything okay?"

"No, not really," said Priya honestly. "How are you?"

"Uh...not great either," said Rachael. "Hayley has sprained her ankle. And now we're not sure we can compete tomorrow."

"That's why I'm calling," said Priya. "I saw it on Dan's socials. Well, my sister did. But that's not the point. The point is that I want to help and compete with you all again."

"Oh my god, Olaf said you can come back?!" Rachael's voice was light with relief. "I'm so glad! Though I didn't think he would. He shouted at Dan when he suggested it."

"Dan suggested it?" Priya's eyes lit up with hope. Then she realized what Rachael had said. "Wait, Olaf actually *shouted*?"

"Um, yeah. He said that what was done was done and is Dan the coach or is he? But how did you get him to change his mind?"

Priya hesitated. "I haven't... Yet. But I was thinking that maybe you could help me! All you'd have to do is tell Olaf that you've found a replacement and you're showing her the routine. Then when I turn up tomorrow morning, he'll be too desperate to say no!"

There was silence on the other end of the phone.

"Rachael?" asked Priya hopefully. "Is that a positive silence or a negative one?"

"I could get in trouble," said Rachael finally. "If it doesn't work, Coach will blame me. What if he bans *me* from practice too?"

Priya lowered her eyes to Pinkie's lurid bedspread. "You're right," she said quietly. "I'm sorry. I shouldn't have tried to involve you. It's not fair."

"It's just…" Rachael faltered. "It's the kind of thing you'd do for a friend. And, well, I don't really know if we are friends."

"What do you mean?"

"You'd hardly ever spoken to me in the two years we've been on the team together," said Rachael slowly. "And then lately, you started opening up and I thought things were changing. But when I saw you crying the other day, you just walked away from me. And then I didn't hear anything from you afterwards. You disappeared. And…I kept expecting a message from you. I mean, you left the team we've both been on for ages. But you never got in touch. It felt like I didn't mean anything to you. Like none of us did."

Priya's face fell. She had no idea that Rachael had seen things that way. But when she put it like that…it all made sense. It was exactly what Sami and Mei had said. That Priya was too wrapped up in herself. She'd never thought she was – she spent so much time trying to make other people happy, how could they call her selfish? But now she was realizing that maybe that *was* the problem. She was so busy trying to please everyone that she wasn't really present. By not opening up to people, she hadn't allowed them to open up to *her*. True friendship was when both people shared and supported each other – not when one person pretended they were fine all the time.

"I'm sorry, Rachael," she said finally. "You're right. I wish you weren't, but you are. I was so focused on me, and how I was coming across to people, that I didn't think about you. But I do really like you. I think you're funny and kind and fun and, honestly? I wish I'd spoken to you more these last two years."

"Wow," said Rachael, taken aback. "I didn't think you'd agree like that."

"I do, I really do," said Priya resolutely. "I made mistakes. But I want to fix them. That's why I want to come and help the team so badly."

Priya could practically hear Rachael's smile. "Okay," she said. "I'll help you. But only because you said I'm funny and kind. Though you missed out beautiful."

Priya laughed. "It's true, I did. And thank you so much – you're the best, Rachael."

"Talk me through the plan. Oh, and I hope you've been practising the routine or Olaf's going to lose his mind. You know Hayley was bottom right for the pyramid? Olaf, um... well, he asked me to take your place on top."

"I can't think of anyone who deserves it more," said Priya firmly. "I'm more than happy to be bottom right. I saw some of your videos on socials..." She swallowed as she remembered the pang she'd felt as she'd seen the team practising without her. "So, I know what I need to do. I'll make sure my part is perfect – I've been working on it all day and I won't stop till we're there."

"What about the individual?" asked Rachael. "You're still preparing for that as well, right?"

"I've done so much on that already that I'll be fine," said Priya dismissively. "The team event is my priority now. Which is why I'm going to need you to tell me everything I've missed so far. But first..." She paused. "Could you maybe just talk me through *exactly* what Dan said about me? Word for word?"

Rachael laughed. "Only if you tell me exactly what's going on between you two. Word for word!"

Priya practised the team routine for the twenty-sixth time that day in her bedroom (she'd pushed her bed against the wall to make space) and frowned critically at her reflection in the mirror. She was getting better, but she wouldn't know if she was in perfect time until she could practise with the others. That was another reason she'd always felt safer doing individual events – the only person she had to rely on was herself. With a team event, anyone could make a mistake and cost them the gold – and it could be Priya. She shuddered at the thought of her plan ending in failure. But then she remembered just how much everyone laughed during practice when things went wrong (well, bar Olaf) and how much fun they all had. The others weren't doing this because they were obsessed with getting gold – they were doing it because they loved it. And Priya loved it too, she'd just forgotten. Her teammates weren't the kind of people who would hate her if she messed up the routine, they'd just be glad that she'd tried. That was the thing about a team event – it was all about trusting and forgiving each other. Things that Priya had never been very good at – especially when it came to herself.

It was ironic after everything that had happened lately, but Priya was realizing that the thing she missed most about gymnastics was being on a team. The laughter, the sense of being in it together, and the pure fun. Every time she watched the videos of them on socials, or the extra ones Rachael was sending her now to keep up her practising, she wished she was with them. She just couldn't believe it had taken her so long to understand this. If only she'd seen it earlier, she'd be with them right now.

But she was still lucky, because Rachael had agreed to the plan. They'd discussed the routine in detail so that Priya would be as up to speed as possible. And Rachael had offered to have her parents pick Priya up on the way to the competition on Saturday morning. They could get to the venue early and spend a couple of hours practising with the rest of the team before they had to compete. It was incredibly risky, but it was the best they could manage.

Rachael had also listened and sympathized when Priya had told her about the Dan situation. It turned out she'd had her heart broken by Simone, a girl who used to be on their team, and Priya had never even realized! She'd been so consumed by her own problems, stressing out about spending so much time in gymnastics away from her friends, that she hadn't even noticed she could have friends *in* gymnastics: her teammates. It was a major oversight and it was not one that Priya would ever be making again. From now on, friendships were her priority. All of them.

She opened up the musketeers' group chat on her phone but there was still no reply to her messages. She wrote another one:

I really am sorry. Please can we talk?

Even though she could see both Sami and Mei were online, neither replied. Priya sighed and exited the chat. She knew how much she'd hurt her friends. Their silence made total sense. But she refused to give up. She was going to keep begging for their forgiveness until the day she died. Or until the day they forgave her. Ideally that day would arrive sooner.

Her phone vibrated and Priya almost dropped it in excitement. A message. From Sami!

I'm not ready to talk. But I thought you should know, Mrs Lufthausen has been sent home.

Priya stared at the message in confusion. Another one arrived. This time it was from Mei.

They're investigating her for being too harsh. Apparently, she's had Katie in detention for 90% of the year. Her dad complained.

Priya's eyes widened. Katie's *dad*?! But she wasn't speaking to him – was she?

Anyway, wrote Sami. *We're still not speaking to you. Just thought you should know this info. Looks like Mrs L might not be coming back.*

Yeah, added Mei. *Apparently she's going through a divorce and that's why she's been extra awful lately. It's not you – it's her.*

But when it comes to us, it IS you, wrote Sami. *Just to clarify. Bye.*

Priya waited for a message from Mei, but all she sent was an emoji of a hand waving goodbye. Well, it was better than nothing.

She sent them a reply thanking them for telling her, with three heart emojis, then put the phone down and leaned against her soft headboard. She couldn't believe that Mrs Lufthausen had been sent home. Her worst teacher was being investigated, and there was a real chance she'd never be back. Either way, it sounded like things were going to change at school. Never again would she be humiliated in maths or forced to explain herself in front of the entire class whilst a furious Mrs Lufthausen yelled at her or stuck her in a week-long detention for admitting she was daydreaming about a boy.

It was good news. And the fact that Sami and Mei had messaged her to tell her was even better news. They were still furious – their messages proved that – but the fact that they'd thawed enough to contact her was a positive sign. It showed that they still thought about her. They cared. Priya smiled – there was hope. The Three Musketeers could get back together again! Then she frowned as she remembered what Mei had said about Katie's dad. Was it a mistake – did she mean Katie's mum? Or was Katie's dad involved? And if he was back in Katie's life, was she okay about it?

Priya shook her head. This was ridiculous. Why was she worrying about Katie after everything she'd done to her? Even aside from the last few months of bullying Priya into doing her maths homework, Katie was the reason that Sami and Mei weren't speaking to her. But...if Priya was being really honest with herself, she knew it wasn't that simple. She'd been the one who had betrayed Sami and Mei, bangle or no bangle. Katie had just been being Katie. It wasn't fair to put all the blame on her. And she was going through a lot. Priya reached for her phone reluctantly. She was the only one Katie had confided in; she couldn't leave her to go through this alone. Without giving herself time to change her mind, she video-called her.

Katie's face loomed on her screen. "What?"

"Hey to you too," said Priya.

"I forgot you existed," Katie said with a scowl, "seeing as you've skipped school for a week."

Priya nodded guiltily. "I know it wasn't the best solution. I just couldn't face coming back."

"Well, stuff has gone down. Some serious stuff."

"I heard Mrs L got sent home," said Priya. "And she's being investigated."

A slow grin spread across Katie's face. "Yup. Comeuppance."

"And I heard that it was your dad who complained…"

Katie's face clouded over. "I'm not talking about this with you."

"Are you sure?" asked Priya. "Because…I'm here if you want to talk. About anything."

"I thought you hated me for ruining your friendships."

"I don't hate you." Priya sighed. "Look, it was my fault too. Although it was a bit your fault."

Katie rolled her eyes. "Right. Well, I guess I'm sorry. For the bit that was my fault."

"I guess I'm sorry too," repeated Priya, suppressing a smile. "For the bit that was my fault."

"Cool," said Katie.

"Cool," repeated Priya, grinning. "So…your dad? Do you want to talk about it?"

"Ugh, whatever, it's not a big deal," said Katie, flicking her hair behind her. "He turned up at home one day with no warning and saw the state my mum was in. And then he called her sister, so now my mum's moved in with her while she gets better. And my dad has moved back in. Temporarily. He still goes to see his new baby mama every day."

"Oh my god! Are you okay? How is that? Being with him?"

"Fine," said Katie begrudgingly. "He cooks me dinners. And he asks me about school. That's how he found out about Mrs L."

"That sounds...good?"

"It's *fine*," said Katie. "Let's not get carried away."

"I'm glad," said Priya softly. "So, things are good?"

"Fine, not good," corrected Katie. "But...yeah. Apart from the fact that Angela is being sent up a year, so she can compete in the right age group for the lacrosse championships."

"Oh, wow," said Priya. "I guess you won't be able to see her as much if she's in the year above. Are you...okay about that?"

Katie shrugged. "Whatever. I'll figure it out." She coughed awkwardly. "So, what about you? Are you okay?"

"I'm still hiding away from the world in my bedroom," said Priya matter-of-factly. "But yeah, I'm okay, thanks. I think I'm going to try and fix things with the gymnastics team tomorrow. And with Dan."

"Whoah," said Katie, her eyes widening. "How are you going to do that?"

"By turning up and forcing my coach to let me do the team event, so then we win gold and everyone forgives me."

"Now *this* I want to see," said Katie. "Send me the location!"

"Are you serious? *You* want to come to a gymnastics competition at eleven a.m. on a Saturday? Won't you be, like, asleep after partying late tonight?"

"Just send it," said Katie impatiently. "You know I like drama."

Priya shrugged. "Sure. Anyway, I'd better go practise my routine. Again."

"Show me?"

"Um, since when you do you want to watch gymnastics routines?"

"Since you got me into those gymnastics TikToks," retorted Katie. "But my standards are pretty high now, so I want to see some triple jumps and tucks, *like you mean it*."

Priya laughed in disbelief as she set her phone up on her desk so Katie could watch her. "It's scary how much you sound like my coach right now."

"Ooh, Coach Katie. I'm into that. Now, let's do this! Come on, Priya, activate those glutes!"

Chapter 24

"Are you *sure* you're going to be okay?" asked Priya's mum anxiously. She looked at Priya, who was wrapped up in her duvet again, sitting on the stairs to wave goodbye to her family. "I hate leaving you like this. You must feel awful missing your best friend's big day."

"I'll be okay, thanks, Mum," said Priya bravely. "Well, at least I hope I will."

"She'll be fine," said Pinkie impatiently. "Come on, or we're going to be late! The invitation said we have to be at the synagogue for nine a.m."

"It's very early for a party, isn't it?" asked their dad, adjusting his tie.

"Sami said it was cheaper to do it earlier," said Priya. "Besides, there's at least three hours of religious readings and speeches before the party." Her dad's face dropped in dismay. "Sorry."

"Pinkie's right," said their mum, wrapping a blue shawl around her bare shoulders. It matched her long silky dress perfectly. "We really should go."

"You look beautiful, Mum," said Priya.

Her mum blushed, looking pleased, while Pinkie frowned. "Uh, and what about me?"

Priya looked at her younger sister, wearing a long-sleeved yellow crop top with shiny green flared trousers. "You look... majorly colourful. Sami will be proud."

"My beautiful family," said their dad, smiling at his wife and youngest daughter. Then he quickly turned to Priya in her duvet. "Uh, you too, *beta*."

"Thanks, but even I know that wearing a duvet isn't a great look for me." Priya smiled. "Anyway, you need to go! Sami will die if you ruin her big moment by walking down the aisle mid-speech." She felt a stab in her chest at the thought. She couldn't believe she was going to miss Sami's initiation into womanhood. But she knew that turning up would just ruin Sami's big day, and that was the exact opposite of what Priya wanted. Besides, she had to focus on her gymnastics plan. One thing at a time.

"Right, come on, come on." Priya's mum ushered them out of the door, waving at her oldest daughter. "Priya, *beta*, I hope you feel better soon."

The door shut behind them.

"Oh, I already do," said Priya to herself, letting the duvet fall to the ground. She was already wearing her sparkly black long-sleeved leotard (perfect to cover up the bangle, seeing as jewellery definitely wasn't allowed in gymnastics competitions) with her grey tracksuit bottoms on top. She grabbed her phone and ran out of the door to wait for Rachael and her parents to show up.

Just then a large maroon car pulled up in her driveway, and Rachael stuck her head out of the window, waving manically. "We're here! Get in!"

Priya grinned at Rachael's parents, who looked exactly like their daughter and were both waving just as manically through the front window, before slipping into the back of the car.

So far, everything was going to plan. She just had to make sure that when she got to the competition, she could convince Olaf to let her perform with the team, do the routine perfectly, impress everyone, get Dan to forgive her, and most importantly, get her spot back on the team. Easy.

"Good luck, girls," said Rachael's mum before heading towards the audience seating.

"No matter what happens, we're proud of you," added her dad.

"Thanks." Rachael smiled. "See you later!" Her parents

walked away, and she turned to face Priya, the smile completely gone from her face. "Okay, are you ready for this?"

Priya's stomach rumbled nervously. "Um. No. But I guess I have to be."

"Good, glad you're feeling confident," said Rachael, failing to hide her own nerves. "It's fine. It's just Olaf. Underneath all his bluster, he loves us really."

"Let's hope so," said Priya, chewing her lip. "Come on."

They walked into the competitors' area, where they saw Olaf standing with the rest of the team – Priya instantly noticed Dan standing with James, looking as cute as ever in his black leotard. Olaf looked around in panic, until his eyes fell on Rachael with relief, and then on Priya with... Priya squirmed as she tried to define his expression. It wasn't exactly fury. Or disappointment. There was some shock in there. And then, well, yes, there probably was fury.

Rachael grabbed Priya's hand and practically dragged her up to Olaf and the team. Priya kept her eyes firmly on the ground because she was too scared to look at her teammates. But she could still see Olaf out of the corner of her eye, shaking his head angrily.

"This had better not be the person you told me you'd trained up to compete with the team," said Olaf grimly.

"It is," admitted Rachael.

"I thought you'd be bringing Simone," cried Olaf. "I specifically said Priya couldn't compete with the team."

Priya squeezed Rachael's hand – she remembered that Simone had broken Rachael's heart. But Rachael stuck her chin defiantly into the air. "Well, Olaf, it's not your choice."

Priya's mouth dropped open. She sneaked a quick look at the rest of the team. All their mouths were wide open too. She could even see Dan's perfectly white molars. Rachael *never* spoke to Olaf like that. None of them did. Well, none of them had until Priya's recent bangle situation. She quickly looked at Rachael's arm to see if she was stuck in a truth bangle too, but her wrists were bare.

"Excuse me?" thundered Olaf. "I'm the coach. It *is* my choice! Rachael – what's got into you? Do I need to have words with you as well?"

"I'm just saying that we're a team," said Rachael, her voice wavering slightly. "We've all worked hard for this event. And I think we, as a team, should get to decide who competes with us."

Olaf frowned. "Like...a vote?"

Priya's eyes widened. This was not part of the plan! What if people didn't vote for her?

"Exactly," said Rachael, confident again. "A vote. And I vote for Priya."

"I don't know if I do," said James. "Didn't she say she doesn't care about us as a team? I'd rather compete one girl down, than with a girl who isn't committed to us."

There were rumblings throughout the rest of the team. Priya's heart sank – it sounded like they were all in agreement with James.

Rachael turned to her. "Priya, you should...explain. Why don't you tell everyone the truth?"

They all turned to look at her. "Um..." Priya tried to think of what truth to tell – what would make everyone like her again? She had no idea! And her mind was spinning too quickly to come up with an answer. Then it hit her. She didn't need to try and make them like her. She just needed to breathe and tell the actual truth. That was all she could do. The rest was out of her control.

She forced herself to look every team member in the eye – even Dan – as she spoke. "I'm really sorry, everyone. James is right. I did say that. It's why Olaf kicked me off the team. I was being selfish, and I was only focused on my individual event, and on winning the prize money. I didn't care enough about the team event."

She looked away for a moment – the disappointment and shock on everyone's faces was too much to bear. But then she caught Rachael's eye, and her friend gave her an encouraging smile. Priya nodded slowly; she could do this.

She turned back to the team. "But I was wrong. So wrong. I just let the pressure get to me, and I forgot about what really matters. Which is, well, having fun! And being a team! I know I haven't always opened up to you much, but I would like the chance to change that. I really do love being on this team. And I've been practising the routine loads these last few days, in the position Hayley was in. I can do it; I know I can. Please let me come back and prove to you that I do care."

Rachael blinked away a tear and gave Priya a thumbs-up. "You nailed it," she mouthed. Priya smiled at her gingerly, avoiding eye contact with everyone else. She was scared that they'd still be looking at her with disappointment.

"Fine," growled Olaf. "Hands up if you want Priya back on the team *for this one event, and this one event only.* Anything else is my decision, because, even if you all seem to have forgotten, I am still the coach."

Priya bit her lip and tried not to look as the team voted. Her heart was beating so fast she felt like she was going to be sick. She stared resolutely at the ground. At her New Balances with their smiley worried faces. Those faces were kind of growing on her – they no longer looked fully anxious to her; they also looked cautiously optimistic.

"You did it!" cried Rachael.

Priya looked up to see that every single person's hands were in the air. Including James's. Dan was even smiling at her. Priya's heart soared.

"Oh, thank you so much! I won't disappoint you – I promise."

Olaf frowned. "Come on, everyone. We still have two hours before we compete. I want us to run through the routine until we're *perfect*. Priya – start with some burpees!"

Priya hit the ground, grinning. She'd never been so happy to do a burpee in her life.

It was time. The team before them were just finishing their routine, and they were up next. The last team to compete in this round of the Nationals. Priya was so nervous she could practically hear her blood pounding. She hated being the last to compete. Especially as the other teams had done so well. She glanced at the scoreboard, with its sixteens and seventeens. There was even an 18.075 – and everyone knew it was unheard of to get a perfect twenty. They'd have to get at least an 18.100 to win. The pressure was on. But she could do this. *They* could do this. Together.

"Hey, Priya?"

Priya whirled around to come face to face with Dan. She gasped, then tried to turn her awkwardness into a smile. He didn't seem to notice; he was too busy frowning and pushing his hair out of his eyes. "I just wanted to say...thanks for coming back. To do this."

"Of course," said Priya. "It's all my fault you were in this position anyway. I needed to make it right."

He nodded. "That's cool of you. You didn't have to. Also, uh, I should apologize. I think I was really harsh with you before. It wasn't fair of me to judge your priorities. I'm sorry."

"It's okay – what I said wasn't cool either," admitted Priya. "Really not cool. I'm just glad I got a chance to apologize to the whole team. And I hope I don't mess up now."

"You won't," he said assuredly. "Just imagine we're practising our flips alone together. We never messed up then."

Priya blushed at the memory. "Okay. I'll try."

The commentator's voice boomed across the auditorium, announcing that they were up next. Priya gave Dan a worried smile, and he grinned back confidently. "We've got this! Let's go!"

The whole team raced onto the mats. Rachael winked at Priya. Laughing, she winked back. Olaf nodded firmly at Priya. She nodded back. She could do this.

As the music started playing, Priya forced herself to breathe slowly. She just needed to focus and breathe. That was it. She remembered Ba's words back when she'd ruined her beam routine two years ago. She'd told Priya just how brave she'd been for continuing even when she'd failed. To Ba, being brave was worth more than winning a gold. And surely her decision to come back and apologize to the team was brave? It had definitely been one of the scariest things she'd ever done. In Ba's eyes, she'd probably already won the gold. Priya smiled – somehow the thought made her feel like she really could do this.

And then they were off. She let her body do everything it loved to do – jump, tumble, roll, dance, stretch and point all over the mat. She almost laughed as she landed her double tuck in perfect synchronicity with Dan's. How had she never realized how fun it was to do all the things she loved so much whilst her *friends* did the exact same things right next to her? She felt like she was flying. Her landings were perfect. She was so aware of everyone around her that it was impossible to mess up her timings – she could feel every person's tiniest turn and movement, so she knew exactly when her body needed to do the same.

Then it was time for the big finale. The human pyramid with Rachael at the top. Priya glanced at Rachael to give her a huge smile of encouragement, and took her place at the bottom right. She felt herself burst with pride as Rachael sprang onto the top of the pyramid and landed in the splits. The crowd cheered. They'd done it.

Priya got up in a daze. She knew that it had been the best performance they'd ever done; she could feel it in her bones, but she had no idea how the judges would score it. She looked automatically to Olaf. He was frowning and mouthing at them to move off the mats while the judges were deliberating, but his eyes were twinkling.

"Olaf?" she asked him. "Was that...okay? I'm sorry I went behind your back. I just really wanted to show the team I do care."

He nodded gruffly. "Yes. I think they've received that message. We'll see you next week for practice as usual. Unless the Teen Olympic team want you."

Priya grinned and threw her arms around him. "Thanks, Olaf."

He cleared his throat and waved the others over. "They're doing the scores now. We're going to need at least an 18.100 otherwise we're out of the game. They're putting up the scorecards now... It's too much to hope for a nineteen, but an eighteen would be— Oh my god, it's a 19.001!"

They'd done it. The applause was deafening as the audience realized this put them in first position. Priya couldn't help laughing hysterically as she turned to the team. She wrapped her arms around Rachael and felt the rest of the team's arms wrap around them both. Priya could barely see a thing other than leotards and jumbled-up limbs, but she didn't need to. She knew that everyone was bursting with as much joy as she was.

"We did it!" cried Priya. "We won!"

Chapter 25

Priya was still riding high as she walked into the girls' bathrooms. She beamed at her reflection happily. She'd done it – she'd helped the team win. Just then the door opened, and Katie walked in. Priya's mouth dropped open.

"Katie? What are you...? You actually came!"

Katie rolled her eyes. "Way to point out the obvious." She was wearing a short black skirt, a dark green satin top that perfectly matched her nails and amazing leather boots. She looked incredible – and completely out of place at a gymnastics competition. "Well done. Nice split jump in the middle. And your double tuck was flawless. You deserved that gold."

"Thanks," said Priya. "I still can't believe you're here. And you made it in time to watch me."

Katie shrugged as she looked at her reflection in the mirror, fixing her eyeliner. "I thought it would be fun to watch IRL. It's even better than on TikTok. Anyway, I want to see this Dan Zhang."

Priya flushed, quickly looking around to check Dan wasn't there to overhear. Then she remembered it was the girls' bathrooms.

"Has he forgiven you yet?" asked Katie. "Is the date back on?"

Priya shook her head. "No. But it's okay, because at least he's speaking to me now! He even apologized."

Katie turned to face Priya, her eyebrows raised. "You literally just won your team gold. What more does he want?"

"I don't know," said Priya, honestly. "But…it doesn't matter anyway. He's not my priority now." She realized just how true that was as she said it. As amazing as it felt to be back in the team's good books, there was something else on her mind. Something much more important.

"He's not?" Katie frowned. "What is your priority?"

"Sami and Mei," said Priya, feeling every cell in her body practically ring in agreement with how true that was. They were the most important people in her life. She had no idea how she'd ever forgotten that. "I need to fix things with them first. I mean, what's the point in winning gold, or even having a date with Dan, if I can't tell them about it?"

"I can think of many points, but whatever," said Katie, folding her arms. "Why don't you just go fix things with them then?"

"I want to, but they're still not speaking to me. They told me again the other day."

"That means they spoke to you," pointed out Katie. "And who cares? Just make them talk to you."

"I can't..."

"Didn't you just force yourself back into the competition here?" demanded Katie. "Why can't you do the same with Sami and Mei?"

"I guess Sami does love big gestures..." said Priya uncertainly. "But I don't know how she'd feel about me crashing her bat mitzvah after she specifically uninvited me."

"Sounds to me like you've already got a plan," said Katie with a smirk. "Crashing a bat mitzvah."

"Priya!" The door swung open and Rachael stood there, grinning from ear to ear. "There you are! I've been looking for you everywhere! Olaf wants to speak to you and Priya – he's got the Olympics scout right there with him!"

Priya gasped. "No!"

"This is your moment," cried Rachael. "If you impress them with your individual this afternoon, then you'll get on the Olympics team! It's amazing – you'll be competing in the actual TEEN OLYMPICS!"

"Cool," said Katie, screwing her eyeliner shut and dumping it in her bag. "I bet you'll get loads of free stuff from sponsors. You should aim for Adidas."

"Uh..." Priya stared at Katie, and then at Rachael, who was

eyeing up Katie suspiciously. "I...don't know. I don't know what to do!"

"Of course, you know what to do," said Rachael. "You need to go and tell Coach yes! Then kick major ass in your individual! But...first, you need to leave the girls' bathrooms." She opened the door. "Come on!"

Priya slowly followed her out into the hallway, with Katie trailing behind her. Olaf and the Teen Olympics scout were right there waiting.

"Priya!" said Olaf, waving wildly. "Meet Soren. He wants you on his team! Well, it'll be confirmed once he's seen you in your individual event – but if you do that anywhere near as well as you did the team routine this morning, then you'll be fine."

"Um, hi," said Priya, shaking Soren's outstretched hand. This was a lot of information to take in – and her mind was still reeling from Katie's suggestion that she crash Sami's BM. Could she really do it? Should she? And more importantly – if she did, would she be able to get Sami and Mei to forgive her?

"It's a pleasure to meet you, Priya," said Soren. "Olaf has been singing your praises for a very long time. He always told me you were more of an individual gymnast, but seeing you in this event, it seems you are a team player too! Which is just what we're looking for!"

Priya stared at him in silence until Rachael nudged her

sharply in the ribs. "Ow! I mean, sorry. That's... Thank you so much."

Soren smiled. "As part of the Teen Olympics team, you'd be joining our other gymnasts at the head coach's training camp once a month, in between training with a private coach closer to home, and you'd travel for competitions throughout the year. How does that sound?"

Priya stared at him. How did it sound? Amazing. Terrifying. Kind of...stressful. She took a deep breath as she realized that her body had suddenly tensed up, and her shoulders had tightened. It might sound good, but...it didn't *feel* good. She'd spent her whole life working up to this, but it wasn't what she really wanted. At least not right now. She just wanted to do what her dad had said and go back to doing gymnastics for the pure love of it – not to constantly achieve.

"Thank you," she said eventually. "It's an amazing offer. But to be honest, all I want is to be back on Olaf's team."

"But, Priya, you can't be on both!" hissed Olaf. He tried to turn his panic into a relaxed laugh. "Ha ha! You'd be on the Olympics team full-time, of course. Much more important than our little team!"

Priya glanced at Katie, who was standing there listening to everything. Katie raised an eyebrow at her, as though she was giving her an unspoken challenge. Priya silently accepted it. "I don't want to be on the Teen Olympics team," she said, suddenly emboldened. "I want to have a life and have sleepovers with my friends on Fridays. I don't want to be permanently stressed and too tired to do my schoolwork. I just want to train with my friends, have fun, and compete. But not to a level that stops me from having a life."

Soren nodded, looking disappointed. "I understand. You are still very young – maybe it is too soon."

The blood drained out of Olaf's face. "Priya...I don't know if you know what you're saying. Maybe we should speak to your parents first – where are they?"

"At my friend's bat mitzvah," said Priya, realizing that was exactly where she needed to be too. "And I already spoke to my dad. He said I can do whatever makes me happy, which is being back on your team, Olaf." His expression softened. Until Priya spoke again. "Anyway, I need to go now. Sorry."

His mouth dropped open. "You can't! You have your individual event."

"I know," said Priya, her voice wavering. She'd spent so much time practising that routine. And the prize money was huge. But nothing was as huge as her love for her friends. She needed to put them first. She nodded decisively. "But I'm going to skip it. I've got a bat mitzvah to go to."

Olaf glanced up at the ceiling, muttering under his breath. "Teenagers. My god."

Soren smiled at Priya. "Enjoy the bat mitzvah. Maybe I'll see you next year and we can have this conversation again? Perhaps with a different answer?"

"Maybe," said Priya. "But…I can't make any promises."

Soren nodded respectfully. "Thank you for your honesty. And Rachael, I look forward to seeing you in the individual as well. Unless you also have a bat mitzvah to go to?"

Rachael shook her head silently while Soren smiled, and walked off with Olaf, who turned back to give Priya one more look of total bafflement.

"Oh my god, Rach, he wants to see your event!" squealed Priya. "That's so exciting!"

"I guess so," said Rachael, dazed. "I still can't believe you did that."

Katie nodded approvingly. "I knew there'd be drama today. I just didn't think it would be you turning down the Olympics for a bat mitzvah."

"Sorry, who *are* you?" asked Rachael.

"She's…my friend," said Priya, "Katie. And this is my other friend, Rachael."

"Hi, I guess," said Katie.

"Hi back, I guess," replied Rachael.

"So, um, I have to go," said Priya. "I'm sorry to leave, Rachael. But you'll tell the team, right? And wish them luck for their individuals? And MASSIVE luck for yours! I bet Soren will be begging you to join the Teen Olympics!"

"I'm not so sure, but it was still cool he said that," said Rachael. "And thanks, Priya. For everything. You're a good friend."

Priya hugged Rachael. "You too. Message me afterwards and let me know how it goes."

"I suppose I'll leave too," said Katie, as Rachael rushed off. "Let you go reunite with your little musketeer friends or whatever."

Priya looked at Katie. It was true what she'd said to Rachael – Katie *was* her friend. Somehow, against the odds, she'd befriended her bully. "You know what," she said slowly. "I'm going to need some help at the bat mitzvah. Moral support."

Katie raised an eyebrow. "Do you mean...?"

Priya took a deep breath. She knew that it was already risky to turn up to Sami's bat mitzvah when she'd specifically asked her not to come. Bringing Katie Wong as her plus-one was practically a death wish. But Priya knew that she had to have faith in all her friends from now on. And that meant having faith in Sami and Mei's big hearts, and in Katie's growing one. "I mean that if I'm going to gatecrash a bat mitzvah, I'm going to need a sidekick," said Priya finally. "What do you say?"

"Why not?" said Katie, trying to hide a smile. "I guess I do owe you, seeing as your fight with Sami and Mei was a little bit my fault... Besides, I bet you don't even have a ride to get there."

The expression on Priya's face clearly showed that no, she did not, and it hadn't occurred to her either.

Katie grinned triumphantly. "Luckily, I have an Uber account linked to my dad's credit card. Let's go."

Half an hour later, Priya stood anxiously with Katie outside the synagogue. "Pinkie should be here! She said she'd come out and meet us."

Katie sighed impatiently. "I really don't get why we need your ten-year-old sister for this. Can't you just walk into the synagogue and go apologize to your friends?"

"Absolutely not," said Priya. "Firstly, my parents think I'm sick in bed. Secondly, Sami will kill me if I ruin her BM by storming in during the speeches. And thirdly, I can't go in dressed like this! Pinkie said she'd bring me my mum's shawl to cover up."

Katie looked Priya up and down. She was still wearing her black leotard with her tracksuit bottoms over it. "Yeah, I can't disagree with point three," she said, looking admiringly at her own outfit in relief. "Thank god I always dress multi-occasion. It means I look good wherever I go."

"I don't look *that* bad, do I?" asked Priya, worried. "I mean, my leotard is sparkly. And it'll be okay with a shawl on top, right? It's pale blue and silky."

"Pale blue, with black?" Katie shook her head, her face showing exactly what she thought. She stepped back to properly appraise Priya. After staring at her for several uncomfortable moments, she turned to her own skirt – made up of black layers of chiffon – and suddenly ripped off the chiffon, revealing a black silk layer underneath.

Priya gasped. "What are you doing? Why did you just rip up your skirt?"

"Take off your tracksuit bottoms," ordered Katie. "Come on!"

Priya was so shocked that she obeyed without protesting. Katie brought the chiffon skirt layers up to Priya and wrapped them around her. She pulled out a thin metal grip from her hair and bent it into a makeshift clasp for Priya's new skirt. She adjusted it, then took a step back and smiled proudly. "There. It's a bit *Black Swan*, but it's kind of cute. And it's way better than the tracksuit bottoms."

Priya looked down at her new outfit – it was like an edgy version of a tutu – and beamed. "I love it! Thanks, Katie. Wow, you're really good at this. You really should go into fashion."

Katie stared at her deadpan. "You think I don't know that?"

"Oh-kay," said Priya. "That's the last time I try and compliment you."

Just then the door opened. Pinkie stood there, holding their dad's black blazer. She nodded at her sister and sidekick. "Nice tutu, Priya," she said. "And well done on the gold. It seems Plan A was a success."

"It was," said Priya. "Thanks for the help. I really had no idea you were such a little...mastermind."

"People often underestimate me," said Pinkie, shrugging. "Anyway. They've just finished the speeches, and now everyone's moving to the hall for the party. So, I think you'll be able to get Sami and Mei alone. Hopefully without the parents seeing. Oh, and I decided the shawl wouldn't go with your outfit, so I brought dad's blazer, for an oversized look."

Katie nodded approvingly as Priya draped it over her shoulders.

"Uh, thanks?" said Priya.

"You're welcome," said Pinkie, propping open the door with her sparkly trainers. "Come on. This way."

Katie walked through first, looking Pinkie up and down as she passed her. "Strong look. I'm into it."

Pinkie – who was about half her size – did the exact same to her. "And I'm into yours. I'm guessing it was you who fixed Priya's outfit?"

Priya rolled her eyes as she followed her younger sister and former bully into the hall. Of course, they were bonding. But now wasn't the time to think about that. She was on a mission to win her best friends back.

Chapter 26

Priya tried to hide at the back of the busy hall. It was packed full of people – their entire class was there as well as most of the local Jewish community, and because of Sami's mum's new boyfriend, most of the local Indian community too – plus there was a DJ at the front playing blaring loud music. Priya couldn't help but smile in excitement for Sami – she'd managed to throw the party of the year, and it was still only lunchtime. She felt a pang of sadness that she'd missed out on the morning, but then she remembered Sami telling her (okay, tearfully shouting at her) that the only bit that mattered was the party. So at least she was showing up for the most important part.

"This is the most uncool party I've ever been to," remarked Katie, looking around in disdain.

Priya shot her a look. "Can you not? This is my best friend's party, and it's the best party *I've* ever been to."

"You need to get out more," said Katie.

"ARE YOU ACTUALLY KIDDING ME?!"

Priya and Katie both whirled around to see Sami standing there with her hands on her hips, absolutely fuming. She was wearing a bright turquoise trouser suit, with an orange crop top underneath, and it looked incredible with her long red hair. Priya gasped in admiration.

"Sami, you look stunning!"

Sami scowled and moved to reveal Mei standing right behind her. She looked amazing too. She was wearing a black vintage lace dress with long sleeves. Priya smiled in pride – her best friends were absolutely beautiful. Well, she hoped they were still her best friends. The expressions on their faces suggested otherwise.

"I know. But I cannot BELIEVE you brought this horrid... *human* to my party," spat out Sami, looking from Priya to Katie with disgust. "And what were you thinking, just turning up like this, Priya? I disinvited you!"

"Um, it's a long story," she said, glancing at Katie. "But maybe, can we just speak privately for a moment? Please?"

"I'll leave you guys alone," said Katie. "I need to ask Pinkie where she got her trousers from anyway."

Priya flashed her a grateful look and turned back to Sami and Mei. "Please can you just give me five minutes to hear me out?" Their faces didn't move. Priya bit her lip. "Even... one minute?"

"No way!" said Sami. "This is my day – not yours."

"She's right," agreed Mei. "You can't just turn up uninvited – and with Katie as your plus-one! It's not okay, Priya. You're completely disrespecting Sami's boundaries."

Priya hung her head. Mei had a point. But she still needed to apologize. "Look, I'm sorry. Bringing Katie wasn't the original plan. She's just...well, it's her stuff to share not mine. But she's not the person you think she is. And more importantly, *I'm* not the person you think I am."

"So, you're not a secret-telling liar who abandoned her best friends?" demanded Sami.

"No!" said Priya. She paused. "Well, I mean, I did do those things. But I didn't mean to!" This really wasn't going the way she wanted. She scrunched her eyes shut and tried to think of something to say to convince her friends she still loved them and would never hurt them again. But then she heard a voice that made her eyes open in slow dread.

"Priya?!"

Priya's mum was staring at her in total confusion. Her dad was next to her looking equally confused.

"What are you doing here?" demanded her mum. "You're meant to be sick in bed!"

"Probably another lie," muttered Mei.

"I...I can explain," said Priya desperately. "Just let me speak to Sami and Mei first. Please. I need to fix things with them."

"Fix what?" asked her dad. "And why are you wearing your gymnastics leotard?"

Priya looked from her parents to her friends in panic. She felt hot tears pricking her eyelids. She didn't know what to do. It felt like everyone was mad at her. How could she repair things? What was she supposed to do?

She desperately tried to think of what Ba would tell her. Of what Ba had been trying to tell her all along by giving her the bangle. About the truth. She wanted Priya to learn to be honest and open up to people, so she could feel more connected and less alone. When she'd done that, things had (mainly) improved. She'd felt closer to Sami and Mei, inspiring them to open up more too, *and* she'd done the unthinkable in telling Dan she liked him. She'd even admitted to her parents how she felt about their arguments, and she'd shown Pinkie that her perfect older sister was actually a mess who sometimes needed her younger sister's help.

But the truth had got her in trouble too. Like when she'd overshared with Katie. Truths that weren't hers. She knew the bangle had been partly at fault, but she had to admit that she'd got overexcited by Katie's attention and had offered up her friends' truths to impress the coolest girl in school. Then there was the other side of things. How *not* telling Sami and Mei the truth about the bat mitzvah had hurt them. How she hadn't been brave enough to admit she'd shared their secrets with Katie until she'd been forced to. And how she'd avoided telling her parents just how stressed she was for years. Her dad kept saying he wished she'd told him earlier – in the exact way he wished she'd been more honest about his awful cooking.

"Go ahead, Priya," said Sami coldly. "There's nothing you want to say to me that you can't say in front of your parents. Or this whole party, for that matter. Why don't you go up to the mic and tell *everybody* why you're here, hm?"

Priya stared at the four frowning faces in front of her. Suddenly, it hit her. She needed to tell the truth – but only her own truth, and on her *own terms*. She couldn't overshare other people's truths, but nor could she try to change her truth for other people. The more she tried to sugar-coat her honesty to make other people feel better, the worse things got. All she needed to do was stand up for herself and her truth, as it was, without worrying about the consequences. In other words, she had to be brave. *Really* brave.

"Okay," she said to Sami. "I'll do that. And then if you're still mad at me, I'll leave. I promise."

She dashed to the front of the stage, where the DJ was, and grabbed the microphone. "Sorry," Priya said to the DJ, ignoring his protestations, "but I just need to borrow this for one minute."

She tapped the microphone to check it was working and stepped into a spotlight on the middle of the stage. Her heart was thudding. She couldn't believe she was doing this. She never spoke in front of people – that was Sami's thing, not hers. The only time she could handle the spotlight was when she was performing gymnastics, in total silence. But this time, she had to do things differently. She had to speak up.

She took a deep breath as a hush fell over the room, the DJ reluctantly fading out the music. "Hi, everyone. I'm Priya Shah. And...I'm here to tell the truth."

She could hear random gasps and whispers from the room – she caught a glimpse of Katie's wide eyes and Pinkie's encouraging smile – and then quickly looked up to the ceiling so she couldn't see any more facial expressions. Instead, she stared resolutely at the disco ball.

"I never used to tell the truth," she began, staring into the mirrored surfaces above her. "I spent my entire life lying. I didn't even realize it *was* lying. I thought I was just being a good friend, a good daughter, a good student, a good teammate and a good sister. But actually, I was hiding things from everyone and it was...lonely. I pretended everything was perfect when inside, I wasn't okay. I was struggling. With gymnastics, with schoolwork, and with stuff at home. I won't go into more details because that's not my stuff to share. I'm only sharing *my* truths from now on.

"Which is that I used to lie. A lot. Until I started always telling the truth, for reasons I'm not going to go into. Let's just say Ba, my grandma, inspired me to do it. And things got better. I felt so much closer to my best friends ever – Sami and Mei. They shared things with me too. I told my crush I liked him. And it turns out he liked me back!" Priya heard "aww" sounds coming from the audience, but she ignored them. She wasn't done. And she had a feeling the "aww"s would disappear when she got to the next bit. "My life started to improve, the more I shared with people. My coach even let me have more time off from training. And I realized that by telling people what I needed, they could actually give it to me.

"But then...I ruined things. I got carried away with all the attention I was receiving. It went to my head. I became selfish, thinking my problems were bigger than everyone else's. And I started sharing truths that weren't mine to keep getting attention. I wasn't kind with how I shared the truth either. I ended up really upsetting my best friends, and I am so, so sorry. People say blood is thicker than water, but it's not true. Sami and Mei are just as much my blood and family as my actual family – who I do also love, by the way. My little sister helped me gatecrash this party, so thanks, Pinkie!

"But, anyway. I just want to say sorry to Sami – and to everyone else I've hurt, really. I promise that from now on, I'm only going to tell *my* truth and nobody else's, and I'll do it in the kindest way I can. Which means being kind to myself too. I'm not going to constantly second-guess myself and try to only say what people want to hear. I'm going to keep genuinely sharing with people. That's how I've ended up being friends with the girl who used to bully me!"

She grinned at Katie who made a cringed-out face but looked secretly touched. Priya continued talking, no longer looking at the disco ball, but directly into the crowd in front of her.

"Sami, I don't know if you can forgive me, but if you can, I promise I'll never betray you again. And I'm going to show you the real me, even if it means talking about really hard things. Okay, um..." Her voice trailed off and she realized she'd been speaking for way longer than a minute. "Yeah, bye. And happy womanhood, Sami – you're the best. Love you always. Even if it's one-sided, like it is right now."

She quickly handed the microphone back to the DJ and ran off the stage. There was total silence and then the audience started clapping loudly. Priya flushed. She didn't want that. She just wanted Sami and Mei's forgiveness. But she couldn't see them. All she could see was a blur of cheering faces. She ran out into the hallway, where she leaned against the wall, breathing slowly. She'd done it. She'd spoken her truth. All of it.

"Priya?" Sami and Mei were standing by her. They had tears in their eyes.

Priya stood up straight, terrified. She had no idea if they were happy tears or angry tears. Or worse, sad tears.

"I just want you to know that I, Sami Levin, forgive you," said Sami loudly.

"Me too," said Mei softly.

Priya burst into tears. She ran up to her best friends,

hugging them tight. "Really? Do you mean it? I'm so sorry, I really am."

"I know," said Sami, squeezing her back. "You just did a three-minute monologue telling my entire bat mitzvah. And you HATE public speaking!"

"It was so brave," agreed Mei. "And inspiring. You know, I think I might tell my parents I'm gay. Even without having a girlfriend. If you can do *that,* then I can definitely tell them."

Priya's mouth dropped. "Really? That's amazing, Mei! I'm so proud of you."

Sami put her arms around them both. "I'm so proud of US. This is why we're the musketeers – we're the bravest warriors I know!"

"I did not sign up to be a warrior," grumbled Mei. "I barely signed up to be a musketeer."

Priya held her friends tight. "Thank you so much for forgiving me. And I meant what I said. I promise I'll try my hardest to never lie to either of you ever again."

The door burst open, and all of three of them turned to look. Katie stood there, scowling at the floor. Sami and Mei frowned at her suspiciously, while Priya raised a hand in greeting.

"What are you doing here?" snapped Sami. "We're having a moment."

"Yeah. Clearly," said Katie. "Look. Sorry to interrupt. I just...wanted to say that what you did up there was really cool, Priya. And it's made me want to tell you that, um, I'm really sorry for what I did to you. I *was* a bully. There's no excuse for it. I should never have treated you the way I did, and I'll never do it again. To anyone."

Priya nodded slowly. "Thank you for saying that, Katie. It really wasn't okay. But I've made mistakes too, so...I forgive you. And I know that it's not all there is to you. You were affected by, well, your stuff."

Katie turned to Sami and Mei. "Context: my dad abandoned us to have a baby with another woman, and my mum's been depressed ever since. Though he's kind of behaving okay now. But it's not an excuse. I should never have taken it out on Priya, or on you guys. So, I'm sorry to both of you too. I used my power for bad instead of good, and I'm over it. You've got my word that I won't be doing it again."

"Oh my god, Katie Wong just apologized to me," said Sami, clutching her chest. "This is serious womanhood happening right now! And of course, we forgive you! I'm also a child of a broken home, so if ever you want to bond over it, I'm here."

"I'm sorry you've been going through such a hard time," added Mei. "I don't approve of what you did at all. Obviously. But I think it's cool you're taking responsibility for it. So, I forgive you too. And, uh, let us know if ever we can help."

Katie smiled shyly. "Really? Thanks. That's...very cool of you both."

The door opened yet again, and this time, they all turned to see Priya's parents standing awkwardly in the hallway with Pinkie. Priya faced her friends. "Hey, um, I think I need to speak to my family. I'll see you inside?"

Sami and Mei nodded, giving her one last hug. Sami linked arms with Katie. "Come on. Now you're here, we totally need a selfie. People are going to freak when they find out KW was at my humble little soirée."

"There is nothing humble about any of this," commented Mei, as they walked back inside. The door closed behind them, leaving Priya alone with her family. She looked at them nervously.

"Um, hi," she said.

"Why didn't you tell us?" asked her mum softly. She had tears in her eyes. "How much you were struggling? And that you were being *bullied*?"

"It's our fault," said her dad, shaking his head. "We made you feel like you had to be perfect. But it's not true, Priya. You're allowed to be imperfect. We're all imperfect. And we love you no matter what."

Priya felt tears sliding down her face too. "I know. I'm sorry. I just didn't want to add to your stress, especially with…"

"Me," said Pinkie, shrugging. "I get it. I take up too much space."

"No, honey," cried their mum, squeezing her youngest daughter. "You don't. You take up the exact right amount of space." She reached her arms out to Priya, enveloping her into a hug. "We just haven't shown you that you're allowed as much space as you need too, Priya."

Priya relaxed into her mum's arms. It felt so good to finally be so honest with her parents, after a lifetime of trying to be perfect. "Thank you," she whispered.

"Thank *you*," said her mum, "for being so inspiring up there. You reminded me of Ba." She hesitated, then faced Priya. "Also, *beta,* I know you wanted to do something for Ba's anniversary. What if we did do a little memorial ceremony for her at home? For her anniversary on August the—"

"Thirteenth! Yes!" cried Priya. "I'd love that. Pinkie and I could organize it? We're a pretty good team."

Pinkie smiled happily at her big sister. "Agreed."

"I think Ba would love that," said their mum. "And I am so sorry I haven't encouraged either of you to speak much about Ba since..." Her voice cracked. "I just... I miss her so much that it hurts to even say her name."

"Me too," said Priya softly. "So much. But it really helps me to talk about her, so maybe it will help you too?"

"Me three," added Pinkie. "I still think about her all the time."

"And me four," agreed their dad, wrapping his arms around them all. "But I do know that she would be super proud of you both. Especially you, Priya, for everything you've just done."

Priya's eyes shone with tears. "Do you really think so? I hate the thought of ever letting her down."

Her mum squeezed her tight. "You could never let her down, no matter what, and it's the same with us. You are enough just as you are. No matter what you do or don't do. You too, Pinkie. My beautiful daughters."

"I'm so sorry, girls," said their dad, letting his arms fall. "I don't think we've always been a good example in terms of honesty." He looked into their mum's eyes. "About our relationship..."

"Yeah," said Pinkie, breaking away from the hug to look at her parents. "You both keep trying to pretend you're happy for our sake, but it's not working."

"Can't you just get a divorce?" blurted out Priya. "We know you're not happy and we just want the arguments to stop! You'll be so much happier alone, both of you."

Their parents stared at each other in stunned silence.

"I...but...girls..." said their mum. "I didn't know you felt this way."

"We do," said Priya firmly. "And we know you want to stay together for our sake, and so people don't speak badly of you, but we don't mind about any of that. We love you both and always will. We won't take sides. We just...want you both to be happy."

"Is it me, or is that the speech we're meant to be giving them?" asked their dad, clearly choked up with emotion.

"They're right though," said their mum softly. "We're not happy. And if they want us to divorce, then..."

"Maybe we could," finished their dad. "But it would mean telling people. Being honest about where we are."

"That's a good thing," pointed out Priya. "Telling the truth has made my life so much better!"

"And who even cares what they think?" asked Pinkie. "Loads of people make comments about my ADHD but I just ignore them. Can't you do the same if people judge you for getting divorced?"

There was a long silence as their mum stroked her youngest daughter's hair, trying not to cry. Then she turned to her husband, her face shining. "Shall we do it?" she asked hesitantly. "Do you really think we could? Divorce?"

His face broke into a smile. "Yes. Let's do it. Let's divorce."

Priya and Pinkie started cheering wildly. They all hugged together tightly, laughing and crying. Priya couldn't remember the last time she'd felt so close to her family.

Suddenly there was a gush of wind. They all turned and saw that the big double doors at the end of the corridor had opened, and there were two people standing there in... leotards. Priya squinted and realized it was Rachael. And Dan!

She stared at them in shock. "What are you both doing here?"

"We came to find you," said Dan.

"Were you just celebrating something?" asked Rachael curiously.

Priya looked at her parents, expecting them to make something up. She knew it wasn't up to her to tell the truth for them. But to her surprise, her mum revealed it all on her own.

"We're getting divorced," she announced happily.

"Um, congratulations?" asked Dan, confused.

Priya's parents smiled, then noticed Pinkie gesturing at Dan and raising her eyebrows, signalling for them to leave Priya alone.

"Let's leave Priya with her friends," said her mum. "Come on, Nish." She dragged her husband behind her, and they followed Pinkie back into the party. Pinkie paused to give Priya a thumbs-up, and then started making kissy faces at her.

Priya glared angrily at her little sister, then quickly turned to Dan and Rachael, hoping they hadn't seen.

"We wanted to celebrate with you," said Rachael. She handed Priya a gold medal. "And give you this."

Priya looked down at her medal, smiling. It was the first time she'd ever won a gold for a team event – and it felt like she was wearing ten medals rather than just the one. "Thank you. I love it. How did your events go? What did Soren say?"

"I got bronze," said Rachael proudly. "He said I'm not ready for the Teen Olympics yet, but he'll keep an eye on me."

"That's amazing," cried Priya. "Well done. And, um, how did you do, Dan?"

"I got a silver," he said. "But no Teen Olympics for now either. I'll be staying on Olaf's team too."

Priya beamed happily at the thought.

"Also, uh, I think this is yours," said Dan. He held up a gold sparkly bangle decorated with rubies and diamonds.

Priya gasped and looked down at her wrist. The bangle. It wasn't there. It was in Dan's hand. "But...how...?"

"It must have fallen off during the routine," explained Dan. "I found it on the mats."

Priya took it from him, in a daze. She didn't understand. The bangle was closed shut again. She tried to open the clasp, but it was stuck. She stared at it in shock. If the bangle had fallen off during the competition, then it meant she hadn't been wearing it when she'd stood up on the stage and told her truth to the entire bat mitzvah. Or when she'd just asked her parents to divorce. None of it had been the bangle. It had all been her. She'd told the truth on her own.

"Also, um, I wondered if you wanted to get that milkshake," said Dan, blushing. "I'm sorry I overreacted before. I, um, I still like you."

Rachael coughed awkwardly. "I feel I shouldn't be here right now..."

Priya laughed. "It's fine, I'll obviously just tell you about it word for word afterwards." She turned to an embarrassed

Dan. "And I feel like the moment for the milkshake has passed."

His face fell. "Oh. Okay. I understand."

"But...I still like you too," she said. "So, how about we dance together instead? Like, right now?"

Dan's face lit up in a wordless "yes". She grabbed his hand and led him back into the party, straight to the dance floor, gesturing for Rachael to follow. They pushed past the crowds to make their way right into the middle of the dance floor, where Priya knew that Sami and Mei would be. Although she hadn't expected to see them teaching their signature dance moves to Katie Wong.

"Pri!" cried Sami. "You're back! And you brought...Dan Zhang?!" She clamped her hand to her mouth. "Oh no, sorry. I mean, um, some guy who you have never spoken to us about."

Dan grinned. "Hey."

Priya's eyes widened and she glared at Sami. But Sami blew her a kiss in response. "You can't be mad because it's my BM and you totally gatecrashed it, then hijacked the stage."

Priya rolled her eyes. "Fine. I'm too happy to be mad anyway – my parents are getting divorced!"

Sami and Mei screamed so loudly that half the bat mitzvah turned to stare. "It's a divorce," announced Sami, as Mei whooped happily. "Mazel tov!" Then Mei noticed Rachael standing awkwardly nearby.

"You brought a friend," she said, staring at her. "A really pretty friend." Suddenly, she went bright red. "Oh my god, did I say that out loud?"

Rachael laughed. "Yes, but I liked it. Do you...want to dance?" Mei nodded, speechless, and threw a look of utter joy mingled with terror at Sami and Priya, who both gave her massive thumbs-ups as she took Rachael's hand.

Dan put his arms around Priya's shoulders, and they started swaying their bodies together. She knew she had an insane grin on her face, but she couldn't stop smiling. She was dancing with Dan Zhang, and best of all, she was surrounded by her friends. She looked over at Sami and Mei – Sami was trying to start a conga line with Katie, who was shaking her head adamantly as Sami grabbed her round the waist and forced her round the room anyway – and laughed out loud. She was so happy right now.

As Dan brought his body closer to hers, Priya rested her head on his shoulder. She closed her eyes and clutched the bangle tight. She whispered internally to her grandma: "Thank you, Ba. You were so right – I'm not alone. And it is okay to not be okay. I'm enough as I am and I don't need to hide my truth any more. I get it all now. But next time – you don't need to trap me in a truth curse, okay? Lesson learned. I love you."

Priya could have sworn she felt the bangle vibrate in her hand. She squeezed it tight and went back to focusing on the fact that she was dancing with her best friends, her new friends and DAN ZHANG, and that her parents – who were dancing happily in the corner with Pinkie – were finally going to get divorced. This was officially the best day of her entire life.

Turn the page for a sneak peek at the next hilariously relatable story with a little twist of magic, from Radhika Sanghani.

Coming soon!

When Sabina had told the Leeches she'd never meditated or done yoga before, she'd meant it. But she'd been wrong. Because when Diva started leading them through some simple stretches, Sabina quickly realized they were the exact same ones she did with her mum! In fact, they were even easier than the ones her and her mum would do, and she noticed the Leeches looking at her with confused appreciation when she managed to stay for a whole minute in a one-legged balance – or a "warrior three" as Diva called it – without wobbling. Neither of the Leeches had been able to stay still for more than a few seconds, and the one time they tried, Felicia went crashing into Alicia so loudly that the whole class lost their concentration and tumbled down like dominoes. Except for Sabina. She had plenty of practice not falling over whilst laughing on one leg.

But the part that Sabina was most shocked by was the meditation. She'd always thought that her and her mum's breathing ritual was something only they did – a private two-person activity with a magic light her mum had invented to cheer up a younger Sabina. But when Diva started to guide them through the meditation, telling them to focus on breathing deeply in and out of their noses, and to imagine a white light in the middle of their eyebrows, Sabina almost cried out in shock. This was EXACTLY what she did with her mum! She opened her eyes then, looking around the room in disbelief as everyone did the same thing she'd spent hours doing with her mum, and when she locked eyes with Diva, she could have sworn her teacher winked at her.

She quickly closed her eyes shut again, and slowly, as she focused on her breathing, she found herself relaxing. Her thoughts started to disappear, until it was just her and the white light, with vague sounds of her classmates breathing far away in the background. She found the same soothing peace that she had with her mum when they did it at home. But then Diva started to mix it up.

"Now we're going to start imagining the colours of the rainbow along our spines," said Diva softly. "They represent the seven chakras. Let's start with red and the base of our spine which symbolizes safety. Breathe into it, let the red grow super bright. And then we're going to move to our tummies, below the belly button, where we have orange – pleasure." She spoke slowly as she guided them through the remaining five.

"Yellow in our centres for power...green in our hearts for love...blue in our threats for communication...indigo in between our eyebrows for insight and intuition...and finally, violet at the top of our heads to symbolize connection to others."

Sabina was so engrossed in the meditation that she didn't even fully associate the words as coming from Diva. They just appeared in her head, and she did exactly what they said, connecting with all seven of her chakras. With each one, she felt the thing it symbolized suffuse her whole body. Like when Diva told them the heart chakra represented love, and

Sabina imagined a green loving light shining through her entire body, until she could feel her toes tingling with love. By the time she reached the final chakras, she felt like she was practically floating, with all the colours of the rainbow radiating around her. She was used to just focusing on one bright light with her mum, but here, there were seven. And Sabina felt seven times as good.

But after a while, something shifted. She felt a sharp sound shatter her serenity. She blinked open her eyes to see the Leeshes giggling at her. Sabina's peace instantly disappeared as she jerked her head around the room to see that everybody was staring at her. Nobody else was meditating anymore and Diva was standing there smiling sympathetically. It didn't take Sabina long to figure out what had happened: Diva had told them to stop meditating, and everyone had stopped. Except her. She hadn't even heard a thing!

"You were like, really into that," said Alicia. "I thought you'd never done it before?"

"I... didn't think I had," said Sabina, embarrassed by the sudden attention.

"You were practically vibrating," said Felicia, edging away from her. "It was...a lot."

"Could I check your stats next time we meditate, Sabina?" asked Faye enthusiastically. "Like, just your heart rate and blood sugar, that kind of thing." Her face lit up. "I could do my next science project on you! To investigate the effects of meditation and whether chakra energy is real!"

"Uh..." Sabina looked from Faye to the Leeches helplessly. She really didn't want to be a science project; she just wanted to get through the rest of Year 8 without humiliating herself, and ideally, making a friend or two. "I was just...breathing?"

Diva clapped her hands again and everyone jumped. "Class is over. Everyone, go and get changed. Sabina, I'd like to speak to you, please. Alone."

Everyone trudged out of the room, including a reluctant Faye who clearly still wanted Sabina to be her new science project. Sabina felt her heart racing as everybody left – had she done something wrong? Was she already in trouble with the only teacher at MG she liked?

But then Diva smiled at her. "You have a gift, Sabina. Your meditation practice is very strong."

Sabina let out a shocked laugh. "Uh, what?! No, I... It's just something I've done with my mum, but I didn't even know it was meditation! And anyone can do it – it's not a gift!"

"Not everyone," her teacher said calmly. "You're a natural. And with a bit more practice and guidance, you can take your meditating to new levels."

"I'm not sure exactly what that means," said Sabina. "But I really don't need more reasons to stand out here."

Diva settled her grey eyes on Sabina's dark brown ones. "Maybe you were born to stand out. Maybe it's in your destiny."

Sabina shook her head quickly. "No, no. The Leeches, I mean the Leeshes, are born to stand out. I'm just...me."

Diva smiled mysteriously and pulled something out of her pocket. She gestured at Sabina to open up her palm, then placed something cold and heavy onto her soft skin. Sabina exclaimed as it caught the light. It was beautiful. A large dark purple stone, with shades of indigo and grey running through it.

"It's an amethyst," explained Diva. "A very powerful crystal that can help open up the third eye chakra – that's the one in the middle of our eyebrows that represents insight and intuition."

"Oh-kaaay? But why are you giving it to me?"

"Because I think your third eye is close to opening," said Diva simply. "If you keep meditating – just like we did today, going through all the chakras – and then you use this crystal when you get to the third eye, it could completely open up." She paused dramatically. "It could change your life, Sabina."

Sabina frowned in confusion. "That sounds like it would just make sure I definitely become Faye's next science project and nobody here ever wants to be my friend."

"Or they'll be so impressed with the powers it unlocks in you that they'll all be queuing up to be your friend." Diva raised her brows enigmatically as she closed Sabina's fingers around the crystal. "Keep it. You'll know what to do with it when the time comes."

Find out what happens next in...

✦ **THE GIRL WHO KNEW IT ALL** ✦

Acknowledgements

I am so grateful to everyone who helped me make this book a reality!

To my lovely agent Chloe Seager, who was so supportive of this idea and has encouraged me every step of the way. Also, for coming up with the wonderful title!

To my editor Alice Moloney at Usborne, who helped me make this book the best possible version it could be. Also for all the "haha"s and hearts in your comments – it made editing this book so much fun!

To the whole team at Usborne who have put so much thought and care into sharing Priya's story with readers – Beth Gardner, Jess Feichtlbauer, Rebecca Hill and everyone else who has been involved – thank you!

To my friends for being excited for me and genuinely caring whenever I told them what was going on with Priya (and Dan...)

To my cousins Prisha and Kaysha Pabari for all your help – especially Prisha for being the first person to read parts of *The Girl Who Couldn't Lie*!

To my dad for buying me endless amounts of books when I was younger and encouraging me to keep reading – and then later, to keep writing.

To myself for actually sitting down and writing this book. And, most importantly, to my younger self for inspiring it ♥

About the Author

Radhika Sanghani is an award-winning features journalist, acclaimed author, screenwriter, influential body positivity campaigner and a 2020 BBC Writers Room graduate.

Radhika writes regularly for the Daily Telegraph, Daily Mail, Elle, Guardian, Grazia, Glamour and Cosmopolitan; was recently featured in Italian Vogue as well BBC Radio 4 Woman's Hour and is a regular guest on Sky News and Good Morning Britain. She is also a TedX speaker on body positivity, a yoga teacher and runs a charity initiative with AgeUK fighting loneliness in older women.

The Girl Who Couldn't Lie is Radhika's first book for children.